13½

-Anthony Legend

DISCLAIMER:

The thoughts, opinions, and expressions herein are those of the author and do not reflect those of Cadmus Publishing LLC. Any similarities to actual events or people are purely coincidental. Names and distinguishing characteristics may have been changed to preserve the identities of any individuals. Published by Cadmus Publishing LLC. P. O. Box 8664. Haledon, NJ 07538

Web: Cadmuspublishing.com

Business email: admin@cadmuspublishing.com

ISBN# 978-1-63751-535-8

Book Catalog Info Categories:

Urban fiction

Cadmus Publishing

CadmusPublishing.com

Acknowledgments

I owe it to the struggle. Through sufferance, I've been granted the chance to achieve. All acknowledgement goes to my distinctive pain and ability to endure. The struggle is beautiful. Also, my queen and mother—thank you both for standing with me.

DEDICATION

I dedicate this book to my brother. And to those no longer with me.

PROLOGUE

May

Raping the innocent street of children's laughter and family gatherings, the sudden eruption of gunfire seized all movement and conversation. Chills ran through the neighborhood, and the acrid odor of gunpowder lingered in the air.

What the witnesses saw was vicious—horrifying. After today, nobody's sleep would ever be the same.

For middle-class families watching from a distance, this was the type of horror they had only seen in movies. But as mothers and fathers rushed their children inside for safety, two bodies lay slumped in a car, unresponsive in the driver and front passenger seats.

Blood stained the interior.

Multiple shell casings decorated the street and sidewalk. The car, riddled with bullet holes, sat on flats. Its windows were shattered.

Suddenly, the driver stirred, regaining consciousness. He pushed open the door, and glass rained down, crashing onto the pavement. Blood trickled from his lip as he struggled to move. Realizing he was dying—too weak to pull himself out of the car—he did the only thing he could.

“Call a fucking ambulance!” he yelled for help

CHAPTER ONE

BOSTON BAGHDAD: APRIL

"Mr. Grant! Pack up!" the correctional officer yelled.

"Shitt—nigga, I'm already packed," Raheem responded.

"So, you ready to go?"

"Nah, I'm ready to go."

The C.O. eyed Raheem, then opened his cell door. "So that's how you wanna leave? On bad terms?"

Raheem looked at him with contempt. Fuck nigga, I came here on bad terms, he thought, holding his tongue. He knew C.O. Dudley was an asshole—the type who got off on writing prisoners up right before they were released, just to make them stay an extra month or two.

Raheem cut his eyes toward the exit, thinking about the free world. Just chill, you'll be out in less than twenty minutes.

C.O. Dudley let out a smug chuckle. "Typical. Typical nigger. You'll be back—y'all always come back. Shit, orange is the new black." He laughed hard at his own joke.

Raheem stopped mid-stride. Fuck a write-up—I'm leaving anyway. He turned, locked eyes with Dudley, and said, "You punk faggot-ass cracker—suck my dick. And I ain't coming back, bitch. Especially not alive."

Then he walked into the unit counselor's office to sign his discharge papers.

"Hey, good morning, Mr. Grant! Take a seat, please. I'm printing your paperwork now. I'll have you out of here in no time," Mr. Hawkins said from behind a cluttered desk. "Must feel great to finally be getting out of this dump," he added.

Shit, I'm not out yet, Raheem thought. "Only if you knew," he said despite his thoughts.

"You got a plan? Any goals?" Hawkins asked.

"You better know it. A man without a plan is a man planning to fail."

"I agree. Well, I wish you the best. Here, sign these documents. Put your name next to every X."

Raheem signed where needed and handed the papers and pen back.

"You're done?" Hawkins asked. "Okay. Follow me."

Raheem followed him down a stairwell and through a hallway he'd never seen before. The air smelled of Clorox.

This must be the freedom route, he thought.

"Well, this is it," Hawkins said, handing Raheem a check. "Here's fifty dollars from the government. Hope everything works out for you—take care."

"Thank you," Raheem replied, shaking his hand.

Hawkins left him standing in the receiving and discharge area, waiting for his ride.

Raheem sat down and reflected on his struggle. "Damn," he muttered under his breath. "Four years, eight months… it's finally over."

The prison term, that is. The struggle? Well, that was far from over. He had to move carefully—watch everything. Sure, he had a shit list of names. But there was also a list with his name on it. Raheem is a thinker. Smooth. Quiet. He felt more comfortable around ten lions than a hundred sheep.

Of average height, he rocked a low, all-even haircut. His eyes were black as a shark's, his pearly whites complimented his smile—a smile that could cast a spell.

He wasn't your everyday street thug.

And soon enough, you'd see why.

"Raheem Grant!" a C.O. called out. "That's you, right?" He stood behind an enclosed counter.

"Yeah," Raheem got up and approached. "That's me."

"Here." The overweight, white C.O. slid a brown paper bag toward him. "Change into those clothes. Your ride's here, but you can't leave in a prison uniform."

The officer chuckled. "Imagine that."

Raheem changed into the provided clothes, leaving the prison uniform crumpled on the floor.

"You done?" the C.O. asked.

"More like ready," Raheem shot back.

The officer smirked. "Then freedom awaits you. Use the door behind you to exit."

Raheem turned and stepped through the last door standing between him and the outside world.

The bright morning sun hit his face. He tilted his head back, gazing into the golden-blue sky.

It was beautiful.

It was life outside of imprisonment.

"Baby! Raheem!"

A familiar voice cut through the air.

Waving her arms wildly, Tia called out. "Baby, over here!"

Raheem squinted until his vision adjusted. When he recognized her, relief washed over him.

Man, this girl is so loyal, he thought, walking toward her.

Tia, however, didn't wait. She ran straight to Raheem and threw herself into his arms. He hugged her tightly, inhaling her scent—freedom.

"Oh my God, baby," Tia said, holding Raheem tight. "You're really real. I missed you so much."

Looking into his eyes, she ran her fingers through his waves.

"I missed you too, sexy," Raheem said, kissing her softly on the top of her lip.

"Boy," Tia said with a playful smirk. "Don't start something."

Raheem licked his lips. "Girl, if I start something, I'ma finish it. I ain't even start nothing yet."

"See, that's what I'm talking about right there," she sighed, then shook her head. "Come on, let's get out of here."

Tia led Raheem to her car.

"How you like our car?" she asked, opening the driver's side door.

"What's this?" Raheem took a step back, looking the vehicle up and down. "A Honda?"

"It's the latest though," Tia defended.

Raheem shook his head, approving. "I'm digging it." He climbed inside, checking out the interior. "Yeah, I'm digging it. You did your thing picking a fly whip, sexy. No bullshit."

"I'm glad you like it, daddy. That means a lot to me."

Tia—who resembled a chocolate China doll with long, silk-textured hair—and Raheem had been together for over eight years. They'd been through it all. It was like they were made for each other—he was the gun, she was the clip. She was the bullet, he was the firing pin.

One without the other? Like a phone with no reception.

It wasn't gonna work.

Tia pulled out of the prison parking lot and headed for the expressway. As they drove toward Boston, they shared a cigar of sweet marijuana, talking about old times.

"This some good bud," Raheem muttered as the high settled in.

"Boy, you know I only smoke the best," Tia said, glancing at him. "Daddy?"

"Hm?"

"You love me?"

Raheem flicked the ashes from the cigar into the tray. "Girl, stop playing with me. You know I love your sexy ass."

“Uhm, you better,” she said, then got serious. “But on some real shit, I need to talk to you.”

“About what?”

“I need you to understand something. And feel me when I say this.” She took a deep breath. “Okay, so—I hope you know I ain’t putting up with none of your games, Raheem. And I mean that.” She pointed at him for emphasis. “And I’m dead ass, so don’t play yourself.”

“Listen!” Raheem waved her off. “Miss me with all that. A nigga ain’t even been out for a full hour yet, and you talking about some silly shit. You know it’s all about us, but—” he blew out a cloud of smoke—“I’ma keep it three hunnit. I ain’t feeling staying at your people’s crib. On dawgs.”

Tia veered into the middle lane.

“I’ll start looking for apartments,” she said as she exited the highway.

“You should’ve been doing that,” Raheem mumbled under his breath.

Tia shot him a hard look, shaking her head. “Like I was saying—I’m on it.”

They rode in silence for a bit.

"You wanna stop here?" Tia pointed at a barbershop. "Get a cut before we go home?"

Raheem glanced out the window. "Dre’s Barbershop," he read. "Yeah, fuck it. I ain’t never been here before, but anything’s better than a jail cut, right?"

Tia laughed as she pulled over. “You handsome regardless.”

“You would gas me up,” Raheem said, getting out of the car.

He struggled with the door latch.

“What the fuck is up with this shit?” he grumbled.

“Boy, let me help you.” Tia pressed a button, and the door unlocked.

Raheem, embarrassed, muttered, “I had it—”

“I know.”

“But good looking.”

He started to step out, but Tia stopped him.

“Wait a minute.” She reached into her purse. “Here.” She handed him some money.

“What’s this?”

“What it look like? Some money for my man’s pocket.”

Raheem leaned over, kissed her full lips, then said, “Thank you, mommy—for everything.”

“You know I got your black ass.”

Standing outside, half in the car, Raheem grinned. "And you know I got us," he said before closing the door.

CHAPTER TWO

Rrrrring...

Mega picked up his cell from the coffee table, checking the caller ID in case it was a female or one of his desperate baby mamas.

Seeing that it was neither, he answered. "Owooo."

"What it do, fool?" the caller said. "You at the crib?"

"Yeah—why?"

"Because I'm downstairs. Buzz me in."

Mega sighed, annoyed. He hated when people popped up unannounced.

"Aight."

After buzzing the guest in, a knock followed at the door.

Mega opened it.

"What's good, dawg?" the visitor said, giving him a three-finger handshake.

"Money, nigga. Come in."

The guest stepped inside, following Mega into the living room and plopping onto the leather couch.

Mega sat at the opposite end, slightly turned so he could face him.

"Nigga, what the fuck I tell you about popping up unannounced?" Mega snapped. "My moms can't even stop by here without calling first. What makes you think it's cool for you?"

"My bad, my nigga, but it's urgent. And you know I don't play the jack, brody."

"Nah, nigga—you know I don't play the phone," Mega corrected.

This nigga always on some extra tough shit, the guest thought.

"Aight—whatever, you win," he said, annoyed. "I'm just tryna put you on to the war report. That cool?"

Mega gave a small nod, letting him continue.

"I got a call this morning from one of the lil homies in Shirley Max—"

"Wait a minute." Mega held up a finger. "Ain't Two-Times in the Max?"

Just saying the name left a foul taste in his mouth.

"Exactly. But the lil homie and Two-Times banged out on sight and got housed in different units."

Elated, Mega laughed. "That's what's up."

"I'm hip. But let me finish. So, I'm chopping it up with the lil nigga, and he tells me dawg touched the bricks two days ago."

Mega shot to his feet.

"You bullshitting."

"I wish I was."

Mega started pacing. "I can't believe I'm just now hearing this. Why the fuck we just now finding out? If I knew ahead of time, I coulda had him smacked the moment he touched soil. Damn! I'm slipping!"

He fell silent.

"You want me and a few of the guys to hunt dawg down and push him?" the guest asked.

Mega thought for a moment.

"Nah," he finally said. "He expecting that. I'ma put a plan together first. We got time. Knowing Two-Times, he chasing paper—and while he trying to come up, we gonna come down... and park him."

"I like the sounds of that," the guest assured. "But yo, put me on—how the whole beef started with this clown? I always been curious."

Trying to remember how it all started, Mega fell into a deep trance.

It was half a decade ago when Mega made a call: "Yo, where you at?"

"Um on Washington Street," the receiver answered.

"Aight, um on top of Northwell Street. As soon as you turn on the street, ya gonna see me on ya right, in front of the gray building," Mega explained.

"Aight, I'll see you in a second."

"Bet," Mega ended the call. A second; we'll see about that. Inwardly, he questioned the truth in the receiver's statement.

"Excuse me, sir, can you spare a dollar?" Stepping from the side of the building and onto the sidewalk, the crackhead begged. Startled by the crackhead's sudden presence, Mega reached for his gun.

"Stupid nigga!" said Mega after realizing he wasn't in danger. "Are you crazy walking up on me like that?" Never removing his hand from his waist, he looked the man over for signs of a disguise and saw none. "Get the fuck away from me—word! Before I spare you a clip."

"Um sorry, please don't shoot me," the crackhead begged. "I didn't mean any disrespect, I swear." Backing away, the man tripped but immediately got up and hurried down the street, disappearing into the night.

Who Mega was waiting for finally arrived and parked. Climbing into the front passenger seat and closing the door, Mega said, "If it ain't Two-Times, two times."

Two-Times smirked. "What's shaking, kinfolk? How you feeling?"

"Um three hunnit, bro. Like, I can't complain, but I ain't bout to settle either," Mega answered.

"I can dig it."

"But on another note, I wanted to link with you and holla at you about a stick," Mega disclosed.

"Okay, talk to me—what is it looking like?"

"Put it like this. I got a big mouth bass on the hook, and all we have to do is reel it in."

"Give me some detail."

"I've been dealing with this Dominican dude named Manny for about a year now," Mega began. "I established his trust, and now he's comfortable meeting me alone. He's an old head, but he's well respected among his people. They'll press play for the old nigga too—so you already know what that means."

"We gotta smack 'em." Mega smiled. "How much bread and work we talking?" Two-Times asked.

"Hold that question." Mega removed a cigarette from his pocket. "You mind if I light this?"

"Yeah—but go ahead."

He lit the cigarette, took a drag, then said, "Now, what was ya question?"

"I said, how much work and bread we talking bout?" he repeated.

"Nothing less than a ticket of boy and plenty bread."

"You sure?"

"Am I sure? Dawg, um talking about a Dominican. Are you listening?"

"Yeah, um listening," Two-Times said, then stared out the window. "When you trying to do this?" he asked.

"Tomorrow."

Shocked, Two-Times said, "Tomorrow?"

"Yeah." Rolling down the window, Mega discarded the cigarette. "Is that a problem?"

"Naw, I just didn't expect us to dive right in so soon—that's all."

"My nigga, what are you talking about? Do the math. We stick him tomorrow, we're rich tomorrow," Mega stressed.

Thinking, Two-Times cupped his chin with his right hand. Why would this nigga call me out of all people to do a lick with him? We ain't tight. We cool, we from the same hood, but I still don't trust him. Shit, I don't trust nobody like that. Mega is different though. He's a slime-ball on the low. I need that money though.

Seeing that Two-Times was thinking, Mega said, "What's on ya mind? Talk to me—you in or not?" The lack of light made it hard, but Two-Times raised his eyes and looked in Mega's: he searched for an ulterior motive. However, he was unable to decloak one.

"Dawg," Mega spoke, getting impatient. "I don't have all night. I'm missing money right now—let me know something."

"Bro, chill," Two-Times ordered, annoyed. "I had to think real quick. But yeah, um all in."

Applauding Two-Times' decision, Mega said, "That was the smartest decision you ever made in ya life. On dawgs, you won't regret it. I'll take care of everything from here and get with you in the A.M. Make sure ya on deck."

"I live on deck."

"Aight, captain," he said with a hint of sarcasm. "Solo!" He exited the car.

The following morning, Mega drove to Two-Times' house. Parked, he squeezed his hand between the driver's seat and door and retrieved his cell phone.

I hate when that shit happens, Mega complained inwardly. He then called Two-Times to inform him of his arrival and to tell him to unlock the front door so he could walk straight into the house. Standing on a porch, waiting for however long for someone to answer and let you inside, could be fatal.

Two-Times' phone rung once then went straight to voicemail. "Fuck it." Mega cursed, grabbed the bookbag occupying the passenger seat, and climbed out the car. Going against his better judgment, he ascended the porch and rang the doorbell. Shortly later, he heard a voice belonging to a woman.

"Who is it?" the voice asked.

"It's Mega! Um here for Two–Times!"

"Oh! Okay, hold on please!"

Mega held on; he didn't have a choice. But while doing so, he clutched the gun under his hoodie, looked over his shoulders, and secured his surroundings. Clear.

When the door finally swung open, Two-Times stood in the threshold with a wifebeater and polo sweatpants on. "Top of the morning. Come in." Two–Times greeted and welcomed Mega inside. From there, he led the way to the basement, which was furnished with a long-tattered couch and a high wooden table.

On opposite sides of the table, they stood and discussed business.

"What's in the bookbag?" Two-Times inquired.

Mega removed the bag from his back and tossed it over to Two-Times. "Ya costume."

"My costume," Two-Times repeated, confused.

"Would you just open it. Damn!"

Two-Times opened the bag, pulled out the costume, and laid it across the table. "Dawg," he said, looking the costume over, "what the fuck is this supposed to be? Like, what the fuck you take me for? Ya a funny dude."

Pressing his hand against his chest, as if offended, Mega said, "How um funny?"

In an attempt to disguise his aggravation, Two-Times laughed half-heartedly. "You just are," he said. "But fuck all that, explain what we doing."

"Aight, peep game," Mega held up his index finger, then covered his mouth and coughed. "Excuse me. So, peep, one night Manny, the Dominican connect, was so thirsty for some pussy he offered me two fingers of boy to fuck this bitch I was with. So, knowing me—I made it happen. But the dumb nigga didn't have a place to hit the hoe at, so he brought the grimy bitch to his stash house and started bragging."

A smile crept across Two-Times' face.

"Look at you," Mega said. "Now you see my vision, huh? Anyway, I arranged to meet dawg in the morning. This morning, I should say—at ten." He gazed at his watch. "It's eight fifty now. I figured we catch him at the stash house, because he's gonna stop there first, then come serve me—feel what um saying?"

Instead of answering the question, Two-Times asked one. "How you meet this dude?" He wanted to make sure he wasn't about to play a role in robbing an undercover agent.

"My man Cisco from New Bedford plugged me in with him. Manny ain't the feds if that's what ya thinking. Cisco is a very careful dude, and plus, I would'a sniffed him out by now."

Before he replied, Two-Times questioned whether he could trust Mega's judgment. "I hope ya right," he finally said. "Let me go grab my blick."

Manny was extremely upset to arrive at his safe house—located in Health Street Projects—and see someone sprawled out on the front steps. The man was obviously a junkie, strung out on drugs.

Thinking, Manny said inwardly: Des last ting I need is a junkie hanging around. Next ting ju know, feds will be kicking doors down and handing out indictments.

"Hey," Manny said, nudging the junkie with his Pledger'Devoe loafer. "Come on, get up—ju have to take dis elsewhere." He demanded, shoving the junkie to wake up. The trespasser hardly budged, which caused Manny to shove the man once more. The junkie showed signs of life and turned over on his side. "Hey! Hey ju, ju"—shocked to be suddenly looking down a barrel, Manny lost his voice.

"Don't move or yell," Two-Times ordered, keeping the .375 revolver steady as he reclined the hammer.

He didn't yell, but he did try to speak; however, fear kept him from uttering a word, and so he inched backward, scanned his surroundings, and prayed for assistance from anyone.

Partly behind him, on his left, he saw a silhouette from his peripheral. Dis mi chance, Manny thought and started to take off.

"Didn't my man tell you not to move." But Mega ruined his plan and shoved the Glock 19 he possessed into Manny's stomach.

"Como este mamagüevo (damn this dick sucker)," Manny grunted.

"You know what time it is," Mega said, grinning. "Take us to the hidden treasure. Now."

Against his own will, Manny led them through a filthy, dark hallway that smelled of urine. They then ascended three flights of stairs, stepping on crack pipes and cigarette butts. Silently, Manny prayed the whole time.

They reached the door to the safe house and ordered Manny to open it.

"Ju making big mistake, mi friend," Manny uttered, and Two-Times hit him over the head with the butt of his gun.

"Nigga, open the fucking door," Two-Times demanded. "This ya last chance and only choice."

"Okay!" Manny squealed, "Okay!" Shaking nervously, he unlocked the door, and together they entered the apartment.

After securing the door, Mega kicked Manny in the lower part of his back and made him fall to the floor—it was time to get to business. On opposite sides, Mega, the betrayer, and Two-Times, his crony, grabbed a handful of Manny's collar and dragged him to the living room, duct-taping his mouth and zip-tying his hands. While doing the same to his ankles, they were caught off guard by the sound of a toilet flushing and froze.

Two-Times' mind raced. "You heard that?" Not giving Mega a chance to reply, he swiftly maneuvered through the apartment, heading in the direction the flushing came from.

Locating where the noise came from, he placed his back against the wall and tightened his grip around his gun. Come on, mutha'fucker, he urged.

First, there was movement; then, the bathroom door flew open, and Two-Times didn't spare a second: he pushed off the wall and stuck the sleek .375 to the Hispanic man's forehead. Surprised, the Hispanic man said, "Mierda loco, ¿qué? (Damn nigga, what?)," and raised both hands in the air.

"Get on your knees. Now!" Two-Times commanded. Slowly, the Hispanic man did as he was told. "Please don't kill me," he begged.

"Crawl to the living room."

"Papa, please. Please, no kill mi."

"Then do as I say when I say it." Now putting his faith in his cooperation, the Hispanic man followed Two-Times' order.

With one foot on Manny's back, Mega watched the Hispanic man crawl through the threshold and into the living room with Two-Times in tow, aiming at the back of his head.

"Who the fuck is he?" Mega asked, aback.

"He's the guy," Two-Times began. "Ya guy was hoping on saving the day." Mega looked at Manny with contempt: stumbling across Manny's drug-sitter was a pure threat towards his life.

Mega kneeled so he and Manny could be at eye level and asked, "Is that true? You were trying to lead us into a trap? Huh, Manny? Huh? That's. What. You. Was. Trying. To. Do?" After every word, just beneath Manny's left eye, Mega poked him in the same spot with the nose of his gun. "Um'a take that as a yes." Standing, he kicked Manny in the side, then handed Two-Times the roll of duct tape. "Duct tape that nigga's mouth and shit," he said, then refocused on Manny. "Now back to you. The games is over. Where's the dope and money?" Partly, he peeled back the tape over Manny's mouth.

"Nothing here, mi friend," Manny uttered.

Mega looked at Manny as if he was pathetic. "You must think I'm stupid," he said.

Two-Times, on the other hand, heard Manny's statement and planned on proving his intelligence. He slid over to the TV—which was the only thing in the room besides an old chair—and turned the volume up to its max. From there, he walked over to the Hispanic man, planted the barrel of his gun to the back of the man's head, and said, "Mega, make Manny face me."

Mega did. Two-Times fired.

Again, Mega peeled the tape back from Manny's mouth and began to speak. However, before he asked a question, Manny puked. Done, Manny said, "It's in di kitchen. Di stuff in di kitchen, papa, under the sink. Ju lift up di floor, it's all dere." Tears rolled down his face. "Please, papa, no kill mi. Mi have family."

Through laughter, Mega said, "Who said anything about killing you? Oh, scary nigga."

After about fifteen minutes, they had finally cleaned out what they had discovered and were cutting through the living room to leave. Two-Times was ahead of Mega and wasn't aware that Mega had stopped until he looked over his shoulder and saw him standing idle, pointing his gun.

Two-Times came to a halt. "What you doing?"

Mega looked from Manny to Two-Times, then back at Manny. "I told you already how this had to go."

When Two-Times and Mega finally got done counting the money and weighing the heroin they robbed Manny for, they had smoked half an ounce of weed in Mega's bedroom.

"Three bricks, one key of cut, and half a mill," Mega said and sighed. "That's what you call a sweet lick. I need a drink." He popped a bottle of Moët.

"Kinfolk," Two-Times began. "Did you say half a mill?"

"Straight cash!" Mega answered.

"That's a lot of chicken." Two-Times couldn't quite comprehend the magnitude of his present situation. It felt unreal. Not even the overwhelming smell of money and opium convinced him. Just yesterday, he was broke. So, to be rich, in his eyes, today was unbelievable.

"Damn," Mega said. "We need some more Backwoods."

"I'm'a go to the store and snatch some. You want me to bring you anything back?" Two-Times asked.

"Yeah, just grab me something to drink."

"I got'cha."

Two-Times looked to his left and spotted a .25 automatic pistol on top of a dresser. "Yo, is that slammer straight?"

"What slammer?"

Pointing at the chrome and black weapon, Two-Times said, "That one."

"Oh—yeah, it's three hunnit."

Two-Times put the pistol in his pocket. "Aight, I'll be back."

Stepping to the side, Two-Times allowed a tall man to exit Scottie's corner store on Northfolk Street before he entered and went over to the cooler, grabbing two Arizona iced teas and approaching the counter.

"Let me get five packs of Backwoods," he said, addressing the pretty young woman behind the counter.

"I.D., please," the cashier requested.

"Are you kidding me? I been coming here coppin' Woods since I was twelve." Reluctantly, he showed her his I.D., and she began adding up the items he wanted to purchase.

"Thank you. Altogether, that will be forty-two dollars and sixty-nine cents," the cashier said and smiled.

"Sixty-nine, huh?" Flirting a bit, Two-Times handed the cashier a fifty-dollar bill. "Thank you too."

She blushed, and he left.

Outside, Two-Times climbed in the rental car he rented and put the plastic bag he was carrying in the back seat. He then turned the car on and started to press the gas, but suddenly, half a dozen unmarked police cars came from different directions and boxed him in.

Simultaneously, plainclothes officers abandoned their vehicles and drew their weapons. "Don't fucking move!" they all ordered, surrounding Two-Times' car. "Don't move!"

Standing outside the driver's door, pointing a Glock at Two-Times, a white officer shouted, "Let me see your hands!"

Two-Times made them visible.

"Now put them on the steering wheel, slowly."

Having no other options, he complied.

Hurriedly, the cop standing outside the driver's door and another officer yanked Two-Times out of the driver's seat, threw him to the ground, and cuffed him. From beneath the knees on his neck and back, all he could do was wonder…

Why now?

Transported to the C-11 precinct, Dorchester District, Two-Times was processed, booked, and then ushered to a gloomy cell. Hesitating at first, he stepped through the threshold, and the metal blue door slid closed, confining him.

Above him, through a dusty vent, cool air blew hard, causing goosebumps to crawl up his arms. It was unbearably cold, and he had nothing—not a quilt, not a hoody, not a thing to keep warm.

Soaked in misery, he pulled his arms through his shirt sleeves and sat on the steel bench.

What the fuck just happened? he thought.

Three hours passed, and Two-Times' condition hadn't changed. What started as a good day had now turned into the worst. With a seventy-five-thousand-dollar bail, he contemplated calling his grandmother and telling her to go over to Mega's house to grab his half of the money.

I know it's blood money, he thought, *and she wouldn't want shit to do with it, but I gotta get the fuck out of here, on dawgs! But what about the work though?* He questioned himself. *I'll just grab my half myself later. God knows I'd never involve my grandmother in no dumb shit, but...*

He pondered long and hard.

"Man, fuck it," Two-Times said after making up his mind. "It's unfortunate, but Grandma-dukes gonna have to come through for me one time, two times."

He picked up the glossy black telephone mounted on the wall and dialed.

After the phone rang six times, Two-Times' grandmother answered and accepted the collect call.

"Hello? Hello?"

"Nana!"

"Yes, baby. What's going on?" she asked.

"I'm locked up," Two-Times disclosed.

"I can see that. But why?"

"I don't have enough time to explain, but they said I was under investigation. Some kind of drug sting. But right now, I'm only charged with possession of a firearm and possession of ammunition."

"Oh God, child. Are you okay?" she asked, worried.

"Yes—but no. Nana, listen, I'm at C-11, and I have a seventy-five-thousand-dollar bail—"

"That sounds serious."

"Nana, please. I know." He shook his head impatiently. "You hear me?" he asked.

"I hear you, boy."

"I need you to make a three-way call to my friend and pick up some money for me so I can bail out." Two-Times closed his eyes and hoped she'd do it.

"Someone gonna lend you that kind of money? What kind of person is this you want me to meet?"

"Nana, will you please? I only have so much time."

"All right, boy. What's the number?"

"617-445-3632. Ask for Mega."

"What kind of name is Mega? Hold on," she said and clicked over.

"Oowooo!" Mega answered.

"Kinfolk! It's Two-Times."

"Dawg—where the fuck are you?" Mega asked.

"My nigga, I'm at C-11, jammed up for the blick. My bail is seventy-five though."

"Bro, that's crazy, you was just here," Mega reflected.

"On dawgs!"

"But fuck all that—what you need me to do?"

"I'ma send my grandma your way. Swing her my half of the chicken."

"Nuff said, I got you."

"Aight, bet. She's on the line now. When I hang up, shoot her your address."

"I got you," Mega assured.

"Good looking, bro. What's a real nigga without some real niggas?"

"A real nigga."

"Nana!" Two-Times called.

"Yes, baby, I hear you."

"I'm 'bout to hang up. Get my man's address and—"

"I already know, boy," Nana said, cutting Two-Times off.

"Okay, Miss Lady, you got it," Two-Times teased. "I love you. See you soon."

He hung up the phone.

Two-Times counted on his Nana. She had been there since his mother was killed—and even before that.

Nana made it to Mega's house in no time and called his cell phone.

"Yo," Mega answered.

Displeased, Nana looked at her phone, then said, "Hey darling, I'm out front. I'm actually at the door." She laughed.

"Aight, I'm coming down," Mega said.

"Okay, hun."

After five minutes turned into ten, and she was still at the door waiting, she decided to call Mega back to make sure he hadn't forgotten she was outside. But the second she pressed send, Mega appeared.

Jumping, Nana held her hands over her chest. "Oh Lord, child, you scared me."

"My fault," Mega said, reaching into his pocket. Pulling out a wad of money, he peeled two twenties off the top. "Ya grandson,

Raheem—Two-Times." He chuckled. "Tell him if his name wasn't Two-Times, he would've only gotten one twenty. But since it's Two-Times, here's two."

He threw the two twenties in the air.

"Now get the fuck off my porch before I turn ya old ass into dust. Oh—and tell that nigga I never liked his black ass since day one. O.T.S., bitch."

Mega's phone rang, snapping him back to reality.

"Yo, you good, gun-smoke? You zoned out real quick," said the unwanted guest.

"I'm hip," Mega said. "I just went back in time. Shit crazy."

"Yeah…? What was so crazy about it? Put me on."

Mega looked at his guest. "Maybe next time—it's a long story. Plus, I got a bunch of shit to do right now, starting with answering this call."

And he wants me to ride and die for him? What am I riding—and possibly—gonna die for? the guest thought. *This nigga got me fucked up.*

CHAPTER THREE

Every night before bed—since Raheem returned home—Tia made sure she felt her man inside her. And tonight was no different than last night.

"Daddy," Tia moaned. "I'm cumming… Cum with me."

Raheem released in her, then rolled over. "Damn, that thing is good," he uttered. "Where that loud at?"

"I got it," Tia reminded him.

"Roll up."

Tia smiled. "I got you, Daddy."

Raheem sat up, giving Tia his lustrous back, and took a deep breath.

"Yo, I need to holla at you," he said.

"What's up, baby? Talk to Mommi," she said, throwing her arms over Raheem's shoulders. "Is everything all right?"

Raheem waited for a moment, then said, "I'm not feeling our situation. And don't get me wrong, I love ya grandparents, but living with them is fucking with my ego. Tiptoeing and creeping around ain't my style."

Oh my God, here we go again, Tia thought, rolling her eyes.

"So you wanna live in the streets instead?" she snapped. "'Cause right now, it is what it is. Like, you make me feel like I'm not taking care of business. I'm on that computer looking for our own shit every day, all day. So don't make me feel like I'm content."

Shaking his head, Raheem stood up. "You just don't get it," he said.

Tia climbed out of bed and stood on the floor.

"What is it to get?" she asked. "Huh, Raheem? What is it to get? I wanna know."

"You don't get how I feel and how this shit is fucking with my pride. I'm twenty-eight years old, staying at my bitch's grandparents' crib. How that sound? Crazy! That's how that shit sound."

"Daddy," Tia said, taking a deep breath. "You're putting too much pressure on yourself. I know you wanna be in your own shit, but you just came home last month. Be patient and let's rebuild while we got the chance. You missed out on a lot, Daddy, and we need to catch up."

Pity begged in her eyes.

He disregarded her plea. "Patience?" he repeated. "What you know about patience? I been patient for five years—the fuck you talkin' bout?"

"And I was patiently waiting for you them same five years—you forgot?"

"My nigga, I don't give—"

Before he said something he'd regret, he caught himself. "At the end of the day, I'm uncomfortable here. Period!"

Tia folded her arms across her chest.

"And you think I am? Huh, Raheem? I want our own shit just as bad as you do. Believe me."

"I can't tell."

"For real, you mad disrespectful. No bullshit."

Feeling unappreciated, she reflected on those lonely nights when she was sexually frustrated, and those long days when she wanted to be held but held out because she cared about the feelings of the man now standing before her, being inconsiderate.

I should've fucked on this nigga. Negative thoughts clouded her mind.

"I'm not disrespectful—I'm fed up. I'm done holding my breath, sneaking around, pretending like I don't exist, like I'm some fucking ghost. And another thing, I'm not 'bout to be in them streets tryin' to get bread, looking out for the dicks and watching out for them kids. I'm done with gang-banging and gettin' money—the shit don't work nor mix—"

"What you tryna say?" Tia interrupted.

"If ya listening—"

"I been listening—"

"Then continue. So like I was sayin', the shit don't mix. So I gotta make changes, 'cause this time around, I'm getting straight to the bag. No distractions. So with that being said, I'm sliding back down South."

Tia's nose flared.

"That was your plan from the start," she screamed. "Nigga, I ain't do that bid with you for nothing," she said, pointing in his face. "You a bitch-ass nigga. I swear to God, on your niggas, I should've been fucked on you—"

"Word?"

"Word! You never was shit. You just like the rest of these fake-ass niggas. *Ain't shit nigga.* And I fucking hate you. I swear I hate you, Raheem."

"Real nigga shit," Raheem said, fed up. "You better watch ya mouth."

"What you say? Watch my mouth?" she questioned. "Nigga, you do a bid with a bitch, and let her tell you that she going down South thirty days after her release—fuck calling her a bitch, you'd try to kill her. So don't stand here and tell me to watch my mouth. I'm hurt! To hear you really say to my face—after all those years of being faithful—that you about to leave a bitch lonely *again*… Hurt. Like, you haven't even paid me back in dick."

Raheem shrugged.

"It is what it is."

"It is what it is, Raheem?" She tried slapping him but missed.

To create distance, he extended his arm and said, "On dawgs—relax."

"I swear on everything I love, the day you walk out of here and go down South is the same day I walk out your life. Your ball, your court."

Tia spun, got into bed, and pulled the covers over her head. The effects of betrayal pierced her heart. She couldn't fathom how the man she loved and put her life on hold for could actually consider being away from her after so many years apart.

Tears fell as she fell asleep.

13 ½ 13 ½ 13 ½

Turning onto the narrow street where Tia's grandparents lived, Hommi spoke through his cellphone.

"I'm on ya strip, cuzo. Come outside."He was excited to see his cousin Raheem.

Hommi and Raheem were blood-related through Raheem's father, who was Hommi's uncle. Hommi was two years older, but still, they were the best of friends.

Hommi spotted Raheem standing on the porch and pulled over to park. *Look at this black-ass nigga,* he thought.

Before exiting the car, he let an oncoming car pass, then got out.

"What's shaking!" Hommi called, crossing the street.

"Them kids when they see me!" Raheem responded, meeting Hommi with a three-finger handshake, followed by a brotherly hug.

Hommi released Raheem. "It's been a grip since the last time we were together," he said. "Look at you. I see you on ya brawlic shit."

"Oh, you see me?" Raheem joked. "Yeah, man, I was in there on my *get big* shit. But on dawgs, my nigg, it really been a minute since I saw you. Those crackers don't play fair. They split us, then smoke us every chance they get."

"No bullshit," Hommi agreed. "But we got eighteen hours to chop it up. Grab ya shit so we can stab out."

"Damn, I'm buggin'," Raheem said, annoyed. "I left my shit in the crib. I'ma go grab it real quick."

While he went to retrieve his luggage, Hommi waited on the porch.

During the wait, an Acura TLX cruised down the street and came to a complete stop in front of Tia's grandparents' house, right in the middle of the road. Hommi tried looking through the tinted windows, but the five-percent tints made it near impossible.

Who the fuck is that inside that car? Hommi questioned, reaching for his waistband. He threw his left arm in the air.

"What's good!" Hommi hollered. "What's sup! You know me?"

13 ½ 13 ½ 13 ½

Gazing at Hommi, the man driving the Acura TLX spoke to himself.

Look at this nigga, bluffin' like he got the hammer. I know you, nigga—you woulda been started firing... I should clap this nigga.

Instead, he cracked the window an inch, letting Hommi get a whiff of the weed smoke.

"I'll see you again," he mouthed, then revved up the car. "And when I do, I'ma burn you."

He sped off.

13 ½ 13 ½ 13 ½

Raheem heard tires screeching and stormed outside just in time to see the back of the Acura before it disappeared.

"You straight?"

"Whoever was in that Acura was on some funny shit," Hommi said.

"You was able to see who it was? Could you recognize the nigga?"

"Not really. The whip was tinted down. Dawg cracked his window, though, and I could tell he had long braids."

Hommi hadn't even been in the city a full day and had already crossed paths with trouble.

"These niggas gonna force a nigga's hand," Raheem muttered, rubbing over his waves. "Help me with these bags so we can flex."

From across the street, while Hommi and Raheem loaded the gym bags into the trunk, Tia stared at Raheem with a disgusted scowl.

"Kinfolk," Raheem called after they were done. "I'ma go holla at wifey real fast."

Raheem stuck his right hand down his pants, pulled out fifty grams of heroin from his boxer briefs, and handed it to Hommi.

"I'ma stash this while you holla at shorty."

Raheem walked over to Tia and tried to hug her.

"No, Raheem," she said, rejecting him. "You get nothing."

"Stop being like that," Raheem began. "You can't fault me for wanting to provide."

Tia placed her hands on her hips. "I don't fault you for that—it's *how* you goin' about it that's pissing me off. But whatever. You gon' do what you want regardless—I can see that."

Raheem palmed his face and took a deep breath.

"I'm not doin' what I want," he said. "I'm doin' what I *have* to do. Again, all I need is two months. That's it. Nothing more, nothing less. I promise."

Pulling Tia close, he kissed her on her full lips.

"Your lips so soft."

As Raheem crossed the street, he looked over his shoulder and saw Tia still standing there. So, he spun completely around and said, "I love you, girl. I'll call you as soon as I touch."

13 ½ 13 ½ 13 ½

Mega met a crony at his favorite restaurant—Flames.

Flames was a Jamaican restaurant that served some of the best Caribbean dishes in Boston. At the restaurant, you, too, were liable to run into anyone.

Over a plate of rice and beans smothered with curry shrimp, Mega's crony explained what he saw in front of Tia's grandparents' house earlier that day.

"So, like I was saying, dawg I caught on the porch was light-skinned."

"He was light-skinned?" Mega asked.

"Yeah. And he was kinda tall with braids. Real skinny too," the crony said.

Mega ate his food, then said, "That's the nigga Hommi."

"Who the fuck is he?"

"He's Two-Times' cousin," Mega asserted. "His name is actually Heron-Homm, but they call him Hommi for short."

"What's the static with him?"

"He give it up for his tribe. Caught a few smacks. But he be O.T. tryna get a couple dollars."

"Hmph—I'm not impressed," the crony said, taking a bite of his food. He then continued, "These motherfuckin' plantains bomb. You shoulda got some."

"Man, fuck those plantains. It's more important shit to worry about." Mega leaned in. "Like, for instance, did you see what type of car the nigga Hommi was drivin'? Did you get the license plate number?"

The crony gave Mega's question some thought, then said, "He had to be pushin' a Chevrolet Malibu—rental though. I ain't sure what state, but it had out-of-state tags."

"Lemme ask you somethin'," Mega said, looking him in the eyes. "Why you ain't clip dawg?"

"'Cause I ain't know who the nigga was. And I only like puttin' dawgs under my belt."

CHAPTER FOUR

Hommi tapped Raheem on the shoulder.

"Two-Times," he called. "Nigga, wake up. We gettin' pulled over."

Rubbing the cold out of his eyes, Raheem asked, "What happened?"

"We gettin' pulled over," Hommi answered, preparing to stop the car.

Raheem sat up and buckled his seatbelt. "Where we at?" he asked. "And what the fuck we gettin' jacked for?"

"We in V.A.," Hommi said.

In the breakdown lane, the car came to a complete stop.

"Now it's startin' to make sense. I bet you it's a redneck jackin' us."

Hommi looked in the rearview mirror. "Sure is. And here he come."

Approaching the vehicle with caution, the state trooper blinded them both with his flashlight. In his mind, he was ready to draw his police-issued pistol at the drop of a dime and shoot them both.

It's dark, and they're Black...

Justified homicide.

The trooper smirked.

Although unsuccessful, Hommi tried blocking the light from his face with the palm of his hand.

"Good evening, officer—"

"License and registration, boy," the state trooper ordered, cutting Hommi off.

Is this cracker crazy? Hommi wondered. *Who the fuck he callin' boy?* He thought about expressing his feelings but bit his tongue. *Redneck lucky I'm dirty, Dawgs.*

Opening the visor slowly, Hommi grabbed what the trooper requested. "Here you go, officer," he said, handing it over.

"It's trooper, boy." The trooper snatched the license and registration and examined them.

"I apologize, sir, but may I ask why you pulled me over?"

"No. But you could stop actin' stupid—you know why I pulled you over."

"Actually, I don't. I was goin' the speed limit."

"Damn the speed limit. It's common sense—you're Black. And to make matters worse, you're drivin' on *my* highway, and ten times outta ten, you boys up to no good." With the back of his hand, he tapped the car door. "You boys sit tight—I'll be back."

"I hate white people," Hommi muttered.

Raheem flipped down the visor and looked in the mirror. Red and blue lights lit up the sky.

"Cuzo," Raheem called.

"Yo."

"This clown called backup."

"Say on dawgs!"

"Nigga, look for yaself."

Hommi checked the side mirror and saw a line of cruisers pulling up along the road, troopers now marching with dogs.

"Fuck, bro. Here they come. Just stay smooth."

I shoulda listened to my bitch, Raheem thought.

One trooper opened the driver's door. "Step out the vehicle," he demanded in a thick Southern accent.

"Step out for what?" Hommi asked.

"I'm sure you already know why. Now step out before me and my brothers help you."

Raheem and Hommi stared at each other, trying to read one another's minds, then reluctantly exited the car.

"This some bullshit," Hommi mumbled.

"What was that, boy?" the trooper snapped. "If you knew what's good for you, you'd shut ya rabbit-ass mouth. You hear me?"

Rather than answering, Hommi assumed position so the trooper could pat-frisk him.

"He's clean, sir!" the trooper confirmed to his supervisor.

"Go join ya buddy at the rear of the cruiser, son."

As Hommi walked to the back of the cruiser, an eighteen-wheeler sped by, honking its horn, nearly blowing him to the ground.

"Yo," Raheem whispered. "Where you stash the work?"

Hommi talked into his fist. "We gon' be straight. If not, I'll take the charge. You just came home."

"That sound cool and all, but if they book you, we both goin' to jail. What the fuck I look like lettin' you go down in Virginia while I go home? That won't sit right with me, dawgs."

"Speak up," said a short, stocky trooper standing nearby. "What happened? Nothin' to say, huh?" He eyed Hommi and Raheem. "What was you whisperin' to ya buddy?"

"I don't know what you talkin' about," Raheem said.

"Yeah, I bet." The trooper dropped the conversation but continued watching them closely.

When the squad of troopers finished ransacking the vehicle, one officer walked over to the supervisor and said,

"They're clean."

The supervisor's face hardened.

"Can't be," he muttered, walking a few feet down the dark road. He eyed Hommi and Raheem. He couldn't see himself just lettin' them go. *Maybe I should plant somethin' on 'em.*

"I see you two sons of bitches are some city slickers," the supervisor said, a mouth full of chewing tobacco. "Now, I don't give a damn if we ain't find nothin' or not—I *know* you no-good half-a-monkeys are dirty as dirt. And I swear before Almighty God, if I catch you drivin' through *my* state again, I won't give a donkey's ass if y'all clean as a whistle—the both of you goin' to prison."

Spit flew from his mouth. "Do y'all hear me?" He waited, but neither responded. "Get y'all Black asses out my beloved state."

As Hommi veered into the middle lane, he worked on easing his nerves.

"That shit was close," Raheem asserted. "I swore we was done, no bullshit."

"I told you we was straight," Hommi replied.

"I'm hip, but no funny shit, my nigga. When I saw all them rednecks with them dogs, I was like—*it's a wrap.* Air-seal or not, I thought them motherfuckers was gonna smell that drop-dead dope."

Hommi laughed.

"Nigga, you laughin'—ain't shit funny." Raheem shook his head. "Where you put the work at, though? Let me find out you had it tucked." He joked.

"Let you find out I had it tucked." Sarcastically, Hommi mocked Raheem. "Where the hell I'ma tuck fifty grams at, you fuckin' weirdo?"

Raheem laughed. "I asked you."

"Ya burnt," Hommi asserted, then continued, "Real shit though, I stashed it in the ceiling."

"The ceiling of what?"

"Of the whip."

"Why?" Raheem asked, looking for a logical answer.

After glancing in the rearview mirror, Hommi explained, "Cause when the dogs sniff for drugs, they never sniff what's over them. They only smell what's in front of 'em and underneath. I know what I'm doin', nigga."

Raheem thought about what Hommi said and couldn't remember one time he'd seen a K-9 sniff the roof of a car.

"Damn, kinfolk," Raheem said. "I gotta admit—that was smooth. I woulda never thought of that."

"That's what I'm here for."

"Word." Raheem agreed.

For the duration of the drive, they filled each other in on their lives. They made no stops except for gas and food until they arrived in Conway, South Carolina.

Turning onto Wild Wing Boulevard, they pulled up to a two-bedroom condo—one Hommi had rented in advance for Raheem's release.

The complex was mostly college students—mixed as far as race—but quiet and well-kept.

One after the other, they entered the condo.

Hommi locked the door. "This it, cuzo," Hommi said, turning around. "You like it?"

Raheem took in the off-white carpet, the 80-inch flat-screen mounted on the wall, and nodded. "Yeah, kinfolk. I'm diggin' it." He smoothed his hand over the stainless-steel kitchen countertop and fridge. "On dawgs."

"You haven't even seen your room."

"Shit, where is it?"

Hommi pointed toward the bedroom. "It's around the corner there."

Raheem checked out the room and returned.

"Yo!" he called. "That room is tough. But that bathroom—bro, the stand-up glass shower, the deep-dish sink with the marble trimming, and that mirror nearly wrapping the entire wall—that shit is stupid hard."

"I'm glad you like it 'cause that's you—you deserve it. But let me call Chief, tell him we touched down, and have him come through."

"Yeah, do that. Tell him to bring some smoke too."

"Got'cha."

Chief was an influential figure. The people of Myrtle Beach called him *The Mayor.* He had the keys to the city, and his hands were in everybody's—who was somebody's—pocket.

Chief was a dark-skinned man with jet-black hair and pearly white teeth. Well-built and tall, he kept a fade so sharp it looked fresh *every* time you saw him. His voice, however, was low; when he spoke, it was as if he was whispering.

Nevertheless, there wasn't anything in the town Chief wasn't aware of, nor was there a damn thing he couldn't find out. His only downfall was his love for cocaine and women.

"Yo," Raheem called.

"What's up?" Hommi answered.

"We might as well start baggin' the work up now while we wait on Chief," he suggested.

"Dawg, we just got off the road."

"What that mean?"

"You right. I'ma grab the wax paper from my room."

Returning, Hommi poured the wax paper out of the box onto the kitchen counter, followed by a digital scale. "You wanna bag up the whole fifty grams in bundles?"

Raheem put down a slip he had just finished applying dope to and pondered.

"Nah," he finally decided. "Let's just bag up half first and put the rest in some rice."

"Bet. I'ma put some music on."

While they inserted the cinnamon-brown, powdery drug into small, square wax slips and listened to a rap artist named *Young Scooter,* a sudden knock at the door startled them.

"I got it," Raheem announced, looking through the peephole. Noticing who was on the other side, he opened the door.

"What's good wit'chu fools!" Chief said, stepping through the threshold.

"You already know!" Hommi said. "This money!"

Immediately, Chief noticed the small amount of heroin on the kitchen counter.

"I see. What y'all got here?"

"That's that drop-dead dope," Raheem disclosed.

"Shittt, I'ma be the judge of that. Let me take a look." Chief examined the merchandise. "Yeah, y'all boys got some fire. Where y'all get this from?"

"Now you askin' too many questions," Raheem said. "The important question is—can you make it disappear?"

"I move mountains, bruh—you know that. How much of it we got to move?" Chief asked.

"Two hunnit bundles," Hommi answered.

Raheem looked at him from the corner of his eye, wishing he never threw out a number.

Raheem trusted Chief—but that was exactly the problem. He always believed that if you had to ask yourself whether you could trust somebody, they probably weren't worth trusting. But in contrast, he knew you always gotta protect yourself from the ones you do trust. Because usually, it's the ones you trust that cross you the worst.

Chief scratched his head.

"Ah, shit. That ain't 'bout nothin'. Y'all do know it's two hunnit a bundle down here, right?"

"Yeah, we already hip," Hommi informed him. "But we sellin' 'em to you for a dollar fifty a bundle."

"Shit, I ain't 'bout to complain. Especially if y'all keep it comin' like this—we'll be rich in a few months."

Raheem rubbed his palms together.

"Ah," Chief continued, "I'ma make some calls now."

"See, cuzo," Hommi started. "I told you this was the move."

"I can't stunt—you did say the boy out here is the wave," Raheem admitted.

"Roll up some smoke, though. I feel a headache comin' along."

Thinking ahead, Raheem tried predicting how much they'd make once they finished flipping the fifty grams of heroin. After considering necessities and possible losses, he concluded their first return should be about seven thousand dollars.

"Aye, ah," Chief said, hanging up his phone. "Let's bend a corner or two. Bring three, four bundles too."

"Aight," Raheem said, grabbing five bundles just in case. The remaining drugs, he put away.

"You drivin', kinfolk," Hommi said, tossing Raheem the car keys. "I drove all the way here."

"You got that. Ya'll ready?"

"Yeah, let's stab out."

13 ½ 13 ½ 13 ½

Outside of Tia's grandparent's house, two of Mega's henchmen sat in a car, waiting. In hopes of catching Raheem coming in or going out, they had been staking the home out for hours.

"Yo—niggas been outside this broad's spot for hours, gun-smoke, and neither dawg nor his Black-ass bitch came out yet. I'm gettin' frustrated sittin' in this car, word!" the henchman in the passenger seat complained.

"Dawg, relax. This takes patience," said the driver.

"Fuck all that *Art of War* shit you talkin'—I ain't wit' this sittin' duck shit. I'm tryna bust my gun. My ass hurt, and some more shit," he said, shifting around in his seat.

"Don't worry, gun-smoke—you gon' bust ya gun," the driver assured him.

"Oh, I know I am. 'Cause I don't care if it's ol' boy or his bitch—whoever come out that house, together or alone, gettin' smacked."

"I just hope you know how to shoot."

The passenger gripped his Glock 40.

"*Know how to shoot?* Nigga, who haven't I shot?" he asked, feeling like his ability to shoot and kill was being questioned. The driver made no effort to answer.

"You just *hope* I know how to shoot," he mocked. "First of all, if you don't shoot a nigga in arm's reach—you fired wrong."

13 ½ 13 ½ 13 ½

During the drive to a small town called Socastee, Chief put Raheem and Hommi on to two young men getting some decent money. He explained how the two had the trailer park in Socastee on lock—and from what he heard, they weren't about to let go without a fight.

"There go the trailer right there," Chief said as they drove by.

"The trailer park right there, right?" Hommi asked, rhetorically.

"Their bando is farther in the back of the park, though," Chief said.

Raheem checked the rearview mirror and glanced at Hommi, trying to see if he was picking up what he was thinking.

"What they fuck with—the white or the brown?" Raheem asked.

"The brown."

"I didn't hear you."

"They doing their thing with the brown," Chief repeated.

"Who are they?" Raheem pressed. "Where they from?"

"Ah, shit, where they from?" Chief asked, scratching his head. "Oh, they outta Lake City. They brothers—twins. Been out in Socastee a while now."

Hommi finally chimed in. "They keep work in the trap with them?" he asked.

"Um, I can't say yeah—but I'm sure they do," Chief answered.

"How much you think they holding in there?" Hommi inquired.

"I'd say dem boys got at least a quarter brix in dere. I'm ninety percent sure. And I say ninety percent 'cause I know these fools. Niggas down my way keep a brix in the trap—that's everyday shit."

"What about their tribe?" Raheem asked.

"Their what?"

"Their tribe—their circle. The niggas they run with. What's up with them?"

"Oh, that's what you mean," Chief said. "Ah, I'ma say this—their camp ain't pussy, but they not cowboys either. Their camp, though, might be the least of ya worries. From what I heard, the twins don't break bread like they supposed to. I put any amount of money on it—if some goons ran them fuck niggas up outta there, took over, and showed love, the rest of them niggas would jump ship or haul ass."

"Yeah, I hear that," Raheem said. "But if we run them out of town, we ain't fuckin' with them afterward. Eagles don't flock with ducks, kinfolk."

Chief pulled out his cellphone. "I respect it," he said. "But pull up to the Super 8 on ya left. Drive around back."

Raheem did as Chief said and parked.

"Let me see two bundles," Chief requested.

Hommi scanned the parking lot, then filled Chief's order.

"I'll be right back," Chief said, stepping out and heading into the hotel.

From the back seat, Hommi leaned forward and tapped Raheem's shoulder. "Bro," he said. "We on these niggas' heels."

"You know that," Raheem replied. "We gon' need some blicks."

"Already got it covered. Right now, I got a .45 Taurus—ya favorite—and a Mac-10, fifty clip." He showed Raheem the length of the extended clip with his hands.

Raheem looked into the rearview mirror to establish eye contact. “Oh, so you already on deck?”

“It’s me you talkin’ to. You know I’m not gon’ be outta state without a few slammers. Where they do that at?”

“I wouldn’t know,” Raheem said, seriously. “But listen, just so you know—when we get our paper up, I’m goin’ back to the city to get at that bitch nigga Mega. I’ll never forget how he played me and disrespected my grandmother—God rest her soul.” He gazed up at the sky for a moment, then continued. “She died right after I got booked. And if that clown woulda kept it real and swung her my half of that bread we stuck Papi for—I woulda made it to the funeral. She ain’t even tell me she was sick, so I wasn’t even prepared for the shit.” Raheem clenched his fist and struck his left palm, hard. “I gotta kill that nigga… I missed her funeral, and it’s all his fault.”

Hommi made a silent prayer, then said, “My gun’s in.”

Raheem knew he meant every word.

Hommi pulled a Backwoods pack from his pocket, took out a rolled blunt, and continued. “We gon’ kill that half-a-nigga, but until then—here, spark this blunt while I call my P.Y.T. Here come Chief too.”

“Good. I’m ready to go.”

Chief stepped back into the car noticing Hommi was still on the phone, he handed Raheem a bundle back and one-fifty in cash.

"They only wanted one bundle for now. I took my fifty off the top," he said.

"That's cool, but what they say about the food?" Raheem asked.

"Ah, mane. Bruh, just put it this way—we rich."

"Shit, then act like it. Hommi, hang up the jack and listen to this."

Chief didn't smoke, so Raheem passed the blunt to Hommi.

"I heard him," Hommi said, ending his call. "That nigga Chief nonchalant about everything."

Chief dipped his pinky between a twenty-dollar bill, raised it to his nose, and sniffed the white powder. "Hommi," he said, clearing his throat, "the shit y'all brought down here is the best dope on the beach."

"You bullshittin'," Hommi said.

"Mane, I'm for real. These fools gon' have a problem as long as that boy y'all got is in the city. Muthafuckas might as well put they shit up 'til we get through—'cause it's gon' go bad waitin' on us."

"I like the sound of that, but where we goin'?" Raheem asked.

"Oh, ah shit—I got another pitch."

"Put the address in the GPS."

13 ½ 13 ½ 13 ½

Chief's tryst wasn't far. The customer—a bare-chested white man with long, unkempt hair—bought a bundle.

"It better be good like you say," the white man said.

Back in the car, Chief said, "Y'all can drop me off at the gambling shack."

Raheem had a question he'd been waiting to ask Hommi for some time. Once they were alone, he finally spoke.

"Why you tell Chief we had two hunnit bundles?"

"Because Chief is used to playin' with a lot of weight—that's what get him goin'. If he thinks he playin' with a lot of work, he gonna try to make bigger deals."

"But we don't have that many bundles. And what if he calls for a big order?"

"Then we'll say we don't have it—this shit ain't gonna be sittin' still."

"I don't think it's any of his business how much we got. If he tryna eat, then he'll make moves."

"What you worried about anyway? Chief is our people—"

"—What that mean?" Raheem cut in. "That ain't never stopped someone from puttin' a nigga on a plate. At the end of the day, our left hand should never know the business of the right."

"But what I told him was a lie."

"Yeah, but he thinks it's the truth. And what I'm tryin' to say—true or false—is that nobody should be able to count our paper. They shouldn't think they know or even have a clue."

For a long moment, they drove in silence down Highway 501.

"You right, cuzo," Hommi finally said. "You heard me?"

Raheem nodded.

CHAPTER FIVE

Frustrated, Tia broke a nail dialing Raheem's number. For hours, she'd been worried, trying to reach him. Seated on her bed, she thought the worst. *So this bitch-ass nigga don't wanna answer his phone? Couldn't even text his wife to let me know he made it safe?* Growing more upset, she pulled her legs to her chest, wrapping her arms around them. *Why do I feel alone? This nigga don't—and never did—care about our relationship. All he ever cared about is them fuckin' streets.* She wiped the tears rolling down her face. *If this clown think he gonna play me, he got another thing coming.*

Tia grabbed her phone.

"Fuck this wack-ass nigga," she muttered. "Let me see what's up with Liya."

Liya was Tia's best friend of seven years. The way they met was different—but when dealing with men in the street life, it was *somewhat* normal.

It was Tia's usual Friday evening, and she was at South Bay County Jail visiting Raheem. They weren't seeing eye-to-eye about something, which led to them arguing the whole visit—Tia leaving upset. But on her way out, a woman called after her.

"Hey!"

Tia stopped.

Catching up, the woman said, "Hey. I don't mean to be nosey or in your B.I., but I noticed you and your man arguin'—and when me and my boo be goin' at it, I be wishin' somebody would ask if I was straight. So yeah—without gettin' in ya mix, I just wanted to make sure you good. I mean *mentally*—'cause I know holdin' a nigga down could be stressful."

Tia was taken aback at first, but when she thought about it—she appreciated the woman's concern. She needed someone she could vent to. She could use someone who'd understand her point of view. Plus, the woman's energy felt genuine.

"Oh my God, girl—was I that obvious?" Tia asked, playing with her ponytail.

"No, not really," the woman replied.

"I hope not. Anyway, yeah, girl, today was one of those days."

"I can definitely relate—oh! By the way." The woman stuck out a delicate hand.

"My name is Liya."

Smiling, Tia shook her hand. "Pleased to meet you. I'm Tia."

"Nice to meet you too. Umm, are you busy this evening?"

"Actually, no. I was headin' home. Why, what's up?"

"Would you like to grab a drink and just kick it? Drinks on me, of course."

I hope this ain't one of Raheem's enemies' bitches tryin' to set me up. 'Cause I like her already—and she don't seem messy—but she is awfully friendly.

Tia hesitated, then said, "Yeah, why not? I'd love to get a drink."

From that day forward, the two had been inseparable.

Tia scrolled to Liya's contact and hit send, putting the phone on speaker.

"Hello, bestie," Liya answered.

"Hey, bitch," Tia replied.

"Shit, tryna get out this house. Why you sound like that though?"

"Stressin' about you-know-who."

"Girrlll, what Raheem do now?"

Flinching from pain, Tia stopped messing with her broken nail.

"He just disrespectful—takin' a bitch for granted," she replied.

"I know how that feel. I'm goin' through the same shit right now."

"But fuck that nigga. I called you to get my mind off him."

"Okay, so what's up?" Liya asked.

"It's nice out tonight—you tryin' to step out?" Tia glanced at her broken nail again.

"Bitch, you ain't sayin' nothin' but a word. Where you wanna go?"

"Let's hit up Blue Hill Tavern."

"That's perfect. I need a drink," Liya admitted.

"Who you tellin'."

Liya laughed.

"Bitch, you laughin' at me? I'm dead serious." Tia laughed too. "But fuck all that—are you dressed?"

"Yeah, but you gon' come get me? My boo got my car."

This girl always lettin' some nigga—I never even met—take her car, Tia thought.

"Yeah, I'll be there in twenty minutes. Be ready."

"Cool! See you soon," Liya said and hung up.

Tia freshened up and threw on a pair of dark blue True Religion skinny jeans, an Ann Taylor button-down long sleeve shirt, and some Jimmy Choo heels to match her leather, Saint Laurent clutch bag.

As she walked out the front door, her hair flowed down her back like a river.

13 ½ 13 ½ 13 ½

The Henchmen sitting outside Tia's grandparents' house were just about to call it a night.

Until patience paid off.

"Look here—we got action," the driver announced.

"I'm on it," his passenger said, wrapping his finger around the Glock's trigger. "Watch how I walk this bitch down."

He watched Tia lock the door and tried to step out—but the driver stopped him.

"Wait." He held his arm out.

"Let's see where she goin'. She might bring us right to Two-Times."

"Dawg, you serious? I'm tryna get this over with."

"So, you think killin' his bitch gon' end the beef?"

"Nah—but I got some new pussy waitin' on me and if you let me clip this hoe, he'll know we on his line—no exception."

"Man, fuck that bitch! If she feelin' you, she'll wait. I'm tailin' this black bitch."

And that's exactly what the Henchman driving did.

13 ½ 13 ½ 13 ½

Liya's sex appeal couldn't be measured—but let her tell it, everything on her face needed some kind of reconstruction. She was insecure, and sometimes her insecurities made her overdo it when dressing.

Liya was five-nine, all legs, with mahogany brown skin, tattoos covering her body. Her soft brown eyes had a piercing stare, and the ends of her dreads—dipped just an inch in red dye—fell just above her little round butt.

Tonight, she was wearing nearly nothing. And just to make sure she was presentable before they headed into the bar, she flipped open her handheld mirror to check her makeup.

Tia started to keep quiet but thought—*what kind of best friend would I be if I didn't say somethin'?*

"Liya," she called.

"Sup, boo?" Liya asked, still touching up her face.

"Why the hell you got on that little-ass skirt? It's a nice night—not a hot one."

Liya looked down at her dress. "What you talkin' 'bout? It fit just right."

"Girl, what you talkin' 'bout? You look thirsty. We just goin' to a bar. I'm only tellin' you this 'cause you my sister, I love you, and you too classy for all that."

"I know, Tia." Liya rolled her eyes. "And I love you for that. "That's why you my sister. "But I'm done—so let's go inside."

"Bitch, you crazy."

13 ½ 13 ½ 13 ½

Parked a block away, the Henchmen watched Tia and Liya cross the street and enter the tavern.

"Damn! Who's shorty she wit'?" the passenger asked.

"How the fuck would I know?" the driver shot back, squinting his eyes to get a better look at Liya.

"I wouldn't know how you'd know. Look at them legs though—I'd love to climb that tree."

"On dawgs," the driver agreed.

"Fuck that, though," the passenger started. "The bitch picked her friend up and led us to a bar, smart guy. So now what?"

Knowing his partner in crime was right, he thought for a second.

"Aight, I got a plan. Just follow my lead. And if anybody ask, your name is Woe."

"Aight, smart guy."

They both opened their door and climbed out the car.

"You shoulda let me smack her an hour ago—you playin'."

"Nigga, just bring yo' ass."

13 ½ 13 ½ 13 ½

The bar smelled like booze, cigarettes, and weed—and even though it was packed, Liya and Tia paid no one any attention. They weren't there for that. Tonight was all about them—catchin' up, ventin', and drownin' out their stress. So, over their second shot of Grey Goose and cranberry juice, they talked.

"Next round on me," Liya promised.

"Girl, I'm so glad we decided to step out. I needed this—no bullshit," Tia said.

Liya downed her shot. "Me too."

Tia sighed. "So why I feel like I held Raheem down five years for nothin'? Like, a bitch was sexually frustrated and loyal all that time just to say, *I did a bid with one of the realest niggas in Boston*? That's corny if you ask me. I don't regret holdin' him down—I did it 'cause I love him—but damn, I was expecting for him to come back home, give me a family, or at least give me back what I put in. I can't believe he really came home and, a month later, left me to go back down South with his cousin. What kinda weak shit is that?" Tia swallowed the rest of her liquor and continued. "That burned…Anyway, I'm fed up, Liya—for real."

Liya could see her best friend was hurting. "I would be fed up, too. But Raheem love you."

"You think so?"

"I know so. You all that boy got—especially after losing his grandmother. You was the only one there for him. Believe me, he'll get it right. It's just up to you if you gonna wait around 'til he do."

Tia sighed, staring at the bar counter. Then, from her peripheral, she saw a silhouette move beside her. She turned her head. "Oh my God, Freaky!" she shrieked, placing her hand over her heart. "You scared the shit outta me! What you doin' here?"

"My fault, I ain't mean to scare you, homie," Freaky said with a chuckle. "But yeah, I just stopped by to get a drink with my man right here." He looked at Liya and caught her staring. He smiled. "Let me buy you ladies a drink."

"That'd be nice of you," Tia said.

"What y'all sippin' on?"

"Grey Goose and cranberry juice."

Freaky waved the bartender over, and quickly, a heavyset white man came over.

"Yes, sir," said the bartender. "What can I do for you?"

"Let me get two shots of Grey Goose and cranberry juice for the ladies, please."

"Comin' right up." The bartender smacked the counter, fixed the drinks, and set them down on separate napkins.

"Thank you," Tia said, scooping up her glass.

Freaky waved his hand dismissively. "You ain't gotta thank me. That ain't 'bout nothin'. But where my nigga Two-Times at? He ain't in the building?"

Tia froze for a second. *Why is he asking about Raheem? He never did that before.*

"Boy, stop it," Tia said. "You know where he at. And you know he don't do no bar."

Freaky's face stayed unreadable. "Nah—I really don't know where he at. I ain't heard from him in a few days." He was lying.

"How he your peoples, and you don't even know where he at?" Tia quizzed.

"I been busy lately—ain't had a chance to catch up with the nigga. That's why."

Tia folded her arms. "Oh well, all I'ma say is he stepped outta town—sorry."

Stupid bitch. That's all I needed you to say.

"That's crazy," Freaky said.

Tia narrowed her eyes. "What you mean, that's crazy?"

"All I'm saying is, he just came home. Wherever I'm going, my wifey would be right beside me. Especially if it's you. Like damn, didn't you do that bid with him? What's his reason for leaving you behind anyway?"

"First of all, nigga," Tia began indignantly. "He didn't leave me behind—I chose to stay. Second of all, I thought Raheem was your man. Why you sayin' this to me?"

Freaky licked his lips. "Because…" he said smoothly. "I'd rather be ya man."

"What?" The hairs on the back of Tia's neck rose. "Freaky, you buggin'. How many drinks you had? 'Cause you outta order." She couldn't believe what just came outta Freaky's mouth. And to stop herself from slappin' him, she told him to leave.

"Listen—thank you for the drinks—but me and my girl need for you to bounce. Like now. And take ya boy wit' you."

"I can dig it," Freaky smirked. "Enjoy the rest of the night."

These niggas outta order out here, Tia thought, shaking her head. She wanted to tell Raheem what happened, but she knew he'd kill Freaky. And she wasn't about to help Raheem get in any trouble. So, she decided to keep it to herself. *Freaky had to be drunk*, she thought, *and blew it off*.

But she couldn't shake what Freaky said about Raheem leaving her after just coming home. She reached in her clutch bag, grabbed her phone, and started typing.

Yeah, nigga—you don't wanna answer my calls. Bet. But you gon' see these text messages.

"Tia, who was that fly, light-skinned nigga with them long-ass braids?" Liya asked. "What is he—Indian or somethin'?"

Still typing, Tia said, "Girl, that ain't nobody but grimy-ass Freaky."

"I'd love to grab them two long braids and ride his face," Liya said, demonstrating.

Tia laughed. "Bitch, you crazy—I swear."

"I'm just keepin' it real. What was he talkin' about, though?"

"He had the nerve to tell me, if I was his girl, I'd be by his side at all times."

She folded her arms.

Liya screwed up her face and put a hand on her hip. "No the fuck he didn't. Ain't he cool with Raheem? These niggas got no loyalty."

"They supposed to be cool. I always tell Raheem, these dudes ain't his boys, but he doesn't listen. I could tell him about his fake friends and how I don't trust them on a Monday—but by Tuesday, he ready to ride and die for them."

"I'll tell you one thing—that clown is disrespectful. You gonna tell Raheem what happened?"

"I'ma keep it to myself. I don't want him gettin' into no bullshit. We don't got time for no setbacks."

"I feel you. But men make themselves look so stupid. 'Cause for one—a real man ain't supposed to have his wifey around certain shit. That is—if he really care about her. And that's all Raheem tryna do—protect—"

"—Excuse me, sexy."

Before Liya could finish, a chisel-faced man cut her off.

"How you doin' tonight?" he asked, his eyes locked on Tia.

Tia sighed. "I'm sorry—what you say?" she asked, wishing she ignored him.

"I said, how's ya night so far?" Chisel-Face repeated himself.

"Oh, my night been just fine, thanks for askin'." Tia answered, covering her nose inconspicuously.

"Can I buy you and ya friend a drink?"

"Actually—that's my girlfriend. I'm a lesbian—sorry."

Liya held back laughter.

"Sorry for what, ma?" Chisel-Face said, smirking. "You like women—and so do I. You don't gotta be sorry, that's just one thing we got in common." Spilling a bit of his drink, a glossy line shone down his fingers. Unembarrassed, he smiled—exposing his chipped tooth.

Inwardly, Tia cringed. "Believe me—we don't even have that in common. Can you please keep it pushin'?"

While Tia went back and forth with Chisel-Face, Freaky and his crony stood across the bar.

"Ayo," Woe leaned over to Freaky, lowering his voice. "How you know Two-Times' girl? And why she think y'all cool?"

"Before I joined O.T.S., I had a rapport with dawg," Freaky admitted.

Woe asked another question—but Freaky wasn't listenin'. His eyes were locked on Tia.

And the conversation he was having with himself. *So, she can holla at that nigga, but not me?* Freaky asked himself. *That's probably why she wanted me to leave—so she could kick it with that lame. Like, who the fuck is that nigga? And I don't know who she think I am—but I'm Freaky from O.T.S.… I don't get dissed.* Freaky pushed off the wall. His blood boiled. Woe called after him—but through the crowd, Freaky kept pushing people outta his way. He moved forward, fast until he reached his target and drew a weapon.

Tia turned around. "Freaky, nooo!" Her attempt to stop what was already written fell on deaf ears—and she went tumbling down.

"Now look at you!" Freaky yelled, swinging the .38 revolver over the head beneath him—over and over.

"Somebody stop him!"

"Shut the fuck up," Freaky growled between blows.

His gun, now blackish-red, kept coming down—again and again. He showed no signs of stopping.

Woe saw the altercation was getting out of hand and tried to pull Freaky back. It took him and a few other patrons to finally separate him. But before they did—Freaky kicked the lifeless body one last time. Then, spat on it.

"Bitch-ass nigga! You niggas got the game fucked up! You fuckin' lame! Ayo, let me go—I'm good."

Still holding him back, Woe said, "You tryin' to body this dude in front of a hundred people—on camera? You sure you good?"

"Yeah, I'm sure. Fuck that scram."

Woe let him go and Freaky shot straight over to Tia and took her by the hand and escorted her—with Liya in tow to her car.

"My fault for knocking you over," he said, helping Tia inside the car. "But what would you have done if I wasn't here? That's exactly why ya so-called man should be. But since that's my man, I got you."

Tia wanted to tell him it wasn't that serious, until he came out of nowhere like some superhero and made a scene.

"Yo, take my number and text me when you make it home," he suggested.

Tia retrieved her cell phone. "What's your number?" He gave her his number and left. Tia looked over at Liya, suspicious. "Bitch, how did that weirdo know where I parked at?"

"Boo, I don't know. But I do know one thing—that nigga is loose, no bullshit," Liya said.

"No funny shit, these Boston dudes crazy as fuck." Tia caressed her temple. "Let's get outta here and go home. I seen enough for one night."

"So true."

CHAPTER SIX

Sprawled across his bed, Raheem slept.

"Two-Times," Hommi called, stepping into the bedroom. "Two-Times."

"Yo," Raheem answered, turning over on his side.

"Here." Hommi handed him a blunt.

"Wake and bake."

"G.L.O." Raheem took the blunt with him to the bathroom and rinsed his mouth out.

"What's good? You tryna go sit on them twins in the trailer park?" Hommi asked.

"Kinfolk, what kinda question is that?" Raheem said, stepping back into the bedroom.

"That's all I needed to hear. Lemme go straighten up."

While Hommi got himself together, Raheem slid on a pair of Champion sweatpants, some Air Maxes, and a white Polo V-neck. Then, he checked his phone for missed calls and texts.

Hommi poked his head in Raheem's room.

"You ready, cuzo?"

"Yeah."

Since Hommi knew the roads better, he drove. Raheem, on the other hand, kept checking his phone and realized he had fifty-eight missed calls and ten text messages from Tia. He opened a text message and read.

From Tia: You ain't shit, nigga. You think shit a game, huh, Raheem? Do you even know where I'm at? Do you even care, daddy? I could be cheating on you right now, and you wouldn't know unless I told you. That's not cool. Your bitch should never have the opportunity to cheat. Why you never here to hold me? Why you not here with me right now? Instead, it's a cornball in my face. *(SMH)*

Is this girl stupid?

Raheem shook his head and called Tia.

"Hello." Tia answered, her voice groggy.

"What these texts about?" Raheem demanded.

"What about them, Raheem?"

"What about them?"

"Yeah, what about—"

"—T, you must wanna piss me off."

"No, actually, I don't. I want you to realize that you have a bitch that loves you, and she don't want you to lose her—Cause she don't wanna lose you. But she's tired of being alone and waiting for you to settle down."

"Okay, I feel where ya comin' from. Umma get it right, I promise. But let me call you back when um done doing what um doing."

"Ya really a bitch," said Tia. "What you so busy doing you can't talk to me? Huh? You faggot!"

"What I tell you about ya fuckin' mouth? You know what—"

He hung up.

"Get focused, cuzo," Hommi urged, driving through the trailer park, trying to locate the trailer home the twins operated out of.

"I'm one-fifty twice." Raheem assured him.

"If I had to guess, that's their trailer right there. You see that line of dopeheads?" Hommi pointed at a trailer home between two others.

Raheem looked in the direction Hommi pointed.

"Yeah," he said. "Yeah, that's it. That's a lot of fiends, too."

They carefully scanned the area.

"Park over there—behind that pickup truck," Raheem suggested. "We could watch who's coming and going without being seen."

Taking Raheem's advice, Hommi positioned them behind the dented pickup, then said— "Yeah, kinfolk—this a good spot. They won't be able to see us from here." Now, as comfortably as possible, they chain-smoked—taking turns critiquing cigars as they watched— Waiting for the twins to make a mistake they could exploit.

"Yo, we been here for a grip," Hommi mentioned, getting restless.

"Um hip."

Raheem took a sip from the bottle of water he had left in the car yesterday. "Them niggas had to run through a half-of-thang."

"Chief wasn't bullshitting, after all."

Another two hours passed before they spotted a white woman pulling up in an off-white Nissan Maxima. She parked in front of the trailer home and spoke on her phone for a moment—then hung up. Not even a minute later, a brown-skinned male, looking to be in his mid-twenties, sporting a close fade, came out of the trailer and climbed into the Nissan.

13 ½ 13 ½ 13 ½

"What's Gucci, Shy?"

Shy wanted nothing to do with small talk. All she wanted was to make this drop, get paid, and move on. She dismissed the twin's greeting and got straight to business.

"The work is in that bag." She pointed at the brown paper bag on the floor by his feet.

"This bag right here?" the twin asked, nudging it with his foot.

"Yes, fool." She responded, irritated.

"Fo' sho." He picked up the bag. "Here you go." Then, he handed Shy some money.

It felt too thin. "Hold up…How much is this?" She shuffled through the bills.

"It's two hundred and fifty dollars. Why?"

Shy rolled her eyes. "Why!" She thought he was joking. "How 'bout why would you ask me why if you already know my price is six hundred a drop? Ya'll makin' all that—"

"—Hold up, ma. Don't count our paper."

" —Money, and can't even pay a bitch right? After all the shit I been through with ya'll. This shit ain't right. Look at all them fiends y'all got waiting in line to get served. Ya 'bout to make my price for business right now, but you can't pay me right? You don't let them come short. I put my life on the line traffickin' this shit, but—"

"—Ya not the only one puttin' ya life on the line. We put"

"—You know what? It's whatever. Just get out my car. And next time you call me, have all mine."

"Aight, shawty. Damn, you ain't gotta scream on a nigga."

"Yes, I do. Or y'all walk over me."

The twin didn't have time to argue and started climbing out the car. But Shy, on the other hand, didn't have any more reasons to care. *It's final—I'm gettin' them. *I'm tired of bein' loyal. *It ain't gettin' me nowhere.* Shy thought as the twin walked back inside the trailer. He had no clue.

13 ½ 13 ½ 13 ½

"Yo, Homm—did you see ol' boy come out with a bag?"

"Naw." Hommi confirmed.

"That white chick just dropped off some work. They ain't gonna have her drop off money—you dig what I'm sayin'?"

"So, what you sayin' is—"

"The money they made this mornin' is still in there, along with the drugs they just got dropped off…These idiots are food."

Through the windshield, Raheem spotted the back of Shy's car and said—"You know what? Follow her, kinfolk."

Shy pulled into a Kangaroo gas station, unaware of her tail. In the life she lived, you always had to stay ahead expecting police or vultures—especially after making a drop-off.

'Cause if you don't— Men like the ones followin' Shy were always around the corner.

Hommi turned into the gas station and parked at a pump—Making sure another gas pump was between them.

Raheem jumped out the car and walked inside the store. Inside, he found Shy waiting in a short line and got behind her. He looked her up and down. *Damn, this white thing is fly*, he thought. *She gotta be mixed with somethin'.*

Shy looked as if she had been dipped in a pool of white chocolate. Her eyes were slanted and as green as a forest. Her long hair, black as a crow, had blonde highlights. And at five feet four inches, she was thick yet curvy.

As Shy stepped forward to pay for her gas, Raheem smoothly eased in front of her.

"Save ya coins, pretty lady—I got'cha," Raheem said, peeling four twenties from the top of his fold. Put forty on pump eight… and—What pump ya whip at, ma?"

"Pump twelve, big shot," Shy answered, studying him.

“You heard the lady. Forty on pump twelve,” Raheem told the Middle Eastern cashier. He smirked—“And I see you peeking with ya peepin’ ass.”

Shy laughed.

“What’s ya name again?” she joked.

“It’s Two-Times, lil mama.”

Slyly, he smiled. “But let me walk you out, if you don’t mind.” He held the door open.

“Well, thank you for paying for my gas, even though you didn’t have to,” she said, walking through the door.

“You wanna thank me?” Raheem grinned. “Then let me take you out—treat you like the beautiful woman that you are.”

Shy smiled ear to ear. “That’s so sweet. You’d do that for me?”

“Love to.”

“You sound different. Where you from?”

“I’m from Boston.”

“Where’s that—New York?”

"Fuck no. Do I look like a New York nigga? I’m from Boston, Massachusetts. Don’t do that.”

“Do what?” She gazed at Raheem, confused.

“Confuse me with a New York nigga.”

“My bad, but I never met nobody from Boston before.”

"Well, now you have. A real nigga at that. What's your name, by the way?"

"Everybody calls me Shy."

"Ya name is dope." Shy started pumping her gas, but Raheem gently took the nozzle from her hand. "I got this, lil mama. You just stand there and look cute."

Shy placed her hands on her hips and poked her butt out just a little.

"I wish I could stand there and look cute every day."

"If you were fuckin' with a nigga like me, you could." Inconspicuously, Raheem checked out her curves. "What's ya nationality?"

"I'm Irish and Honduran—why? You tryna figure out where I got all this ass from?" Shy laughed, knowing exactly what Raheem was thinking.

"Ya too much. But yeah, I did wanna know. You got me."

"I knew it."

Raheem placed Shy's left hand between his palms. "Dig this though, sexy—Put my number in your phone." His confidence made her vulnerable. Rather than just taking his number, Shy wanted to take him home. But for now, she saved his number and gave him hers.

“Make sure you answer for a G, Two-Times,” he said, holding up the deuces.

“You just make sure you call, so I could.”

“When the best time?”

“It don’t matter. I’m on ya time—Two-Times.”

“That was cute. I’ll call you later. Aight.” He gave her a hug, then walked off to rejoin Hommi. They both watched Shy exit the gas station.

“Yo, that was a bad white bitch,” Hommi muttered.

“I’m hip. She not even straight white. She’s Irish and Honduran.”

“She’s something special.”

“Real shit,” Raheem agreed.

"I thought she was gonna gun you down," Hommi admitted.

"Come on, dawg—where we from? And she’s biting."

"I hear that. But fuck all that. You got some work on you?" Hommi asked, changing the topic.

"Yeah, why?"

"Chief called me. He said he needed a few bundles—somebody want 'em."

"Aight, I got a few on me. Where Chief at anyway?"

"He’s at the barbershop."

"Perfect. We both could use a haircut anyway."

"Speak for yaself, nigga—bitches love me with braids."

CHAPTER SEVEN

BOSTON BAGHDAD

While Raheem and Heron-Homm were in South Carolina pursuing a vision, a war was still in motion in Boston between S.O.L.O. (*Soldiers Only Live Once*) and their sole adversary, O.T.S. (*Only The Shooters*).

Mega used to be a member of S.O.L.O., but after crossing Raheem, he formed O.T.S. and recruited a fair number of gun-mad individuals.

S.O.L.O. is where Raheem is from. The name started as a concept, but that was before his best friend Dre was murdered. Then it became a way of life. A lifestyle. A reason to live and apply pain—and a reason to die while doing so.

"Did you see the O.T.S. kid in the barbershop?" Driving by the shop, an older member of S.O.L.O. asked a younger member, named Riot.

"Yup. The light-skinned nigga in the third chair, right?" Riot said.

"Bingo."

"Aight, let me out so I can do my thang," Riot said, eagerly. "Why he had to go to this barbershop? This strip is hot."

"Why does it matter? Just get in, clap him in the head, and get out. Simple." The older member stated and pulled over around the corner from the shop. Riot got out of the car. *This little nigga better get through. I should do the shit myself*, the older member thought.

As well as being fatherless, Riot was also motherless. And he didn't have a care in the world. Numerous times, he asked himself— *Why should I? Don't nobody care about me.* All he wanted to do was smoke weed and enjoy the smell of his gun's own discharge. The value of life meant nothing to him. And this was his way of thinking— At the precious age of fourteen. It's sad, too, 'cause Riot was actually a handsome young man with plenty of potential. But he wanted to be the only thing he thought he could be—A gangster. Short, brown-skinned, with shoulder-length cornrows and hazel eyes, all the girls in his neighborhood adored him.

During a normal, cool afternoon, he strolled down River Street with something to prove. The fifteen-round .9mm Sig tucked between his waist was so heavy, his jeans kept falling.

Pulling them up, he hoped the small crowd of civilians standing at the bus stop across the street wasn't paying him any attention. He tried tightening his belt—that didn't do him no good. Making up his mind, unnoticed—he took the pistol from his waist and stuffed it in his front hoodie pocket. Better.

Although Riot had done this plenty of times, his heart thumped hard as he continued descending River Street. Every car that drove by, he glanced in, checking for undercover police.

And, keeping in mind that the man from O.T.S. could have someone picking him up from the barbershop, he also checked for rivals.

The closer he got to the barbershop entrance, the more he anticipated the inevitable. He thought about waiting for his foe to finish getting his haircut and gunning him down when he came outside.

That was until two Black men with fresh haircuts exited the shop. Quickly, he dismissed the idea and threw his Antonio Ansaldi hood over his head.

Swiftly, he slid into the shop, walked straight to the third barber chair, raised his gun, and aimed at his rival, who was still seated in the chair. The entire space—only eight people inside—Was caught off guard. But the threat of danger forced clients and barbers to duck and find cover. Everyone except for the barber cutting the O.T.S. member's hair ran for cover.

The barber stood there frozen in fear, watching Riot in a huge hoodie, struggling to keep aim.

This nigga caught me drippin'. I knew I should'a never came here. Those big windows gave me up. I'm not letting this little nigga smoke me—fuck that! The O.T.S. member thought, and lunged at Riot.

Unfortunately for him, he accidentally stepped on the bottom of the apron and fell forward—on top of his own gun.

Riot stepped to the side and shot him. Repeatedly.

He, too, considered the barber an enemy. In his young mind, anybody who interacted with an O.T.S. affiliate—in any way—was a foe.

Which is why he aimed at him next. Under the gun, the barber thawed. He thought he witnessed hell in Riot's eyes.

"Man, I don't got nothin' to do with this." His voice cracked, and a dark circle appeared in his pants.

"Yes, you do." Riot corrected—And pulled the trigger.

Click.

Nothing happened.

The trigger didn't budge.

He fingered it again.

And again.

But the trigger was stuck.

Realizing the gun jammed, he took off running.

On the way to the getaway car, he heard police sirens nearing and spotted an oncoming cruiser. Immediately, he switched from running to walking normal. *Fuck, I was in there too long,* he scolded himself. Walking a few more feet, he took a left up a side street and was glad to see the getaway car still waiting. He sped up, and once he reached the car, unseen, he opened the back door, jumped in, and said, "Touchdown."

13 ½ 13 ½ 13 ½

Raheem and Shy were spending a lot of time together. Shy was head over heels for Raheem, which was unusual for her. Raheem was trying to keep it all business, but she was making it hard. She knew how to treat a man, plus the sex was addictive. She was already causing conflict in his relationship with Tia. What Tia would never consider doing, Shy was volunteering to do— and Raheem was loving it. Truth be told, he was loving it too much. It got to the point where he wasn't paying Tia any attention at all.

What can I say? A good bitch will have you doing shit like that, Raheem thought.

Raheem invited Shy to one of his favorite restaurants in North Myrtle Beach, called America's Greatest. Tonight couldn't have been more perfect. The moon was full, the sky was clear, and the weather was just right.

America's Greatest was a popular spot, usually overcrowded, so Raheem called ahead and reserved an isolated table for two. It was pricey, but the privacy was worth it.

"How's your Long Island iced tea?" Raheem asked.

"It's pretty good. They're not cheap with the alcohol, for sure," Shy replied.

"They take pride in their customers having enough of everything they serve."

Shy knew she shouldn't have been drinking, but the liquor had her feeling good inside. Liquor always made her horny and emotional. She was ready to let her guard down for Raheem. And she had been feeling like this for a few weeks now. She told herself years ago she would never give her heart away, but she wanted to give Raheem the keys. Something about this man sitting across from her was different. He was one of a kind.

Either that or he had the gift of gab, Shy thought.

Whatever it was, she was ready to express how she felt. And she had something important to share with him. Knowing what made him happy, she couldn't wait to tell him.

"Baby," Shy called.

"I'm listening," Raheem said.

"I just want you to know that for these last two and a half months of knowing you, life for me has been amazing— and it's all thanks to you. I appreciate you so much. You wasn't lying like the rest of these dudes when you said you wanted to show me what it's like to feel like a queen."

Raheem smirked.

"I love ya smile."

"You're not alone," Raheem said. "But anyway, I wanna thank you for giving me the chance to make you happy. I look at it as a privilege."

Shy gazed into Raheem's eyes. Her own eyes became watery. "Baby," she uttered. "I don't know what to say… You always do, though. Fo real, if you wasn't real, I woulda made you up."

Raheem studied what Shy just said and wondered where all this mushy stuff was coming from.

He started to ask but brushed it off.

The state Shy was in—that's exactly where he wanted her. So, nonchalantly, he stayed in character and placed his hand over hers and said, "That's deep." Raising her small, soft, manicured hand to his lips, he kissed the back, then continued—"Why you telling me all this, though? What's really on ya pretty mind?" He couldn't help it. He had to ask.

Breaking eye contact, Shy dropped her head. “I wanna tell you something,” she whispered.

Raheem reached across the table, and with a hooked finger, he tilted her chin up. “Talk to me,” he urged. “Stop acting like you can’t tell me anything.”

Shy inhaled. Then exhaled. “Okay,” she said. “How can I say this?” She bit her bottom lip, thinking. “Umm… you know what? Fuck it. Um just gonna say it. Two-Times. Pa. Um—um in love with you.”

Raheem froze. “That’s crazy.”

He looked off to his right, watching a waiter rush past. he rubbed his hands over his waves.

“Damn, this conversation got so deep we haven’t even touched our food.”

“Okay, but what you gotta say 'bout what I just told you?”

Raheem hesitated. Then blurted out— “I’m in love with you too. And how I feel for you—I never felt for a woman in my life.”

Shy swallowed the lump in her throat. “Are you serious?”

“I wouldn’t have said it if I wasn’t.”

Shy hesitated. “So… does that make us a couple?”

Raheem smirked.

“Naw… we a unit.”

Shy didn't say nothing, but her body language said everything.

"You done with your food? You ready?"

"I am."

Raheem raised his arm and caught the waiter's attention. "Check, please!"

They were cruising on their way to a hotel when Raheem pressed the automatic sunroof and let the thick smoke from his blunt escape. The song *No Love* by August Alsina featuring Nicki Minaj blared through the speakers, making the moment even more memorable.

Enjoying the weed's pleasant taste, Raheem took another pull, then blew a streak of smoke up and out the sunroof. *What a night,* he thought. *I got a bad bitch in my passenger seat, the streets are empty, and the stars are bright. This is what you call freedom.*

Enthralled and turned on by Raheem's charisma, without warning, Shy hovered over his lap, unbuckled his Gucci belt, freed his semi-hard dick, and slid it into her warm mouth.

Raheem swerved.

She then slipped her hand between her moist thighs and played with herself at the same time.

When Shy was finished, they had already pulled up to the Landmark Hotel on Ocean Boulevard, and both of them came. Raheem in her mouth, Shy on her fingers.

Now in the hotel room, Raheem sat at the round table, rolling another blunt, while Shy sat on the bed, deep in thought.

The room wasn't grand, but the beachfront view, the light Febreze scent, and the tranquil vibe made it feel comfortable. The only light in the room came from the full moon shining through the sliding door, casting a dim glow over everything.

Raheem noticed Shy was uneasy. Something was on her mind.

While trying to figure her out, his thoughts wandered. *Who is this bitch? And what's up with her? This shit is crazy. Here I am breaking my wifey's heart for a chick I barely know, and at the end of the day, it might not even be worth it. I feel disloyal, but I can't lie—this shit feels good.*

"Ma, what's wrong?" Raheem asked. "Why you looking like that?"

"I'm fine," Shy said.

"I *know* you fine," he replied matter-of-factly. "What's on your mind, though? Don't make me feel like you keeping secrets."

Shy hesitated, then finally said, "A lot is on my mind." She rubbed her damp palms over her skirt.

Raheem stared at her for a minute. “What the fuck is ‘a lot’?” he finally asked. “What does that even mean? Break it down for me.”

Nervous, she ran her hand through her hair. “I been lying to you,” she confessed in a low voice. “And I got something to tell you.”

Raheem crossed his right foot over his left. “About what? Huh, Shy? About *what*? And do—matter fact, fuck that—what you got to tell me? I don’t like being kept in the dark.”

“I know.”

“Obviously not.”

“I’m sorry,” Shy said, pinching the bridge of her nose, trying to keep from crying. “I lied about what I do.” She couldn’t hold the tears back. They started falling down her face. “I’m not a registered nurse. And I’m not a bank teller.”

Raheem walked over to her, rubbing her back for comfort. “Shy, you can talk to me about anything. I get it—you couldn’t trust nobody before, but you can trust me. I ain’t never gonna judge you. You my girl now.”

“It’s just hard… I don’t want you to look at me different.”

“Shy, nobody’s perfect. I’ma love you regardless.”

“You mean that, Pa?”

“I wouldn’t have said it if I didn’t mean it.”

Shy paced the floor, debating whether she could trust Raheem enough to be completely honest.

"Pa," she called, looking up at him.

"I traffic drugs for different people—for money."

Raheem smirked slightly. *Finally.*

"That's it?" he said. "That's what you was hiding from me? You made it seem like you was selling pussy—and even if you did, I still wouldn't judge you."

Shy was touched by his words. *He really loves me,* she thought and hugged him tight.

"I love you, Two-Times."

"How much?" he teased.

"Two times." She kissed him. "I love you so much, I'm gonna have ya baby." She waited for his reaction.

"Wait," he said, confused. "What did you just say? *Have* my baby? You meant, you *want* my baby, right?"

"I *mean*, I'm gonna have ya baby," she smiled.

"I'm pregnant."

"What?" Raheem stepped back.

"I'ma father?"

"Yup."

Raheem playfully tackled her onto the bed, got on top of her, and kissed her all over her face. "I love you, girl. We gonna be a family." He wasn't aware, but those simple words just *stole* Shy's mind and heart.

Raheem got up and grabbed the blunt he had just rolled. Then, he turned to her. "Answer this for me. Is everybody you dealing with treating you right? Niggas ain't trying to take advantage of you, are they? Not only is you my wifey, you my B.M. now. And if anybody playing you…" He placed the Backwood between his lips and lit the blunt. Blowing out smoke, he continued—

"They playing *me*, and I'm not having it."

Shy exhaled slowly. "It's crazy that you asked, because there *is* someone… but I'ma tell you all about it *after* you give ya baby's mama some dick."

She grabbed Raheem by his pants, undoing his belt. Once she freed him, she hungrily shoved him in her mouth, devoted to the task.

Meanwhile, Raheem kept smoking, watching her perform. *Ain't nothing like good weed and some bomb head,* he thought.

Shy sucked the tip of his dick seductively, then kissed the top. "Come on—I wanna feel you inside me," she whispered, wrestling out of her skirt, sharing her little secret.

She was pantiless.

Now nude, Shy laid across the bed, spread her legs, and slid her fingers over her dripping pussy.

"It's hot and ready," she moaned. "Come put the fire out, please."

Raheem sat his blunt down, came out of his trousers, and pulled his shirt over his head. Shy parted her legs wider, exposing her shaved pussy, and Raheem slid inside her.

"I love you," she moaned, wrapping her thighs around his waist. "Please don't ever hurt me."

"I won't," he said, pumping into her. "But you gonna have to prove ya love for me."

"I—I will."

Raheem pulled out, flipped her over on all fours, and slid back inside.

She met his strokes, matching his rhythm. Feeling the urge to cum, he pulled out and nutted all over her heart-shaped butt. Still on her hands and knees, looking over her shoulder, Shy smirked.

"Get it all out." Just to make sure, she spun around and sucked him dry.

"I don't know why you ain't just nut in me."

Raheem collapsed back onto the bed, exhaling. "Pass me my blunt," he said.

Going above and beyond, Shy grabbed it, lit it, and handed it to him as she lay across his chest.

"So," she said. "Where was we? Oh yeah—about them fools playing us." Raheem gave her his full attention. "It's these twins I be making drops for in Socastee…"

For the rest of the night, Shy told Raheem *everything*. From how much the twins were selling, to where they kept their money and drugs.

Tonight, under the full moon, *a single conversation was about to change everything.*

CHAPTER EIGHT

The phone rang…

Raheem checked the caller ID, then accepted the incoming call. "Yo."

"Pa, it's Shy. You on deck?" Always skeptical, Raheem listened closely into the phone and heard the wind blowing in Shy's background, which told him she was mobile.

"Who you with?" Raheem asked.

"No one—um, by myself," Shy asserted.

"Oh, aight. But yeah, I'm always on deck," he assured her.

"Right, I know that. Well, anyway, the twins need me to pick up."

Damn, this is really a bad time, Raheem thought. Fuck it. "You remember the spot you dropped me off at the other night? The spot off King Highway?"

"Yeah, I remember."

"Pick me up from there."

"I'll be there in fifteen minutes."

Fifteen minutes later, just as Shy said, Raheem joined her in her car, and together they drove to Lake City.

"Shy, you sure nobody gonna be at the house except for the one person that's supposed to be there?" Raheem double-checked.

"Yes, bae. Ya Gucci, believe me," Shy reassured him.

"How you so sure?" Raheem asked. "How you know when you pick up, they don't have someone watching you?"

"Pa, believe me, ya Gucci. Nobody gonna be there. And they sure as fuck don't have no one watching me. I mean, maybe they did at first, but I been doing drops for the twins for a while. I know them. You have nothing to worry about."

Raheem let Shy's words sit in his head. You better be right, because if not—B.M. or not—Im'a push you first.

They arrived in Lake City twenty minutes past twelve o'clock in the afternoon. Since they were in a rural area, plains of grass stretched for miles, haystacks dotting the land. Every so often, they'd pass a farm of cows or a barn full of pigs.

"The house is around the corner from here," Shy said.

Raheem climbed in the back of the car and lay flat across the seats. He then texted Hommi and asked if he was ready.

Hommi texted back: When am I not ready?

Suddenly, the car came to a complete stop.

"We're here," Shy said before exiting the car and heading to the porch. Looking over the lip of the car door and out the window, Raheem could only see the upper half of Shy as she stood at the front door and waited. Timidly, she peeked over her shoulder to see if Raheem was watching her, but she couldn't tell whether he was or not.

This ain't right, she thought. When I said I wanted the twins to get robbed, I didn't mean their people too. I wish I kept my mouth shut.

Finally, the door swung open, and Raheem watched Shy disappear into the dull yellow house. After waiting a few minutes, Raheem casually stepped out of the car, ascended the loose, cracked wooden steps, and trespassed onto the porch. Standing before a dark brown door, he pulled out the .45 Taurus he had concealed, holding it in front of him with the nose pointing toward the floor.

Soon, he heard light footsteps approaching and tightened his grip around his gun. When the door cracked open, he forced it all the way with one hand while raising the .45 Taurus just above his hip, waving it back and forth between the two women inside.

The mixed lines of anger and fright masked the twins' mother's face; however, she didn't seem surprised and automatically looked at Shy. "You dirty white bitch," she uttered. "I knew I shouldn't have trusted you. Y'all been robbing us for years. And look, like always, you got a nigger to do your dirty work."

"Back up," Raheem ordered. "Now!"

The twins' mother thought about rebelling and hesitated, but then did as she was told. Raheem eased into the house, closing and locking the door behind him.

Immediately inside, to the right, a set of stairs led up to an additional floor. The living room was to the left, and the room next to it, accessible from the living room, was the dining area. Tall black leather chairs and antique wooden carvings decorated the living room. In the dining room, a long polished table surrounded by chairs occupied the center of the floor. Along the wall stood a China cabinet. The cabinet looked like it could use some attention, but the silverware inside sparkled.

The twins' mother was sixty-eight years old—nothing more than wrinkled skin and bones. Her shoulder-length hair was thin and completely white. And although she was basically harmless, the dark rings encircling her sunken, bigoted eyes made people feel uncomfortable around her.

Raheem backed the twins' mother into the kitchen. "Now get on your knees," he demanded.

On her knees, Raheem zip-tied the twins' mother's hands and feet. I'm going to hell for this one, Raheem thought. Surveying the kitchen, he spotted a dog bowl on the floor and listened for signs of a dog. He heard nothing.

Wondering, he asked himself: Why didn't Shy tell me nothing about a dog?

"Ay, Grandma, where the dog at?" Raheem asked.

"Why would I tell you?" the twins' mother answered.

Raheem grabbed a handful of the twins' mother's hair and pressed the nose of his gun against her temple. "Because if you don't, I'ma turn you into dog food, and that mutt of yours gonna have you for dinner."

"It's in the back," Shy blurted. "She always put him in the back when I come by."

"I wish I didn't," the twins' mother said dryly. "Y'all not gonna get away with this, Shy. My boys gonna get you."

Shy thought about the reality of the threat. She's right. I'm not gonna get away with this. The twins done had people killed for less. Much less. I should leave.

Raising the gun as if he was about to strike the twins' mother, Raheem said, "Listen, you old bitch, I think you should choose your words wisely." Kneeling, he whispered in her ear, "Let's not make this harder than it has to be. Just tell me what I want to know. You do know what I want, right? Of course, you do. But like I was saying, tell me where you're hiding the dope at so I can go on my merry way and leave you in one piece. You have options. You can tell me where the drugs and money at, and I'll leave you in one piece. Or, I could cut you limb by limb until you tell me—and leave you in pieces."

"I'm not telling you a damn thing. The Lord is my shepherd," said the twins' mother.

Raheem's nose flared. "You know what? I got something for you." He pulled his phone out of his pocket and called Hommi. Meanwhile, Shy crept off.

"Yo," Hommi answered.

"Ayo, this old hooker over here ain't talking. Time for plan B."

"Nuff said. I'll call you back."

13 ½ 13 ½ 13 ½

Hommi ended the call with Raheem and climbed out of the car. Scanning the trailer park, he made sure no one was watching him as he had been watching the twins. The day was still early, so those who worked should be at work, and students at school—but you never know.

After making sure the coast was clear, Hommi snuck around the back of the twins' trailer home and peeked through a disfigured blind. Instantly, above the back of a small couch, he saw the backs of both twins' heads. They appeared to be playing a video game.

As Hommi returned to the front of the trailer, he called Raheem and got no answer. *What the fuck is this nigga doing?* Hommi asked himself. After waiting a couple of seconds, he called again.

"Dawg," Hommi said as soon as Raheem answered. "What are you doing?"

"Waiting on you," Raheem answered.

"Put the phone to that bitch's ear." Switching hands with the phone, he pulled his right arm through his jacket sleeve and held a MAC-10 close to his side, under the jacket. Ready, he knocked on the trailer home's door. Not long after, the door opened, but the twin who answered wasn't the same one Hommi and Raheem had first seen a few months ago. This twin was slightly taller, with dreads and a scar running down his forehead.

"What'cha want?" the twin with the dreads asked.

Pretending to be a drug addict, Hommi said, "Uh, sorry for bothering you, but my partner sent me here to, um, cop off you. He did say you might not serve me because you don't know me."

The twin sized Hommi up and thought he saw something in his coat, but due to complacency, he brushed it off. "Who sent you?" he inquired.

"They on the phone. They said once you hear their voice, you'd fuck with me. Here." Hommi stuck the hand holding the phone out. The twin took it and put it to his ear.

"Aye, mane, who dis?" The twin's heart skipped.

"Momma."

Right away, Hommi pointed his gun at the twin's stomach. His eyebrows furrowed as he said, "Pussy, get the fuck in the trailer."

Following the twin inside, he looked to his right, catching sight of the other twin in the corner of his eye as he sprang for the .380 SIG lying on the table.

"Naw! Naw, mane, chill! They got Momma!" the twin with the dreads announced, stopping his brother mid-stride.

"What you say, fool?" asked the twin with the fade.

"They got Momma, bruh."

"Yeah, nigga, we got ya Momma," Hommi said. "So listen to ya brother and follow suit. Now, both of y'all, get on ya stomach."

Neither wanted to chance losing their mother, so they complied. Once flat on their chests, Hommi snatched his phone from the twin with the dreads and swept the trailer. Old discarded boxes of takeout food and miscellaneous trash were everywhere—on the table, on the arm of the couch, and scattered along the floor.

There were even chicken bones beside an overflowing trash can. The wallpaper had peeled, lapped, and within the air, there was an awful odor, but Hommi endured.

Satisfied with his survey, he ordered the twin with the fade to get up and zip-tie his brother's hands and feet. Doing as Hommi said, he made himself a promise: *If this fuck nigga lets us live, he's dead.*

When he was done zip-tying his brother, he laid back down on his stomach, and Hommi secured him too. But Hommi wasn't through—taking precautions, he checked the twin with the dreads' zip ties. Sure enough, like he thought, they could be loosened.

"Come on, mane," said the twin with the fade. "You don't have to check over me. I tied him up good. I'm not gonna play with you when I know you got my Momma hostage."

"Nigga, if you don't shut—" Furious, Hommi couldn't finish his sentence and fought the urge to shoot the twin with the fade. "Who's who?" he asked after calming down.

"I'm Bugg," the twin with the fade confirmed.

"And I'm June," said the other twin.

"Ain't that cute. June and Bugg. June-Bugg. Y'all some real silly-ass niggas," Hommi said.

"Aye, mane, what's up with our Momma?" June asked.

Standing between the twins, Hommi spoke. "Ya mother is straight. But her fate depends on y'all. So with that being said—where the goods at?"

Fuck, this ain't good, Bugg thought. *I'ma have to tell this fool where the stash at. This shit ain't worth my Momma's life.*

"It's under the couch," Bugg said first. "When you lift the couch, you'll see a flathead screwdriver. Use it to lift the tile up, and everything you're looking for is there."

Hommi walked over to the couch. "How much is supposed to be here?"

While Hommi waited for an answer, Bugg thought about how, after today, his relationship with his brother would never be the same. *I gotta do what I gotta do,* he concluded.

"It's twenty-five thousand and two hundred and fifty grams of boy," Bugg confessed.

June replayed what he just heard in his head. *Twenty-five thousand and two hundred and fifty grams?*

"Aye, fuck nigga!" June called, angry. "I thought you said we was out of work."

Bugg ignored him.

"Huh, fuck nigga? You was gonna play your own brother? You robbing Momma too. You do know that, right?"

June tried to scoot over and bite Bugg, but Hommi jumped between them.

"Aye! Aye! Chill the fuck out before I clap the shit out of both of you," Hommi warned, then went back over to the couch and confiscated the drugs and money. He even took the .380 Sig. "Aight, fellas," he said, strolling over to the twins. "That's everything. I guess y'all not as dumb as I thought. I didn't even have to kill one of you." Thinking he heard something, he looked over his shoulder at the door. *It's about time I get outta here before someone pop up,* he thought.

"Aye, mane!" June called. "Can I speak to my momma now? You got what you want." Knowing how stubborn his mother was, he worried she was already dead.

"You sure can," Hommi said and called Raheem.

"Oowooo," Raheem answered.

"Cuzo."

"How we looking?"

"Everything is everything on my side," Hommi disclosed.

13 ½ 13 ½ 13 ½

"I'm still trying to get shit situated on my end. I'm telling you, dawg, this old lady is something else," Raheem told Hommi.

Coming back from searching the house, Shy re-entered the kitchen. “Pa, I didn’t find nothing,” she said.

“Nothing?” Raheem asked Shy in disbelief.

“Nothing,” Shy answered, feeling as though she failed him.

“Shit crazy,” Raheem said and walked over to the twins' mother. “Aye, granny, here’s ya chance to do the right thing. Where is the stash?”

Through piercing eyes, the twins' mother looked up at Raheem. “Um not telling you shit, coward.”

“Ya choice,” Raheem said and pressed his phone to his ear. “Kinfolk, you there?”

“Yeah,” Hommi answered.

“I’m putting the phone to her ear.”

13 ½ 13 ½ 13 ½

Hommi studied the two specimens on the floor, tied up like hogs... He then, holding the phone close, aimed.

“No! No! No!” Bugg screamed but was quickly silenced by shock. He couldn’t believe his brother was just shot and killed before his eyes. *But for what?* was all he wanted to know. “Aye, mane, what was that for?” he asked.

"Your mother ain't playing fair. You might want to tell her something," Hommi suggested and bent down, holding his phone an inch from Bugg's face.

"Momma!" Bugg spoke into the phone. "Momma, please stop playing with these goons and tell them what they want to know. June is dead, Momma. He killed June in cold blood. Whatever they take, we'll get that back. Give them what they want—please."

13 ½ 13 ½ 13 ½

Tears stained the face of the twins' mother. She heard the gunshot. Now, all she could hear was Bugg's plea and what he said: *June is dead, Momma. He killed him in cold blood.* She couldn't imagine her son, her baby, lying dead because of her stubbornness.

"You ready to talk?" Raheem asked.

It took a moment for the twins' mother to answer, but finally, she said, "It's behind the stove in the wall. When you move the stove, peel off the wallpaper, and you'll see the front of the safe." *Unbelievable. This woman put me through all that shit, and the whole time the stash was under my nose,* Raheem thought while doing exactly what she said.

Seeing that the safe was digital, Raheem said, "What's the passcode?"

"9-6-0-5-7-0-3-8."

Raheem punched in the code, and like magic, the safe popped open. "That's what I'm talking 'bout," he said and turned around to tell Shy to put everything in the safe in the garbage bag. But come to find out, she was gone. *Where the hell this girl go?* Wondering, Raheem called her. "Shy! Yo, Shy!" Not getting an answer, he went into the hallway and called her again.

No answer.

Let me find out this hoe left me, Raheem thought.

The thought of Shy ditching him worried him very much, and for many reasons, so he stepped over to the front door to peek outside. Cracking the door open, a thin line of light beamed through, momentarily impairing his vision. However, before he could open the door any further, he heard footsteps and wood crackling from behind him. He turned around—immediately spotting Shy coming from the second floor.

"What was you doing up there?" Raheem questioned instantly. "You didn't hear me calling you? What was you doing?"

"No, um, sorry. I didn't hear you. I was using the bathroom," Shy explained, cringing in fear.

Raheem looked for any sign of infidelity. *I swear this hoe is lucky she's carrying my seed,* he said inwardly.

"Come on," Raheem demanded. "I want you to put all the stuff in the safe in the bag."

13 ½ 13 ½ 13 ½

Hearing the commotion on the other end of his phone, Hommi worried something terrible happened.

"Bro, you straight over there?" Hommi spoke into his phone. "Cuzo! Ayo, bro, you hear me?"

"Yeah, yeah, I hear you," Raheem got back on the phone. "My fault, something just threw me off real quick."

"Aight. So what's up? Is everything, everything?"

"Yeah, bro, the light is green."

"Bet, I'll see you in a second," Hommi said and hung up.

For Bugg, the tension instantly rose. "Aye, mane, did my momma cooperate?" His voice was shaky, and he pronounced *cooperate* wrong. "I apologize for her. She's just old school."

A devilish smirk appeared on Hommi's face. "And ya breaking news," he said and nailed Bugg to the floor. "Five," he counted the current number of murders he committed.

Shy handed Raheem the garbage bag of merchandise. "That's everything," she said.

"Our seed gonna be smooth now," Raheem said, making Shy blush.

"I know ya gonna kill me," the twins' mother announced. "And to be honest, um fine with that. When ya a mother, you can feel when something happens to ya children, and I can feel it in my heart that both of mine are gone. There is no life without them, so I'd rather be with my boys in heaven. I done seen enough anyway. But I promise you, this ain't it. There is a life after death, and we will see each other again. Mock my words."

Fed up, Raheem shot the twins' mother in the head; her blood colored the wall.

Shy clutched her stomach. "What the fuck!" she screeched. Wide-eyed, she looked at Raheem. "Two-Times, what did you just do?"

Again—blank face—Raheem fired his gun. And to be sure he ended Shy's life, he stood over her and fired some more. "I would've never been able to trust you," he murmured.

Back in Conway, Raheem tailed Hommi in Shy's car to the back of an abandoned building and got out. Hommi, too, got out of the vehicle he was driving, went over to Shy's car, and lobbed his tracker-phone through the driver's window. From there, Raheem doused the car with gasoline, sparked a match, and threw it. The car engulfed in flames.

Leaning towards stepping off, Hommi said, “Come on, cuzo, let’s go count this fucking fred.”

CHAPTER NINE

BOSTON BAGHDAD

Rico approached Honest while she sat on the bed and handed her the outfit he picked out.

"Iron this for me."

"Alright," Honest said, accepting the task as an opportunity to cater to her man.

Honest was Rico's main girl. They been a couple for almost four years now and rented a two-bedroom apartment together in Dorchester.

With no makeup, Honest was beautiful. She's the same complexion as candy caramel and looked as though she tasted just as good, with long, thick curls. Being so short, with big round eyes and dimples on both sides of her cheeks, she carried an innocent air. But only Rico knew better.

"Bae, you want me to iron the pants too?" Honest asked. "They already look done."

"The whole fit," Rico answered.

"Your wish is my command."

Rico entered the bathroom, turned the shower on, and allowed the water to heat up while he used the toilet and spun a cigar replete with marijuana. Raised up after his older brother Raheem, he was too affiliated with the S.O.L.O. gang. And as he was well respected, he was adequately known by the ladies. They loved his chestnut skin complexion and how he articulated the latest designer clothes on his six-foot figure. But what truly drove them crazy was the slight gap between his two front teeth and the scar above his right eyebrow, which he endured in the midst of a gun battle. Nevertheless, besides being a gorgeous gangster, Rico was arrogant.

Very arrogant.

But Honest didn't let his arrogance bother her. Neither did it bother her that she was going against the grain and breaking sensitive street laws. She loved Rico, and nothing would come between how she felt and the life she wanted with him. A while ago, she came to terms with herself that living is easy; it's the choices we have to make that make life hard.

13 ½ 13 ½ 13 ½

Freaky stood in the basement of another one of Mega's apartments he referred to as the "Dog-Pound." His purpose for being there was to relay the latest war report. However, he hated the place. It smelled of shit and bleach, and he was surrounded by multiple pit bulls that weren't fond of nobody except Mega.

"So… what's shaking with the bitch?" Mega asked.

"Shit, really," Freaky answered.

"She didn't tell you what town or state dawg slid to?"

"Naw, she didn't say. Gun-Smoke, the bitch ain't dumb. She's not gonna just tell me where the nigga is at." Freaky was becoming frustrated with Mega trying to figure him out.

And Mega felt the vibe.

So, he released one of the dogs from out its cage.

The tiger-striped pit bull—which was now prowling back and forth—made Freaky nervous. But that was the whole point. Freaky kept an eye on the animal, thinking, If this fucking mutt tries to bite me, um'a shoot the shit out of it. Then um'a clap this nigga and every other dog down here.

"Didn't you say she texted you, right?" Mega continued probing.

"Yeah," Freaky answered.

"What you plan on doing? I mean, are you gonna try to infiltrate and win her over? You know, because it could be beneficial." He played on Freaky's intelligence.

Is this nigga serious? Freaky thought. This nigga must think um slow. Real niggas don't tell the next nigga what they're up to.

"To keep it all the way a buck," Freaky began, "I wasn't planning on doing shit. I figured when you thought the time was right, you was gonna give me the light to clip her."

Mega's gut told him Freaky was hiding something, but rather than mention it, a thought came to mind: game-face him. So he did.

"That's why I fucks with you, Freak. Real shit."

13 ½ 13 ½ 13 ½

After a hot shower, Rico dried off, relit his cigar, and returned to the bedroom, leading an S for a shape of smoke. Wearing nothing more than a purple tank top and a thong, Honest's ass swallowed the thong completely as she stood over the ironing board and pressed a steaming hot iron against a shirt. The sight caused the towel wrapped around Rico's waist to rise some.

Feeling Rico's presence, Honest turned around to tell him his clothes were done and caught him gazing at her butt. "Bae!" she said. "What are you looking at?"

"It's more like, what um looking for. Ya ass is so fat, it looks like you don't got on no drawers in this motherfucker," Rico said.

Blushing, Honest's dimples appeared.

"Boy, ya crazy. Here, take ya clothes. I'm done, nasty."

Rico started to remove his towel but was interrupted by his cell phone ringing.

"The fuck."

Annoyed, Honest said, "Phone a damn hotline. Answer it."

"Yo!"

"The fuck you yelling for?" the caller asked. "You straight?"

"Um always straight."

"Aight, whatever," the caller said, brushing off Rico's slick remark. "Um'a be there in a minute. Be ready, or um keeping it pushing."

Chuckling, Rico said, "Aight, tough guy. Solo." Hanging up, he refocused on Honest. "Now, where were we?" He grabbed her by both butt cheeks and drew her close.

"What you want from me?" Honest asked, batting her long eyelashes.

"Stop playing with me. You know what ya man want." Catching the hint, she pushed him gently, and he flopped onto the bed. She then knelt between his legs, opened his towel, and proceeded to plant soft kisses around his pelvis.

"This what you want, bae?" Rico didn't answer. He didn't have the chance. His dick and balls were in Honest's warm, loving mouth before he could utter a word.

While in heaven, his phone vibrated from hell. Not wanting the moment to end, he let the phone vibrate some more and would've let it go to voicemail had Honest not stopped.

"Answer it," she demanded.

Rico sucked his teeth indignantly. "Yo."

"Um out front. Come on," the caller stated.

"Aight, um coming out now."

"Hurry up," the caller said and hung up. Rico, on the other hand, let the phone fall onto the bed, palmed the back of Honest's head, then guided it to his lap.

Hurry up. Lil nigga got me fucked up, Rico thought.

Climbing in the front passenger seat, Rico closed the door and reclined the seat. "What's good, lil bro?"

"Naw, dawg, miss me with that 'what's good, lil bro' shit. What was you doing? I told you to be ready. I been waiting in the middle of the street for a grip. And I got the slammer on me."

"That make both of us," Rico disclosed.

"Two joints is always better than one," said Rico's brother, Darian, who was wheeling through traffic.

"My fault though, baby boy," said Rico. "Wifey was bugging before I left."

Yeah right, Darian thought.

Darian, known on the streets as Knoxs, is another one of Raheem's brothers. Though he is the youngest, he is also the biggest of the three and, for good reason, has a chip on his shoulder.

Plenty of times, the dark-skinned giant was mistaken for a model. Women lusted after him, imagining grabbing onto his abs like they were projecting rocks and climbing him like a mountain. And adversaries, needless to say, badly wanted to knock him down like a tree.

All his life, he kept a low, even haircut. But to add character, he had his barber put three Adidas stripes on the side of his head. Besides a neatly trimmed mustache above thin lips and jet-black eyebrows that arched slightly at the corners of sharp eyes, he kept no hair on his chiseled face.

Noticing Rico searching through his car like he lost something, he investigated: "Kinfolk, what you looking for?"

"You know what um looking for," said Rico. "You think ya slick."

Darian laughed. "How you gonna tell me I know what ya looking for?"

Rico opened the console. "Cause, nigga, what um looking for is right here." He took the Gucci glasses from the console and put them on. "No funny shit, you was really gonna beat me for my glasses, you slime ball." He shook his head. "Cold dirtbag."

"You know the rules. You leave it in the whip, it's no more ya shit," he reminded his brother.

"Yeah, aight, nigga. That rule doesn't apply to me. Weak-ass press game. You got a Backwood?"

"Nope."

"Stop at a store so I can snatch a pack."

"I got'cha. Let me bust this trap first. I had this geeka waiting for a hot second—and he owe."

"Get'cha Fred."

13 ½ 13 ½ 13 ½

Across the street from Ashmont Station, in an unmarked cruiser, Detective Griffin waited outside Dunkin' Donuts for his partner.

Detective Griffin is the sixth generation of Irish migrants who sailed to America for equal liberty.

Don't listen to none of that garbage. I'm Bostonian—100%, Griffin thought.

Anyway, despite the detective's opinion, he is full Irish, tall yet lanky like some cables, in his mid-thirties, pale white, with hair the color of sand and gray, skeptical eyes. His nose was bone-thin and sharp at the brim, and his face suffered from persistent acne.

No woman wanted him, but he could care less. He was part of, and belonged to, the Boston Gang Unit. He and his partner were assigned to an immense list of street gangs throughout the city, but his main focus—and, frankly, obsession—happened to be the S.O.L.O. gang. He was responsible for patrolling their area in Dorchester, and taking them down was something he took pride in. Seeing them prosecuted was a sight he would never get enough of.

It was personal for him.

So personal, it was beyond his co-worker's understanding. So personal, he was considered the best on the force. So personal, the community called him a piece of shit and a dirty cop under their breath. He didn't lose a wink of sleep, though. Who he was and how he performed—he believed in his case—was justifiable.

Returning, Detective Griffin's partner, Tom Stratton, eased into the cruiser carrying two large coffees. "Here, buddy," said Stratton. He passed Griffin his beverage and closed the passenger door.

Tom Stratton was African American, born in Boston but raised in the inner city by his foster parents, a white couple.

Stratton was in his early thirties, short and stocky, kept a clean baldy, and sported a keen goatee. He had a prominent jaw made of glass, and it had been proven time and time again. Regardless, he enjoyed a physical altercation, and his light skin complexion marked with scars was proof.

"Just how you like it, bro," said Stratton. "Iced coffee, extra sugar, no cream. Fucking disgusting, but you like it, I love it."

"Thanks, pal. Just how I like to start a shift," Griffin gloated. "Hey, Tom—did I tell you about the new break I came across involving the shooting on Washington Street, in front of Dorchester Court last week?"

Stratton gave the question some thought. "No. No, I don't think you did?"

"Well, let me bring you up to speed. I spoke to one of my reliable C.I.s and got some juicy info. I learned that I was right. The shooting was indeed between S.O.L.O. and O.T.S., and I have real good reason to believe Rico, a S.O.L.O. member and an impact player, was one of our trigger men."

Stratton lowered his cup from his mouth and held off from drinking. "What makes you so sure?" he asked, aware of his partner's obsession.

"It was on your day off, but the hat we found on the scene—"

“What about it?” Stratton interrupted.

“I’m try’n to tell ya. Anyway, I saw that gap-tooth bastard Rico wearing it one day when I pulled him and his buddies over and searched their car for weapons.”

“I think you’re thinking narrowly.”

“How the fuck so?”

“The manufacturer didn’t discontinue making the hat after this kid Rico purchased it.”

“I know that, but I know it’s the damn hat—I can tell.”

“You’d know better than me. I wasn’t fortunate to see it. I wasn’t there. I was there for that shooting, though. We responded to it. Them punks started shooting right out front of the courthouse, and that female lawyer caught a stray. I bet she’ll be a D.A. by next year.”

“It irks me them animals ain’t behind bars somewhere, brushing their fucking teeth with toilet water,” Griffin said, scowling.

“Matter of fact, Griff—patrol their area.”

13 ½ 13 ½ 13 ½

Outside a known druggy’s apartment, Darian waited for his brother. Vexed and glancing in both side mirrors and the rearview mirror regularly, he wondered: What's taking this dude so long to make a play? He knows I hate staying in one spot for too long.

It wasn't much longer before Rico appeared. Darian grilled him hard as he walked over to the car and got in.

"What's up!" Rico said. "Why you grilling me like you want some blow?"

Pulling off from the curb, Darian said, "Let me find out you was in there busting ya geeka down." He assumed. "I put any amount of money on it—ya horny ass was in there hitting ya fiend. I know you."

Through laughter, Rico said, "Yeah, aight, nigga. I wouldn't fuck a clucka with ya dick. The bitch couldn't find her money, and when she did, she gave me mad change. That shit took a lil second to count." He lied.

The real story went like this: The drug addict called Rico for a twenty rock but only had thirteen dollars of the purchase price. So, to compensate for the difference, Rico told the young addict he'd accept oral sex.

And she accepted the deal.

"Yeah, whatever—tell me anything," Darian said. "But anyways, where to?"

"Slide to Ray's. Niggas need some Backwoods."

13 ½ 13 ½ 13 ½

DT. Griffin's dick almost got hard as he got near Ray's convenience store and spotted Rico leaving, talking on his cell phone, not paying any attention.

"Hey, look at our boy, shit-for-brains," Griffin said.

Rico jumped back inside the car and hung up the phone. "Yo," he began. "Go to the honeycomb hideout. We might as well save some gas and go fall back. You feel me? Roll up and wait for some Fred to call."

Darian turned from looking off to his left and looked at Rico—who immediately noticed something was troubling his brother.

"Knoxs, you three-hunnit? Why you look like that?"

"The dicks. They drove by grilling you stupid hard. And I think they're busting a U-bone."

Darian looked in the rearview mirror, and just like he thought: The unmarked cruiser made a U-turn.

"Here we go." Burning rubber, he took the first right onto Crowell Street and floored it.

13 ½ 13 ½ 13 ½

In the midst of making a U-turn, Griffin observed the Dodge Charger pull off in a hurry. Automatically, he and Stratton fastened their seatbelts. He then threw on the sirens and stepped on the gas.

13 ½ 13 ½ 13 ½

"They catching up, Kinfolk." Rico announced, looking through the back window. Thinking, he pulled an MP .9MM from under his shirt. I should dump on these faggots.

While Rico contemplated holding court in the streets, Darian was doing 70 mph on a side street. From the side of the road, miscellaneous waste papers caught wind and floated in mid-air as onlookers stood in their yards and on their porches, watching the two cars fly by.

"Let me see ya joint," Rico demanded.

"What?" Darian snapped, trying to focus on driving.

"Swing me ya blick and pull over. I'ma get little."

"Naw, bro, hold up."

"On my threes, you better think of something fast then. Because if not, I'ma start dumping," he warned.

"Then let me think!"

Fucking idiot. Think, Knoxs.

After barely dodging a collision, he bent a sharp corner. Think, Knoxs.

Several police cars joined the chase, and they were determined to apprehend the two suspects. Darian knew it was only a matter of time before they found themselves boxed in.

Think, Knox. Fucking think.

Lifting the E-brake, Darian took an unexpected turn and hit the gas. The tires screamed, causing a little girl with pigtails crossing the street to look in the direction of the noise. Seeing the Dodge Charger appear from a cloud of white smoke, she quickly ran for safety. Darian glanced in the rearview mirror and saw the leading cop car now making the turn.

That's enough time, he thought.

Reaching under his left thigh, he grabbed a .45 ACP, gave it to Rico, then said, "Throw both the slammers out the window on my call." Rico didn't reply, but he did show that he comprehended by wiping the guns down with his sleeve and rolling the window down.

Darian took a left onto Carruth Street, then immediately pulled the E-brake and took the hard right. "Toss 'em!" he said, and Rico threw both guns out the window, one after the other.

After putting some distance between them and the guns, Darian ended the chase and surrendered. Once surrounded, the doors of the cop cars flew open systematically, including Griffin and Stratton's. Red and blue lights illuminated the sides and roofs of a row of houses.

Now using their doors as shields, an army of officers aimed ready Glocks at the idle Dodge. "Put ya goddamn hands up for us to see 'em, you motherfuckers!" Griffin ordered, taking lead. "Let's go—put 'em up!" Rico and Darian pressed their hands against the ceiling. Holstering their weapons, the men and women in blue swarmed the muscle car and snatched Darian and Rico out of it. As soon as their chests met the pavement, they were placed in cuffs—tightly.

"I got this one," Griffin said, emerging from the crowd. The posted officer walked off. Unholstering his Glock 19, Griffin knelt beside Darian and shoved the gun into the side of his neck. "You fucking fucker, you could've killed me and my guys back there." Mad, his eye twitched. "I should blow your fucking dickhead off for that stunt you pulled. Why were you running? Huh!"

"You ain't gonna do shit, so move ya gun," Darian uttered.

"Why were you running?!"

"My driver's license is in my back pocket, registration in

the glove box. Now do your job, bring me to the station, and book me so I can bail out."

"Oh yeah?" His eye twitched. "You little punk."

"Yeah, nigga. The fuck. You know where I'm from, so miss me with the chit-chat. Bust ya gun or book me."

"I'ma bust ya. And when I do, ya gonna wish it was my gun. Get up." With little help from Griffin, Darian stood up. "Take him in."

13 ½ 13 ½ 13 ½

After making a phone call, Darian returned to a cold, seedy cell with Rico.

"What's the word?" Rico inquired.

"We smooth. I called my bitch, but she didn't answer, so I called Tia and told her to hit kinfolk and see if he can wire her the chips so we can make bail," Darian explained.

"It's wild funny that we both can't reach our bitches. What's the point of having chicken put up if you can't reach no one to grab it for you and come bail you out? Or is it more like, what I have a bitch for? Yeah, I think it's the latter."

"Real talk," Darian agreed.

The two brothers were still holding a conversation when Darian noticed a white, muscular cop with a scruffy beard mugging them as he strolled by.

"What's up?" Darian said. "What you looking at?"

"You. What you gonna do about it?" the officer retorted.

"Take ya badge off and come in here, and I'll show you what I'd do."

"Chill, bro," Rico said.

"Nah, he's tough. Come in here."

The cop smirked. "I'll see you around," he threatened, then kept going.

Darian slammed both fists down on the wooden bench. "I'm tired of these cops, I swear to God."

"I'm hip—me too," Rico agreed.

"For real, dawg. These racist-ass crackers think they can do whatever they want. They come to our hood and act like we did something to them." Rico listened as his brother vented.

"Yo," Darian continued. "You ever wonder what Ma would have to say about us being in the streets? Or how life would've turned out if she hadn't died?"

Shaking his head up and down, Rico said, "All the time. But why you thinking about that right now?"

"I don't know." But that was far from the truth. He knew why. His mother's death affected him beyond words, and he always thought about that night. That pivotal, infamous night she was separated from him, his brothers, and earth.

*If only I would've...*Dwelling, Darian again re-visits the past as if he can redo what has already been done.

"Darian." His mother called after noticing he was awake and attentive. Entering the bedroom, she spoke low, hoping not to wake Raheem. "What you doing up? Didn't I say for you to take ya butt to sleep?"

"But um not tired, Mommy." Darian whined.

"Boy, yes you are." She tucked him in bed. "Now take ya lil' ass to sleep before you wake up ya brother. And um not playing with you."

She started to leave but stopped at Darian's call.

"Mommy?"

"What, boy?"

"Why you got ya tall shoes on?" Unable to fight it, a smile crept across her face. *This lil' nigga always got questions—like he's my pimp or something,* she thought.

"Because," she began. "Santa might stop by, and I wanna look nice for him. So you better be good and go to bed, or he won't come."

The mention of Santa—and the thought of him not showing up to bring the presents he'd been begging for—got his full attention. "Okay, Mommy. Good night. I love you."

Hearing her son say he loved her made her heart swell with emotions. Her kids were her world and the main reason she chose her profession—there was nothing she wouldn't do for their love and security.

Retracing her steps, she gave Darian a kiss on the forehead. "I love you too, baby... Now take ya ass to sleep."

And with that, she left.

An hour later, Darian woke up to a disturbing noise. He jumped out of bed and rushed over to Raheem.

"Raheem," he called, pulling on his brother. "Raheem, wake up. Wake up, Raheem."

Raheem shoved him. "Get off me," he demanded, agitated. "What do you want, Darian?"

"Listen to that noise… Do you hear it?"

"No—go back to bed, ya dreaming."

"No, um not. Listen." He paused for a moment. "You heard that? It sound like Santa hurting Mommy."

Raheem, as far as Santa went, had no clue what Darian was talking about. He'd already told him Santa was fake. However, he did hear something. It was hard to distinguish that thin line.

Is it pleasure?

Or is it desperation?

The screams were faint. The screams were muffled. And the feeling in his gut was real. He was confused, worried, and, needless to say, overwhelmed with fear. Regardless, he climbed out of bed.

Raheem and Darian were both familiar with, and used to hearing their mother play-fight with her many boyfriends that stopped by—but tonight's sound was totally different.

Under his pillow, Raheem kept a butter knife. Retrieving it, he and Darian tiptoed across cold tiles toward their mother's bedroom door. Their hearts raced.

As Raheem picked at the lock with the butter knife, he shook violently. His sweaty hands lost grip once or twice, but he kept at it. Soon, the door cracked open. Slowly, with his forearm, he pushed it open completely—instantly, tears spilled over the edge of his and Darian's eyes.

What they were witnessing wasn't for any child to ever bear, let alone seeing it happen to their own mother.

Lying in bed, her leather skirt was hiked up. Her bare, motionless legs—spread apart. And between them, a pasty-white, black-haired man with bottle-cap glasses and fresh red lines on his back was strangling their mother—although she had already surpassed.

"Knoxs. Knoxs. Yo, Knox, snap out of it," said Rico.

"Yo. Yo. What's good?" Darian answered, a little startled.

"Bail. We made bail while you was daydreaming."

"I was thinking about Ma."

"Dawg, no funny shit, you gotta stop thinking about that shit. It happened. It's over with. You gonna drive yaself fucking crazy."

"Nigga—that's easy for you to say. You wasn't there. So watch what you say to me, dawg. And don't tell me shit 'bout what I should be thinking about. Word up."

Brushing by Rico, he left.

Inconspicuously, as Rico and Darian walked out of the police station and onto Blue Hill Avenue, across the street from the station, B3, DT Griffin, and Stratton watched in disgust from behind limousine-tinted windows.

"You know," Griffin began, "I sure wish I could do our city a huge favor and put a bullet in their fucking heads. Look at 'em." He jutted his jaw at Darian and Rico. "Them cowards think they're above the law. I can't wait for the day we bury them with an asshole full of time. Especially their brother."

"I'm with you on that one," Tom agreed.

Griffin turned the headlights on. “Let’s see who bailed them out. Plus, I wanna see where they’re going. While it’s night, we might as well take advantage.”

13 ½ 13 ½ 13 ½

Rico got out in Franklin Field Projects. His mistress, a Cape Verdean beauty, rented an apartment there, which was beneficial because, in a completely different apartment, he employed a S.O.L.O. associate he thought was capable of distributing his drugs for a fair percentage. He wanted to check on him.

Rushing through the filthy hallway, he stuck his face in the corner of his arm and blocked his nose from the stench of urine until he reached the dope house and applied a coded knock against the door. Seconds later, the door opened and revealed Riot—wearing an Adidas warm-up suit and Top Ten Adidas sneakers.

“What’s shaking, big homie?” Riot said, giving Rico a handshake that consisted of three fingers.

Stepping into the apartment, Rico said, “Ain’t shit, baby boy—how you?”

“Um, three double-oh. Just getting to the bird food.”

What Rico liked about Riot so much was that not only was he a shooter, but he listened—and he was monetarily productive. You rarely came across young men with all three qualities.

The dope house consisted of three bedrooms. When you first entered, there was a long, narrow foyer adjacent to the front door leading to the kitchen. Throughout the foyer were four rooms. The first space, on the right side, was the living room. Then, further down, a bedroom. On the left side, near the middle, was a bathroom. A few feet down, another bedroom. The last bedroom was past the kitchen, directly across from the back door.

When Rico turned into the living room, he immediately became aggravated at the sight of someone he'd never seen before, sitting on the raggedy couch.

"Yo, Riot—who's ya man?" Rico asked, pointing at the unfamiliar teenager.

"Oh. Um." Riot glanced at his friend, then back at Rico. "That's my man, Tank."

"Tank?"

"Yeah, Tank—he's solo."

Thinking, Rico looked Tank over. *I can probably find something for this little fat nigga to do.*

"Next time, let me know ya gonna have somebody over. Especially if I don't know them."

"You got it—my bad."

"I still love you. Don't sweat it." Noticing the guns on the coffee table, pointing in every direction, Rico went on. "But yo, what's really good with all those blicks? The two of you don't need five tones in here."

"We from an army block. You can never be too safe," Riot responded.

Proud, Rico smirked.

"Word," Tank chimed in. "Who's to say we won't need them all?"

"Hold up—who are you again? You know me? Exactly. Ain't nobody talking to you."

Rico redirected his focus back to Riot. "Like I was saying. I ain't mad at you, baby boy. You just better use those bitches when it come time."

"Go without said. On dawgs."

"Aight, I'ma slide upstairs. Today was crazy, so I'ma end the night early and get up in some pussy. Did Nina set you straight?"

"Yeah, that sexy Cape Verdean bitch already hit me. I'm good for the night."

"She a bad bitch—"

"—what's that pussy like?" Riot asked, cutting Rico off.

"Water. But anyway, call me if you need me."

Rico left, and Riot locked the door behind him.

One day, I'ma be known just like Rico. And it's gonna be me fucking bad foreign bitches, Riot thought and went back into the living room. Seated, while Tank pulled on a blunt, he continued thinking. *Watch. My name gonna ring bells like church. Whole city gonna smell my gun smoke.* Snapping out of his thoughts, Riot looked at Tank.

"Ayo, Tank," he called. "Why you in the streets?"

Shrugging his shoulders, the ash from the blunt fell as he said, "'Cause I wanna be… what about you?"

"'Cause these streets the only thing that ever loved me… And it's all I got."

The conversation was over, and the sudden knock at the door supported that.

"I'll get it," Tank said and handed Riot the cigar. He then got up, strolled over to the door, and looked through the peephole. Recognizing the addict on the opposite side, he let her in.

"What's goody? What you want?"

The woman standing before Tank—scratching—resembled Whitney Houston at her lowest. Whenever she didn't have enough money to purchase what she wanted, for laughs, the local drug dealers made her sing.

"I want…" The Whitney Houston lookalike began. "Lord, what do I want? Um… okay, let me get one white, one brown. And can I get my free one? This my third time coppin' today."

Tank stuck his hand down the front of his pants, pulled out a plastic sandwich bag full of crack and heroin, and retrieved what the Whitney Houston lookalike asked for—minus the free one. The free one, he planned on pocketing.

"Hey," she said, looking in her palm. "Where's my freebie?" Now she was staring at Tank. "This my third time coming to y'all today. Um supposed to get a freebie."

"I don't know what ya talkin' bout—now beat it."

Shoving her out the apartment and into the hallway, he shut the door in her face, then locked it and returned to the living room.

Passing Tank the blunt back, Riot picked up one of the guns on the coffee table. He slid the clip out and decocked the P85 Ruger. A bullet spit out the chamber and landed in his hand.

Mesmerized by the weapon and the power it possessed, he stared at it for a bit.

You are my mother… and my father. In his head, he spoke to the piece. It was sudden, but a feeling came over him, and he pointed the gun at the wall.

13 ½ 13 ½ 13 ½

Stepping out the shadows, Griffin and Stratton announced that they were Boston police and brandished their badges, compelling the person of interest to halt.

Standing still, the woman shook.

"Ma'am, you don't have nothin' to be afraid of. Calm down," said Stratton. "That building you just came out of—what apartment you coming from?"

Still shaking, she kept quiet.

"Ma'am, listen to me. I'm sure if me and my partner search you, we'll find something you not supposed to have. And once we do, you goin' to jail. You wanna go to jail tonight?"

She shook her head no.

"Good. So, I'ma ask again—what apartment you came from?"

She told him.

"Who's in there?"

She told him.

"And they sold you drugs?"

She hesitated.

"Yes or no?"

She told him.

"Aight. Get outta here."

Whitney Houston lookalike scurried off, thinking: *I don't even care. Treating people messed up don't pay off.*

13 ½ 13 ½ 13 ½

"I can't wait to catch another one of those kids," Riot said, looking down the nose of the gun with one eye open as he aimed. "His people gonna have to put on their best suit in the closet… for the worst day of their life."

"On everything," Tank agreed.

"Matter of fact—what's good with ol' girl you be kickin' it with? I thought you said she had the drop on one of them niggas."

"You already know the bitch on my dick. But on that other shit, I'm workin' on it. I'm not tryna be too obvious, 'cause the last thing I want is for her to know where it came from when dawg get clipped. If she pillow talk with me, she'll do it with the next nigga she fuckin'."

"But she did say one of them niggas lived—"

Banging at the door cut Tank short.

"BPD! Open the door!"

Getting low to the floor, Riot and Tank looked at each other.

Fear now dwelled in the whites of their eyes.

"Bro, that's the boys," Tank whispered first. "What we gonna do?"

Riot swept up the clip he ejected earlier and stuck it back in the Ruger.

"Bro, you heard me?"

Cocking the gun, a round eased into the chamber.

"Dawg, we gotta get outta here. Say something."

Gun in hand, Riot moved from around the table, and in a trance, headed for the front door.

13 ½ 13 ½ 13 ½

"Shots fired! Shots fired! Get down!" Griffin shouted, dropping to the floor.

After a couple more shots, the shooting ceased, but the two detectives gave it a second before climbing to their feet and checking themselves for wounds.

"Dude, I'd rather had taken a shell instead of lyin' on that disgusting-ass floor," Stratton muttered.

"I agree, but it is what it is now. Come on, help me kick this door in."

Once they gained entrance, the apartment was empty.

Neither Riot nor Tank was there.

They were long gone.

"Son of a bitch." Cursing, Griffin turned red. "Call it in, Tom. I'll do the paperwork. Fuck!" His eye twitched. "That fuckin' crack whore ain't say they had guns. Fuckin' cunt."

Holding the walkie-talkie to his mouth, Stratton asked Griffin a question: "Before I call it in, what about the shooter—or shooters? Do we know who the suspects are?"

"We have an idea… but we gonna keep it to ourselves. Payback is a bitch."

13 ½ 13 ½ 13 ½

"Yo," Tank said between deep breaths. "What just happened?"

"I don't know, my nigg, but I hope I hit something." Riot said and began going through his pockets, searching for his cell phone. "Kinfolk, I can't find my jack."

"What you mean?"

"I think I dropped my phone or left it in the trap. Either way, I fucked up." In dismay, he shook his head.

13 ½ 13 ½ 13 ½

Rico woke up to gunshots followed by loud thuds and hurried over to the window, peeking through the drapes.

The forlorn street was ominously dark, and the shadow cloaking the unmarked cruiser almost made it impossible to perceive. However, Rico spotted it.

That's the same Ford that chased me and Knoxs earlier. They must've followed me here.

Scurrying back to his side of the bed, he reached in his pants pocket and grabbed his phone.

"Baby, what you doin'?" Nina said, turning on her side and clasping onto Rico's arm. "Come back to bed and hold me."

Shrugging her off, Rico said, "Chill. Go back to sleep." And called Riot's phone.

13 ½ 13 ½ 13 ½

Griffin heard a phone ringing and followed the chime to the couch. He then stuck his hand between the cushions and recovered a T-Mobile cell phone.

Noticing the name on the screen, he answered it. "So, you shootin' at cops now?" Griffin questioned as Stratton stared, wondering who he was on the phone with.

"Who's this? And what the fuck you talkin' bout?" Rico asked, both annoyed and confused.

"You know what the hell I'm talkin' about, you prick. Don't worry, though, your days are numbered."

Griffin ended the call.

13 ½ 13 ½ 13 ½

Rico stared at his phone, stunned.

Why this dude on my dick so hard?

As he wondered, he also contemplated breaking his phone—and actually began dismantling it—but before he removed the chip, it rang.

"Hello." Immediately, he answered.

"Kinfolk, it's Riot. I'm using Tank's phone."

"Fuck all that—where are you?"

"I'm on American Legion Highway, hidin' in Franklin Park."

"Don't move. I'm sendin' someone to come snatch you right now."

"Aight, bet."

Ending the call, Rico dropped his head in distress.

"Fuckin' lil' homies."

CHAPTER TEN

The aroma of some strong marijuana claimed victory throughout the whole condo while Young Jeezy played in the background.

Raheem and Heron-Homm sat at the dinner table. Raheem was counting money, and Heron-Homm was packing up the drugs they robbed the twins for. They both pictured a promising future from here on.

"Yo, cuzo, pass me the compressor," said Hommi.

Handing Hommi the compressor, Raheem said, "Ya dumb lazy. You see me over here doin' somethin', but yet you still keep askin' me to pass shit."

"Ya still countin'. Let me find out ya classroom was in that basement," Hommi joked.

"Yeah aight, nigga. I woulda been done if it wasn't for you interruptin' me." *Funny-ass nigga*, Raheem thought.

As he continued counting, he reflected on the promise he made to Tia:

All I need is two months, mommy, I promise.

It's goin' on five, though. No bullshit—I feel disloyal as shit. I wonder… am I considered a fake nigga for not keepin' it real with my bitch? I promised this girl a better life when I came home and ain't done nothin' toward creating one. Instead, I'm doin' the same shit I went to jail for—only difference—I'm doin' it in another state. I gotta stop lyin' to my baby girl and get my shit together. She was the only one there for me when I lost my Nana. And during my bid, she held it down.

I owe her… but I'm not gonna front—I deserve to live. I did just do five long years in the max. Yeah, after I live a little, I'ma tighten up. I just gotta find a way to buy some more time.

And I gotta remember:

Real niggas change money from hundreds to thousands… they don't let money change them. Get in and get out.

Randomly glancing at Raheem, Hommi pondered:

Look at this nigga in his head, thinkin'. All he do is think, think, think. What the fuck he thinkin' about now? I hope he don't get stuck up there one day.

"Yo, here." He passed Raheem the blunt, purposely breaking his concentration. Despite Hommi's effort, Raheem stuck the cigar between his lips, counted the last of the money, and applied a rubber band around the fold.

"We up to bat," Raheem said and filled a white foam cup halfway with 1738 Remy.

Although ecstatic, Hommi remained calm, extended his arm, and stuck out three fingers. Raheem did the same, and they interlocked fingers as Hommi said, "You see what a lil' bit of aggression get us."

They were *one hundred and thirty-seven thousand dollars* richer and now had *one thousand and seventy-five grams of heroin.*

"Cuzo, we gotta stick to the script and get quiet money. The dog that bark draw attention."

"You can say that twice."

"I would, but we gotta divide this paper."

In the midst of dividing the money equally, a conversation surfaced in Raheem's head that he needed to tell Hommi about.

"Oh yeah, I almost forgot to tell you. I chopped it up with Rico today."

"What cuzo talkin' about?"

"He basically gave me the war report. Said him and Knox got into a police chase and had to toss two joints."

"Okay… and?"

"And guess who bailed them out." Raheem folded his arms across his chest and waited.

"Hold up, they got booked?"

"For a bunch of traffic violations." He said and resumed waiting.

"Nigga, who bailed them out?" He asked anxiously.

"Freaky."

"Yeahhh," Hommi said, taken aback. "You bullshittin'. You just now findin' out about this today?"

"Yeah. I don't know why they called that nigga to bail them out—I woulda wired the bread."

"That whole thing ain't sittin' well with me, on dawgs. I thought Freaky moved outta state after he got touched."

"I thought the same. But yeah, bro—Freaky bailed them out for seventy-five altogether."

"He gettin' a lil' chicken too, huh."

"But that's just the beginning." Raheem paused, hit what was left of the blunt, sipped his cup of Remy, then proceeded. "So, after the chase and bailin' out, later that night, Rico's trap got raided. He had a lil' nigga runnin' it, though, so he wasn't there. Matter fact, you heard of the young boy. His name Riot—but fuck all that."

Dismissively, he waved off the irrelevance.

"The lil' nigga clapped at the boys through the door and ran up outta there, leavin'—I think—four or five slammers behind."

"Time out," Hommi said, making the hand signal. "Why the lil' nigga have that many blicks in there in the first place?"

"I don't know. You askin' the wrong person that question. I like the lil' nigga, though."

"Now we gotta ASAP them some blicks," he concluded.

"I'm hip."

"They gon' need 'em. They in the field. I'ma call Chief and tell him to swing through—he gotta pick up anyway. Speaking of that… how much work you think we should swing him?"

Raheem pondered, then said, "Give him two-fifty. Enough to make him feel like he doin' somethin' since you said he like that. I think it's important that we bird-feed him. You know, keep things from gettin' messy. But in case it do, we'll be on top of it and clean it right up."

"I like how ya thinkin'. When he get here, I'ma see what's good with the hammer connect."

"Sound like a go… oh yeah, I spoke to Ugly already. She on deck. I'ma have her drop five hundred grams on Money-Makin' Rich in Baltimore, too."

Ugly and Raheem once shared an intimate relationship. She was a few years his junior, but he took her under his wing. That was eleven years ago, the first day she was introduced to the street life and its amenities. He taught her everything she knew.

Ugly was actually attractive—her name meant the complete opposite. Nothing about her was ugly, not even her feet. Peanut-butter complexion, shoulder-length hair, hazel eyes, full lips, and a slight gap between her two front teeth—that's why Raheem started calling her *Ugly*.

She was cute and she knew it. She stood five-foot-seven, kept an athletic shape from playing high school basketball, and carried herself like she knew the world was hers.

Not too long after she met Raheem, he got arrested for a shooting. She moved on, got pregnant, and relocated to Salem, North Carolina with her father.

Raheem, however, didn't hold her decision against her. With a child involved, their relationship wasn't the same. But they were still close.

While serving his latest sentence, Raheem met Money-Making Rich in the middle of an altercation.

Shirley Max – Unit P-2, the metal doors slid open for breakfast. Like always, Money-Making Rich took his sweet time getting dressed and leaving his single cell.

An attribute his peers were aware of.

An attribute they were about to use against him.

While Money-Making Rich laced his sneakers, two mean-mugging men entered his room—subtly.

"You might as well not even tie those," said one of the mean-muggers.

"Why not?" Money-Making Rich asked, looking up at them.

"Because we takin' those too."

“Oh, this what this is?” Standing up, Money-Making Rich stood tall. “Niggas ain’t takin’ nothin’ from me.”

Walking by and paying attention to his surroundings, Raheem heard what was taking place.

Sucker-ass niggas preyin’ on the weak.

The thought alone irked him. But hearing Money-Making Rich stand his ground?

That made Raheem change his initial plans.

Raheem stepped into the cell.

“Aye, why don’t y’all ease up on dawg? He don’t bother nobody,” he said.

“Two-Times, this don’t got nothin’ to do with you,” said one of the mean-muggers.

“Nah, it don’t—but I want somethin’ to do with it. I don’t respect y’all move. Y’all only pressin’ dude ’cause he from C.T. and he don’t fuck with nobody. But now he do, so y’all can stab out—or get stabbed up.”

He removed a makeshift knife from his waistband.

“Bro, niggas ain’t stuntin’ yo knife.”

From that moment forward—

All you heard was sneakers screechin’ and men gruntin’.

The altercation was eventually broken up.

But first.

A lot of blood spilled.

Raheem got stabbed in the arm and the back of his shoulder.

Money-Making Rich took four stab wounds— One in the wrist. One in the hand. Two in the chest.

The two men who tried robbing him? They had to be rushed to a hospital outside the prison.

From that morning forward, Raheem and Money-Making Rich were brothers and before Money-Making Rich was released, they exchanged information.

After trying Massachusetts, Money-Making Rich relocated to Baltimore. And frankly—he was making a decent life for himself selling weed. But when Raheem called and offered him a business proposition, he thought it was a great idea. The heroin trade in Baltimore had a huge market. And he wanted a piece of it. "Whatever you send, I'll cover."

13 ½ 13 ½ 13 ½

When Chief received the phone call from Hommi, he was at a hotel with six of his friends—rotating a plate.

On it?

Lines of cocaine that sparkled.

"Aight." Chief spoke into his phone. "Ah shit, I'll be right there… I'll call him and see what's up…"

While Chief was talking, his friend Chubb picked up on the seriousness of the call and he started eavesdroppin'. He avoided making eye contact with Chief—even held a conversation of his own—but he was locked in.

"I'm leavin' now," Chief said, ending the call.

"Got damn, fool. What's up? Ole lady want you home?" Chubb asked.

"Picture that. That was my peoples from up top. They got somethin' for me," Chief confessed, rubbing his palms together. He imagined the look on the faces of the people who counted him out.

"What you mean they got somethin' for you?" Chubb asked, jealous.

"I mean exactly what I said. Da fuck this fool talkin' 'bout?" Chief wasn't speaking to anyone in particular.

But his words gained everyone's attention in the room.

"Man, who are these fuck niggas?" Chubb raised his voice. "Talkin' 'bout ya folks from up top. Dem niggas out here gettin' money?" He pointed to the floor. "Dat was a stupid question, huh? 'Cause knowin' you, I bet you brought dem right to da money."

"Fool, until you start touchin' some paper, don't worry 'bout all that. Always complainin' like some kinda bitch. Sound worse than my ole lady. Got damn, talkin' 'bout takin' ya money—you don't even get money."

Finding himself wastin' time arguing, Chief walked to the kitchen and grabbed the keys on the counter.

"You got a GPS, fool?"

"You know I got a got damn GPS."

Chief headed toward the door.

"Put some gas in my ole lady too, muthafucker!"

As Chief stepped outside, a warm ocean breeze passed through, carrying the sea's salty fragrance—

A smell he always loved.

Scanning the packed parking lot, he spotted Chubb's car.

A Impala.

He climbed inside.

Closing the door it squeaked.

"Cheap-ass Impala," Chief muttered, turning the key. Sputtering, the car started. He put his destination in the GPS and pulled out the parking spot. He knew how to get to Wild Wing Boulevard. But while under the influence, it was best to focus on driving, and let the GPS do the work. Had he tried to do both? There was a good chance he woulda ended up in a ditch.

13 ½ 13 ½ 13 ½

BOSTON BAGHDAD

In the D Street projects, located in South Boston, Mega smoked a Newport in the dimly lit hallway as he waited at the bottom of a staircase for an O.T.S. affiliate—who he loaned drugs to—to bring him his money.

When the O.T.S. affiliate appeared, another ten minutes had gone by, and Mega was fuming.

"Gun Smoke, what's goody?" the O.T.S. member said, sticking his hand out to give Mega dap.

"Nigga, do I look like ya bitch?" Mega snapped, leaving the man's hand in the air. "Don't ever have me waiting this long again. Matter fact, don't ever have me waiting, period."

"My fault. I just wanted to make sure the count was correct."

"Yeah, well, you better figure out a way to do that before I get here."

"I got'chu."

"Anyway—have you seen Freak?"

"Naw, not lately."

Mega pondered, then said, "I want you and the rest of the guys to keep y'all ears to the streets. If y'all hear about any activity concerning Freak, let me know. And if someone sees him—watch him."

"Done."

"Aight. See smoke, gun smoke."

"Always."

13 ½ 13 ½ 13 ½

The sit-down with Heron-Homm and Raheem went well. Chief adopted the responsibility to open a new dope spot in the trailer park in Socastee and redirect the twins' clientele. The task was simple; he had done it plenty of times. But what wouldn't be as simple was convincing his crew to join him. How Chief saw things and how his partners saw things were completely different. He understood business and could care less where someone was from. The only thing he was interested in was making serious money. He could never understand his partners' petty way of thinking. While he drove back to the hotel, he asked himself, *How do you ever expect to turn old money into new money if you're not willing to network and make moves with new people?* He thought about the question for a second, then reminded himself, *This game is a big risk in itself, and shit, for those who don't take 'em, don't make it to their full potential.*

That doesn't just go for the game, though—that goes for life in general.

Chubb was standing outside the hotel, smoking a Black & Mild cigar when Chief pulled into the parking lot. Parking, Chief got out and walked over to Chubb, handing him the car keys.

"Chu fill her up?" Chubb asked.

"You know I put gas in dat hoe. I wouldn't be here if I didn't. Chu knew what chu was doing by letting me take da car on E. Chu fat, black, big-lip sucka," Chief said.

Chubb laughed. "Aye mane, chu know ain't shit free."

"Remember that when you want some of my powder," Chief said and entered the hotel.

Flicking the cigar, Chubb strolled over to his car and plopped in. Curious why Chief wanted to know if he had a GPS, he checked the recent destinations, scrolled down, then stopped on an unfamiliar address. A wicked grin formed across his face. *These fuck niggas gotta go,* Chubb said inwardly. He didn't mind Chief getting money—that's his boy—but what he couldn't stand and wouldn't stand for was out-of-towners coming to his city, taking money out of their mouth, fucking their women, and flaunting in their face.

It's not happening. It's not fucking happening, Chubb thought.

13 ½ 13 ½ 13 ½

After returning from meeting the gun connect, Chief introduced him to Hommi, who sat a duffle bag replete with firearms on top of the dining table.

"Now, how you wanna do this? I copped twelve tones. You wanna send all twelve to the tribe? Or keep a few and send Kinfolks the rest?" Hommi asked.

"Let's go with ya idea—keep two and send the rest up top. They need them more than we do. Ugly will be here soon, too," Raheem said.

"Aight, cool. Oh yeah, one more thing. What you wanna do? You wanna send niggas some work?"

Raheem negotiated, then said, "Yeah, fuck it. We do it for the tribe anyway."

"Dawgs!"

"We can send them three hundred grams along with the blicks," Raheem continued. "I'll tell them to hit the work and turn it into five."

"If they do the right thing, we'll up it next time."

"That's the plan, then."

13 ½ 13 ½ 13 ½

When Ugly made it to Raheem and Hommi's place, it was still early in the next day (1:50 AM), but it was great timing for trafficking.

Raheem and Hommi didn't waste any time loading the car. Raheem then gave Ugly the addresses where Money-Making Rich and Rico wanted her to make the drop. Eager to get the job done, Ugly got right back on the road.

Not long after Ugly left, Raheem called Money-Making Rich and Rico and told them to be ready. He knew better than to give them a specific time because you could never be too sure. And on the flip side, you can never be too safe. One thing you don't ever want to do in the game is put someone you love in a situation that can harm you or break your heart, which Raheem understood. He knew the less you tell a person, the less they have over you when the Feds come.

Raheem looked over his shoulder and saw Hommi sitting on the couch critiquing a Backwood. Hommi gave him a head nod.

"Shit, you tell me what's up?" Raheem said.

"What you want me to tell you, cuzo?"

"Dawg, let's step out, hit up a club—something. I'm tired of chilling in the spot. I haven't done shit since I been home."

Hommi didn't care for the nightlife. A good night to him was the same kind of night Raheem was tired of—sitting in the house, listening to music, smoking, and drinking. As long as Hommi was adding money to his safe, he was satisfied staying home.

"I'm trying to get some new pussy, I'm not gonna front. And to keep it all the way real, we deserve it," Raheem said.

"Where you wanna go?" Hommi asked, lighting the cigar.

Smiling, Raheem said, "I was thinking Secret's. That strip club be jumping."

"Aight, fuck it. You right, we deserve it. Plus, what's the point of ballin' if ya not gonna play ball?"

They both went to their separate rooms to get dressed. Neither one said anything, but they both had the intention to out-dress the other. An hour later, they pulled up to Secret's, drove around back, and parked. The parking lot was lively, and when they got out of the car, all eyes were on them.

To complement him, Raheem wore a tan and brown Hermès button-up, blue stone-wash vintage Polo jeans, a big-buckle Hermès belt, and a pair of Rag & Bone soft bottoms. For jewelry, he decorated his wrist with his new all-gold Cartier. Not too loud, but then again, not too quiet.

Hommi, on the other hand, sported a red and black Polo rugby shirt with the big Polo logo the color of wheat, all-black fitted Yves Saint Laurent jeans that rested perfectly on top of scuff-proof, wheat Timberlands. To hold his pants up, he wrapped a Versace belt with the Medusa head around his waist. As for jewelry, he put it in his mouth. So whenever he smiled, you couldn't help but see the gold encrusted in diamonds guarding his teeth.

Raheem and Hommi smelled and felt as good as they looked.

As they entered the club, gold diggers schemed while intrigued onlookers whispered among themselves. Inside, the club was vast and surrounded by huge mirror walls. Two stages occupied the floor for the exotic dancers. The first stage dwelled at the front near the marble-top bar, while the second stage was further in the back. Above both stages, exotic dancers covered in body paint danced in cages. Everywhere you turned, you saw beautiful, half-naked women. The place was crowded—shoulder to shoulder—and smelled like perfume over sweat. From midair, money fell and joined the surplus on the floor.

Finding an empty, clean table by the first stage, Raheem and Hommi settled down.

"From here, we can see the front door too," Hommi said.

Acknowledging what Hommi had said, Raheem glanced at the entrance and shook his head.

Not long after, a slender, curvy, dirty-blonde white woman with round breasts swayed over to their table, braless.

"Can I help you gentlemen?" the dirty-blonde waitress asked, yelling over the music.

"Yeah," Raheem announced. "What's the secret?"

"Huh? What you say? You got to speak up, handsome," the waitress said.

"I said—yeah, actually, you could. We," Raheem pointed at himself and Hommi, "would like two bottles of Ace of Spades and five thousand in ones."

"Do you want me to take the money out of the five thousand to cover the bottles?"

"Did I say anything about taking anything out of anything?" Raheem asked and looked at Hommi, who chuckled.

"Naw, we straight," Hommi answered. "Here, ma." He gave the waitress fifteen hundred dollars. "That should cover the bottles, plus some."

"—Plus some pussy," Raheem mumbled.

"Okay, I'm sorry for assuming. I'll be right back." After apologizing, the waitress left to fulfill their order.

"That pink-toe got a nice little ass on her for a bunny, huh, kinfolk?" Hommi asked, watching the waitress walk away.

"Word, she does," Raheem agreed. "And you know I love me some pig feet." They both laughed.

"I'm glad you talked me into coming out. It's poppin' tonight, no bullshit," Hommi stated.

Raheem embraced the extravagant atmosphere the club had to offer. He felt good about where he stood in life, but where he stood today was just the beginning.

Sticking out of a bucket of ice, the waitress returned with two bottles of Ace of Spades and five thousand in ones.

"Separate a thousand ones for us five times, sexy, and set the money across the table," Raheem instructed.

"No problem," the dirty blonde replied politely, then focused on the task. Once finished, Hommi threw her two hundred dollars.

"Thank you, handsome."

As soon as the waitress moved along to serve another patron and the money on the table was visible, exotic dancers flocked over to Hommi and Raheem.

"Heyyy boys," said a succulent dancer. "What can I do for y'all?"

"You can start by bending over and touching ya toes," Hommi said.

"Okay."

Lap dances: they accepted a few. Money: they threw a bunch of it on stage and in the cage above. And bottles: they bought two more of Moët. They were having a good time, but it wasn't until Raheem set eyes on an exotic dancer he had to have that the pandemonium—for him—slowed down.

The woman he couldn't turn from was Native American, brown-skinned with a reddish tint, had long eyelashes, light brown eyes, and long black wavy hair. And her body? Well, let's just say her body wasn't one you'd see every day. But Raheem wanted to. He wanted to see it every day and night. Which is why, when she was in the process of passing, he gently grabbed her hand and said, "Excuse me, sweetheart, but do you have a minute?"

Curious who attempted to court her, the Native beauty looked Raheem over.

"I'm sorry, honey, I don't," she answered.

"Why not?"

"Cause I'm busy."

"What's ya name?"

"It's Rose."

"Ya real name," he pressed.

"Oh my God, why?" Rose asked, annoyed.

"Because she matters."

Rose rolled her eyes. "Rain. My name is Rain."

"Now we gettin' somewhere. But since ya busy, how 'bout I give you a call so we can chop it up later?"

"Oh no, I don't hook up with men outside the club. Sorry, I really have to go now."

"Aight, aight, hold up." He went in his pocket, pulled out two one-hundred-dollar bills, and wrote his cell phone number on both of them. "Here," he handed Rain the money. "You call me."

Rain looked at both bills under some light and was confused. "Hey," she called. "Why did you write ya number on both bills?"

"Because," Raheem said, "I'm Two-Times. And I'm twice the nigga."

13 ½ 13 ½ 13 ½

Back in Boston, under two different hair dryers, Tia and Liya sat in their favorite hair salon. It wasn't twelve o'clock yet, and the place was crowded with women under hats, scarves, and dryers. Tia and Liya had made arrangements last week, so they were fortunate to be almost done and not stuck in the waiting area.

"So, how you and Raheem making out?" Liya inquired.

"We good as of now. I spoke to him last night. I gave him an extension, but he got a couple more weeks to get back to me. I swear, girl, I'm not hearing no more excuses, forreal." Tia said.

"I feel you, but at the same time, I'm happy to hear that y'all in a better place."

"Thank you, Liya."

"You know ya welcome, boo."

"Aye, you wanna hear some real shit, though? If it wasn't for you, bitch, I woulda been gave up on that boy."

"Noo. Don't say that."

"Why not? It's true. You remind me how much I love him during the times I forget."

"That's what I'm here for." To get more comfortable, Liya shifted some in the chair. "My butt starting to hurt."

"You know what they say, 'beauty consists of pain.' But anyways, hopefully, me and Raheem can figure something out while I'm in Myrtle Beach. Because you know a bitch deserve to be held every night by her man. Especially after being a good girl for all these years."

"Tia, you not about to tell me you been a good girl your whole relationship, so you can just stop."

"Liya, seriously. I ain't never gave Raheem's pussy away."

"Well, if that's the case, shit, I'll marry you."

They both laughed.

"So, how long you staying in Myrtle Beach for?"

"Until I get pregnant."

Not saying a word, Liya raised her cell phone up to her eyes and concealed the envy that dwelled in them as best as possible. *I'll do anything to switch places with this girl. These bitches kill me with this 'it got to be my way' perfect relationship shit. Only thing perfect is a dream.* She thought.

Ding! The hair dryer alerted them that they were finished.

"Thank God," Liya announced.

"Forreal though. Let's go get a bite to eat. I'm hungry," Tia said.

"Let's do that. I'm hungry too."

After they paid their stylist and thanked them, they strutted out of the salon, complimenting each other.

CHAPTER ELEVEN

BOSTON BAGHDAD

Lately, if you saw Freaky, you saw Rico. After bailing him and Knoxs out of jail, Rico honestly felt like a friendship with Freaky was worth sowing. A friend with Freaky's characteristics was the kind of company he wanted to keep. He trusted Freaky. And he believed a relationship that is sowed in the fabric of trust is parallel to a good gun that never jams—*they're reliable.*

Out of jealousy, people spoke negatively about their bond:

"Freaky is Rico's right-hand now—what is this world coming to?"

"Dem niggas don't even know each other like that."

"Fake love shit. Rico probably game-facing dawg. He so grimy, I don't know how Freak trust him."

Rico and Freaky heard the whispers, but they were all said in the dark. And as the saying goes, *everything that is said in the dark will one day come to light*, so they waited to see who the light would illuminate. *He who radiates darkness will swiftly consume.*

So that Honest could buy herself lunch, Rico parked in front of her job on Dorchester Avenue to drop off some money.

"Big head," Rico spoke into the cell phone. "Come outside. I'm right out front."

"It's nice as shit today," Freaky said, seated in the passenger seat.

"You ain't lying," Rico agreed.

When Honest appeared from the brick building, she was caught off guard by the sight of Freaky. *What is Rico doing with him?* she thought. Freaky was clueless to who Honest was, but she knew exactly who *he* was—and him being around her man was a little too close for comfort.

Rico got out the car. "What's up, big head?" he said. "Why you look like you saw a ghost or something?"

Snapping out of a trance, Honest said, "I'm sorry, bae, I was thinking about something pertaining to work."

"Everything good, right?" Rico asked, concerned.

"No, everything ain't good," she said with a little sass. "Your wife is hungry."

Smiling, Rico said, "That's why I'm here. I brought you a sausage. Now I want you to take ya time when you eat dis muthafucker, I'd hate for you to choke."

Playfully, Honest punched him.

"Aight, aight—here, crazy. Fifty dollars."

Honest accepted the money. "Thank you, punk."

"Watch ya pretty mouth, sucker. Give me a kiss so I can flex."

She gave him a kiss, then went back inside the building, thinking of the perfect plan.

Approaching a red traffic light, Rico brought the car to a complete stop. As he and Freaky waited for the light to change, he checked the rearview mirror as usual and immediately noticed a gray Honda Accord with a familiar license plate number. Rushing, he scrolled through his cell phone to confirm his suspicion, and just like he thought—the exact same license plate number was logged in his phone.

Like the weather, his mood changed.

To see who was behind the tints, Rico tried to take advantage of the sun and make out exactly who was in the car, but his vision was still impaired.

"Yo, Freak," Rico called, tapping him on the leg.

"What's good?"

"You see the gray Honda Accord behind us?"

Freaky looked and inwardly said, *fuck.* "Yeah, I see it, kinfolk. What about it?"

"That's dem kids, bro," Rico asserted.

"You sure?" he asked, trying to dilute the surety in Rico's observation.

"Nigga, I'm positive!"

Freaky was in a tough position…

Only a tough decision would get him out of it.

"So, what you trying to do?" Freaky asked.

"You mean—so what *we* bout to do," Rico corrected, staring at Freaky awkwardly.

"You know what I meant."

When the traffic light turned green, Rico let the Honda get in front of him.

"I'ma tail them until we get to their destination. Once there—we smack 'em," Rico explained.

"Could you see who was in the whip?"

"Barely, but it looked like a yime and a nigga. I know the whip belongs to that kid Flames' girl. I figured that's her driving. And the nigga has to be dawg."

The Honda took a right onto Talbot Ave. Remaining two cars behind, Rico did the same.

Freaky searched the car, thinking, *I need something to cover my face with.*

"Yo, you don't have a ski mask or a hoody in here?"

"There should be a hoody in the back on the floor," Rico said.

Freaky reached in the back, snatched the hoody off the floor, and put it on.

With Rico still two cars behind, the Honda ascended Miller Street until it yielded at a stop sign. After allowing cars to pass, and once it was clear, the Honda made a left onto Harvard Street, crossed a bridge, then stopped for a red traffic light.

What the fuck! Dumb-ass lights, Rico cursed inwardly.

Suddenly, the light turned green, and the Honda made a right onto Glenway Street, drove for three blocks, then pulled over and parked.

"Pull over right here," Freaky urged, pointing. "It's not too close but not too far."

Agreeing with Freaky, Rico pulled along the curb and parked. Clutching a .357 long-nose, he immediately got out of the car. Hunching over, gun on his side, concealed, he crept, along the line of parked cars.

Meanwhile, on the sidewalk, hunched over too, under a hoody, Freaky groveled while gripping a .45 Colt revolver. As they both advanced, they blocked out everything…

> The children across the street playing basketball in the driveway.
>
> Who their transgression may affect.
>
> Potential witnesses.

Even life in prison.

Rico made it to the Honda first. The woman that was previously driving had the door cracked open and was about to climb out the car. But when Rico suddenly appeared, she jumped, and Rico raised the pipe to her head.

The cylinder spun six times.

The passenger was rising out of the car when Freaky fired, and a slug slammed into his chest, forcing him to fall and lie awkwardly between the car and the door. Seeing that, Freaky kicked the door completely open and aimed downward with both hands.

The passenger gazed at who was about to take his life and was shocked—the man standing over him had once spent plenty of time in his home, had called his mother *Mom*, had even called him *brother*. But in the eyes that stared back at him, there wasn't a trace of acknowledgment.

From the passenger's facial expression, Freaky could tell he knew who he was; the hood couldn't deceive him. So he pulled it back.

"Secrets are best kept when only one can tell it."

A flash was the last thing the passenger saw.

13 ½ 13 ½ 13 ½

Chief was excited. It had been a while since he felt like he was needed. But now that he was in the process of regaining wealth, he was feeling somewhat like his old self. He had made a promise—swore he would never again allow fast money to get the best of him. Instead of being a liability this time around, he was gonna add value to the ring.

For instance, it hadn't even been a week yet, and he had already gotten rid of the drugs Hommi and Raheem first gave him and was ready for more. He also had the amount of money they wanted back in return.

After scrolling through his cell phone and landing on Hommi's number, he called.

Ringing twice, Hommi answered. "Yo."

"Aye, mane, what's up wit it? It's Chief."

"I'm hip, my G. You the only one that call me soundin' like you whispering and shit."

"Ya a funny muthafucka. But aye, I need to see you one time, two times."

"Where you at?"

"The trailer park, in Socastee."

"Aight, I'll be there when I'll be there."

"Don't come here," Chief said. "Meet me at the smoke shop on the Bully (Ocean Blvd). I gotta grab some wax paper."

"I'll see you there. Out." Hommi hung up.

Chief grabbed Chubb's car keys from off the arm of the couch and told him he'd be back.

"Aye, mane, where chu goin' with my ole lady?" Chubb asked. With the TV remote in hand, he pretended to be looking for something to watch.

"Bend a corner real quick."

Chief didn't have to tell him where he was going—Chubb already knew. He was listening in on Chief's call, and beneath the surface, he was fuming. Thinking, he said to himself:

What is dis nigga, a secret squirrel? Nigga hidin' dem fuck niggas like we ain't good enough to meet 'em. Who the hell are they, God? My boy turned into a cold dick-rider. I'ma keep my mouth shut and get dis money though.

13 ½ 13 ½ 13 ½

Seated at her desk, Honest tapped her foot on the floor repeatedly. Her head hurt from thinking so hard. She just couldn't grasp what her eyes captured today. *What was Rico doin' with that dude?*

She massaged her temple as her mind ran on.

Is Rico already aware of who Freaky is? He can't be. I know my man.

Honest felt helpless and wasn't sure what to do. She wanted to tell Rico, but how? She combed through her hair with her right hand, trying to find a way to disclose what she had to say without Rico asking her a million questions, but she came up with nothing.

She then thought about keeping it to herself—staying out of it.

I can't, she told herself. *My man's life might be in danger.*

In frustration, Honest threw her pen across her desk, folded her arms, and leaned forward in her chair. She felt sick and hated the feeling she was experiencing. Stuck between a rock and a hard spot, she didn't know if she should tell her lover or tell her—

"Excuse me, ma'am," said a young white man standing at her desk. "I have an appointment with Dr. Myrie."

13 ½ 13 ½ 13 ½

For asylum, Rico and Freaky went straight to a home in Hyde Park. Because other S.O.L.O. members frequented the house, there were already a bunch of people hanging out.

Neither Freaky nor Rico said a word about the shooting.

Hoping to learn more about the aftermath, Rico sat in a chair, stone-faced, and watched the news.

Coming from another room, Freaky entered the living room and pressed his back against the wall.

"Yo, bro," Freaky called.

Rico looked at Freaky. "What's goody?"

"I need to holla at you," Freaky said.

"Talk."

"Not right here—the bathroom."

Getting up, Rico followed Freaky into the bathroom and closed the door. The friends they isolated themselves from didn't mention it, but they *did* think it: *What the fuck they got going on?*

Rico turned on the water, letting it run in the sink. "What you need to holla at me about?" he asked.

"So, ol' boy I clapped—he wasn't who we thought he was," Freaky explained.

"What you mean?" Rico asked, screwing up his face.

"What you mean, *what I mean*? Dawg wasn't who we thought it was. It was his younger brother."

"And the yime?"

"The bitch was Flame's girl, like you said."

"How you know all this so soon, Freak?" Rico looked in his eyes for a trace of deception.

"Come on, bro, you know the streets talk. And I fuck with mad bitches that's in the loop. You know that, bro."

Rico cupped his chin. "So that was ol' boy's lil' brother?"

"Crazy, huh?"

"Naw," he said without hesitation. "No bullshit, I don't give a fuck. On dawgs. What is a war without casualties? I'm countin' the bitch and the lil' brother. The bitch probably brought the kid Flame to do a mission, or he probably called her after one to pick him up. And the brother—shit, I'm sure we woulda had to clip him someday anyway. Fuck 'em both. Two field goals." He smirked. "But fuck all that, they dead, we livin'—so let's talk about Fred. How'd ya like to get money with me and my peoples?"

"I'd love to, my nigga."

Freaky stuck three fingers out, and they shook hands.

"I fucks with you."

CHAPTER TWELVE

BOSTON BAGHDAD

The sun's head was poking over the horizon when Ugly finally made it to Boston. She felt a huge sense of relief once she parked outside the last address.

Sipping her coffee carefully, she checked her surroundings. The street was clear and quiet. The birds chirping—sounding like music to Ugly's ears—was all you could hear.

It's nothing like the city, Ugly thought.

Too bad she was only in town on business. She wanted to stay awhile, surprise some of her loved ones, but she had to get back to North Carolina. Her father had her daughter, and she told him she only needed him to watch her for a few days. And too, she had work tomorrow night.

Calling Raheem, she told him she was outside the address in Boston. In response, he urged her to sit tight.

After a boring ten minutes, Rico came out of a sky-blue house and stepped onto the porch, looking up and down the street. Sensing Rico was who she was supposed to be meeting, she thought it was kinda funny that she could see him, but he couldn't see her.

To get his attention, she flashed her high beams. Rico proceeded over to the car while she rolled down the passenger window.

Outside the passenger's front door, Rico kneeled down and said, "Every day."

In response, Ugly said, "Is Dre Day," confirming her relation.

"Now that we got that out the way," Rico carried on, "park ya ass in the yard right there, pretty lady." He pointed at the open yard adjacent to the sky-blue house.

Did he call me pretty? Ugly asked herself, backing into the yard and parking.

"Pop the trunk!" Rico ordered. She hit the release button. Looking for the tools to take the car apart, he dug through the trunk.

Ugly rolled her window down. "The tools are under the spare tire," she said, hoping to speed up the process. *I'm tired,* she thought. *I need to take a nap, or I'ma kill myself on that highway on my way home.*

"Excuse me?" she called out to Rico.

"What's up, ma?" Rico asked after coming from behind the car.

"Um," she smiled nervously. "What's your name again?"

"I never told you my name," he declared, wondering why she wanted to know.

"Okay—so what is it?" she asked, hoping she wasn't crossing boundaries.

"Names are unnecessary, ma," he retorted. "What's shaking, though?"

This nigga rude as hell. I don't even wanna ask him shit no more, she thought. *Girl, forget ego trippin', you need some rest.*

"Can I take a nap inside while you do what you gotta do, please? I'm tired as hell, and I gotta drive straight back to N.C. from here."

Rico almost said no, but then he thought about it. He could already tell Ugly was gonna get on his nerves. He wasn't interested in small talk. Even though he thought Ugly was cute, he had a job to do, and he could do without her in his face while trying to work.

"You know what," Rico began. "Yeah—you can do that. Come on."

Ugly climbed out the car and followed Rico around the back of the house. At the back door, she removed her shoes and entered the dwelling. As Rico guided her through the apartment, she looked around, surprised at how clean the living space was.

No dishes in the sink. No grease or oil over the stove. And the living room—very neat and clean.

Silently, she applauded his cleanliness. *I wish I had a man that carried the same qualities.*

In the hallway, adjacent to the living room, Rico grabbed a blanket from the closet and gave it to Ugly.

"You can chill here in the living room," he said.

Ugly took a seat on the couch. "Can I have something to drink?"

This woman got me fucked up, Rico thought.

"It's soda and water in the fridge, cups in the drainer. Help yaself." With that, he left.

"Wow," Ugly uttered. "Whatever happened to hospitality?"

13 ½ 13 ½ 13 ½

The following morning.

After undergoing multiple surgeries, family, friends, spectators, fake friends, and those who didn't even know his real name—but now that he was dead, swore they were best friends—mourned in Boston Medical Hospital.

The dead's parents had questions that no one could answer. No one but the killer.

And God.

Flame cried uncontrollably after witnessing his brother under a white sheet, smudged with red fingerprints, being wheeled out of the surgery room—going who knows where.

Trying to calm him, Mega hugged him, letting him vent.

"It's all my fault. Because of me, he's dead, bro. Niggas killed my lil' brother, on dawgs. Why, bro? Why? He ain't have nothing to do with shit." Stepping back and out of Mega's embrace, Flame stalked the floor. "My lil' brother is dead. On dawgs, I'ma kill these niggas."

Mega shook Flame by the shoulder. "Gunsmoke, did lil' bro say anything to you before he died? Did he say he saw who did it? Was you able to get any information out of him?" Flame shook his head. "What did he say? Dawg, focus. Tell me what he said. You gotta snap out of it and get focused if you tryna get some get-back."

Flame pulled himself together.

"I asked Cory did he see or know who shot him, and… and he couldn't talk. But he shook his head yes," he disclosed. "On everything I love, I'ma kill everybody. I'ma body niggas' mothers, sisters, girlfriends, brothers—anybody that anybody love—I'm killing. They took my girl and my brother. Everybody is dead."

While he rambled on, Mega thought about the phone call he received the other day.

"Yo!" Mega blurted. "I think I know who's behind this. But listen to me—ya buggin' talkin' about all that killin' in here. You don't know who's listening. And let me put you onto some real shit. It's one thing more important in war than killing… and that's surviving. So let's survive today and find out exactly who smacked bro, so we can kill tomorrow."

13 ½ 13 ½ 13 ½

Inside the kitchen, Rico weighed the heroin wrapped in plastic while Darian stood near.

"Three hundred grams," Rico disclosed.

"We should hit it and turn it into five," Darian said.

"That's exactly what we're gonna do. Bro said that anyway. But we're gonna cut it with the fentanyl and turn it into six."

"Sound smooth. How many hammers they sent?"

Rico picked the duffle bag full of pistols off the floor and set it on top of the table. "He said him and Hommi kept two for themselves, but they sent niggas ten blicks." He unzipped the bag and reached inside. "We got ourselves a pistol-grip .357 phantom," he said, setting it on the table before continuing. "A snub-nose .38 special. A 9mm Beretta. A .45 Millennium. A Glock 19. Oh, look at this baby." He pulled it out of the bag slowly. "A MAC-11."

"Nothing like it," said Darian.

"Nothing!" Rico agreed, then revealed another gun. "This is a .22 TEC. The clip is clear, you see that?"

"Let me see that lil' sucker. This muthafucker like that," Darian said, examining the weapon.

"Kinfolk, fuck that dumb-ass gun and check out this long-nose .44 Bulldog."

"Damnnnnnn—that look like the Joker's gun."

"Hold up, we're not done. We got a .40 cal and a .380 Bersa." Rico turned the bag upside down. "That's it." With all ten guns lying on the table, he looked at them with lust in his eyes.

"How much do we owe for the food?" Darian asked.

"Five hundred."

"Five hundred what?"

"Bro said all he want us to do is give Tia five hundred dollars. He's flying her out to S.C."

"Shit, for all this, I'll throw her another five, on Gee'z." They both laughed in agreement.

After putting the guns back inside the duffle bag, Rico said, "Um'a call Freaky real quick."

"For what?" Darian said, confused.

"Tell him we need to meet up so we can talk about our next move."

"Why would we need to chop it up with him? What does he got to do with it?"

"He's getting paper with us."

"What makes you think I want to get money with him? I don't even trust ol' boy, to be real." Truthfully, Darian was offended. He didn't appreciate how Rico undermined his volition and involved Freaky without giving him a chance to make a decision for himself.

"You don't have to get money with him then. He'd get gwop with me," Rico said.

"You really fuck with this guy?"

"Yeah, I really do. Why?"

"Because I don't. Like, my nigga, dawg, you don't even know that dude no more. How could you trust someone that gets clapped, moves O.T. for a few years, then comes back out the blue like he never left? Ya tripping."

"Naw, nigga, ya tripping. The nigga showed nothing but loyalty. I give it back. That's my kinfolk. I fuck with the nigga, and um done rapping about the shit. Fuck I look like talking about another nigga like some hoe." With nothing more to say, he stepped off to use the phone.

One thing Darian realized about his brother was that he gave too many people a chance to harm him if they decided to. Personally, he believed Rico trusted too many people and put too many people on his level. But what could he do or say? Rico was grown. All he could do—and would do—was try to protect him by all means. And if something were to happen to him? Kill. That's what family is for. Like their mother used to tell them: "Without family, you have nothing. And without family, you are nothing."

13 ½ 13 ½ 13 ½

Raheem was a little early, maneuvering through the crowded airport in search of Tia's departure gate. Her plane was scheduled to land at one o'clock p.m., and he couldn't wait to see her.

During his search, he happened to walk by a group of authority figures. Some maintained a K-9. However, in passing, Raheem overheard them talking about someone being suspicious and their description. He wasn't able to hear much, but he did hear that whoever they were looking for was short, Latino, and a woman with a large designer bag. Raheem hoped the best for the woman, but the conversation was of no importance to him.

That was until he noticed a Latino woman, obviously nervous, carrying two large Chanel bags, waiting to go through customs. Raheem couldn't imagine not warning her, especially knowing there was a chance she might go to jail. Quickly, he surveyed the area. He didn't see cops, so he headed over to the woman and nonchalantly stood beside her. Up close, he saw that she was Mexican, quite gorgeous, and had long, chocolate-brown hair. Sweating profusely, her forehead glared as she shook.

Due to the height difference, Raheem bent some and whispered, "I don't know you, and you don't know me, but I do know for sure the police is on to you. And if I was you, I'd abort mission." The Mexican woman took a glimpse of Raheem before he turned his head and checked his surroundings. The police were partly of his concern, but he was mainly worried about Tia. The last thing he needed was for her to see him talking to another woman. Nevertheless, when he turned back around, the Mexican woman was gone. She had disappeared among the crowd of people.

When Raheem heard someone call his name, he was back on the move. That's my baby girl, he thought and looked for her. Spotting her at the baggage claim, he smiled. That's mine, he said to himself and strolled over to her, hugging her tightly. He then kissed her.

"I miss those soft lips," he admitted. "Let me get ya bag for you." He grabbed the suitcase off the treadmill, and together they headed for the door.

The hotel room was twenty-four stories high, had a beachfront view, and was equipped with a jacuzzi, which dwelled partly on the balcony.

The hot water thrusting from the jacuzzi felt good against Raheem and Tia's bodies as they relaxed and indulged in a tall bottle of Grey Goose. Now this is how life is supposed to be spent, Raheem thought. He also wished that someday soon he could spend every night with Tia like this. Wishes do come true, but he knew it was going to take sacrifice. He just had to get Tia on the same page, which wasn't going to be easy, but she was gonna have to come to terms and play ball. That is, if she wanted to continue playing ball in his ballpark—on his team.

Without warning, Tia wrapped her petite legs around Raheem's waist, and through her teardrop-shaped eyes, she stared into his. "Raheem," she said, "why do I feel like you don't love me the same?"

Instantly getting a headache, Raheem pinched the bridge of his nose. "Tia," he uttered, "is this really what you want to talk about? Like, we're supposed to be enjoying the night, the stars, each other. I can't even believe you questioning my love for you. We been together since we were lil' niggas."

"So," she retorted. "And yup, this is what I want to talk about. Us being together since we were young don't have nothing to do with how I feel now."

"Why though? Why do you want to talk about something so irrelevant right now?"

"First off, it's not irrelevant, nigga. It's real important to me. It's how I feel, and it's steady on my mind. Plus, you know me—I'll feel fake as shit acting like everything's all good when it isn't. Now answer my question."

As he casually took a swig of Grey Goose, she waited.

"What's the question again?"

"Yo, you think I'm a fucking joke," she snapped. "You know what the fuck I asked you. Why do you have a bitch feeling insecure about how you feel about me?"

"Mommy, relax. It's not that serious."

"Tell me my feelings aren't that serious one more time and watch me slap the shit out of you."

To prevent a fight, Raheem decided to entertain the conversation and address her question. "You feel the way you feel because of ya thoughts," he began. "And all the frivolous shit y'all women think about. Ya thinking process is negative, and let's not forget ya friends and what they say. If you believed in me completely, you wouldn't think the way you do. But you don't, and that's why you feel the way you do. You know, instead of second-guessing the love I have for you, you should be appreciating what I'm trying to do for us. This conversation we're having is a conversation for a couple that just started dating, not a couple that's going on a decade together."

"You know what," Tia began. "You're somewhat right, but I don't let no one put nothing in my head. And I don't keep negative company around me that would even try to put toxic thoughts in my head. I don't play that. It's nothing no one could tell me about me and mine."

"So if it's not ya friends, then who is it?"

"I told you already, Daddy—it's you. You're the only one that can make me feel how I feel."

Spontaneously, tears came down her face. "I just don't ever want to lose you. I love you so much."

Raheem wiped her tears away with his thumb. "I'm never leaving you. Stop thinking like that. I love you too much for all that." Wrapping his arms around her, he held her close and tight. Against each other's chest, their hearts beat at the same time; they were truly a match.

"You promise, Daddy?" Tia uttered.

"Yes, Mommy—I promise," Raheem answered.

Hungrily, Tia kissed him. From the depth of her vagina, electricity ran through her entire body. Her levee was ready to cave, and her natural juices, which leaked from her camel toe and mingled with the water, was proof.

As Raheem applied soft kisses on Tia's elegant neck and along her collar, she tilted her head back in ecstasy and gazed at the midnight sky.

The stars sparkled in her eyes.

And the misty breeze felt like it came from heaven.

"Daddy," she gasped. "I want to feel you."

Raheem lifted her out of the water and sat her on the edge of the jacuzzi, then began tongue-kissing the pearl between her folds. Furthering his journey, Tia cooed as Raheem toured her love tunnel.

After relishing in Tia's fruit basket, Raheem got out of the jacuzzi and helped her to her feet. He then guided her naked body over to the rail and whispered in her ear, "Who does this pussy belong to?"

"You. It has always been yours," she said, and Raheem parted her sea and entered her after bending her over. Straight ahead, the black ocean shifted and glistened. It, too, represented their love: robust, immense in width, and endless.

In the midst of enduring the mixture of pleasure and pain, Tia uttered, "Daddy—until death do us part, right?"

"You know that," Raheem grunted.

They spent the rest of the week together pretty much the same way they spent tonight. They were enjoying each other's company so much, they lost track of time, and before they knew it, it was time for Tia to return home. After such a great week, Raheem thought they were parting on good terms, but little did he know, the week they spent together only made the situation worse.

Tia wanted him to come home and assumed that he would have known that without her having to say so.

Seated in her assigned seat on the plane, a thought came to mind: He's supposed to want the same as me. He can't possibly love me like he says. For the whole flight, Tia thought about her relationship with Raheem. Her feelings were conflicted, but once she landed, she concluded:

"I'm done coming second. If he wants that life, then fuck it, he can have it, but I'm good."

13 ½ 13 ½ 13 ½

It took persuading, but when Darian finally did agree to sit down with Freaky, he saw him in a different light coming out of the meeting. Before ending the meeting, they decided to modify Norfolk Terrace and use the small complex to sell their drugs.

CHAPTER THIRTEEN

BOSTON BAGHDAD

It was yet again another hot summer day, and Thetford Ave. Park was still the go-to destination on days like today. The whole neighborhood and people from neutral neighborhoods hung out in the park.

In the playground area, there was a man-made green frog that was nothing more than a sprinkler. To keep cool, some of the kids played in the water, while the other children ran around, slid down the slides, swung on the swings, and hung from the jungle gym. Nearby, parents smiled broadly as they watched on.

On the basketball court, separated from the playground by a tall, black-wired fence, a full-court game was in motion. On the sideline, the onlookers made side bets and talked trash.

Then—adjacent to the basketball court—was the tennis court. But since no one played tennis in the ghetto, at least not this one, the space was used to host a dice game.

A forty-ounce bottle of Old English pent down sixteen hundred dollars while a mass of women and men encircled and watched two men gamble for the pot. Their names were Casino and Shocka. Shocka was forty-one years old, tall and dark-skinned with cornrows—a street legend.

Casino, however, was twenty-one years old, average height, light brown with long braids, and not much of anything in the streets. But what difference did it make to the dice? They were indifferent to either factor.

Kneeling, Casino shook the dice as a ball of sweat rolled down the side of his face. *Come on, baby,* he thought and released the three dice, letting them roll…

"Trips!" He jumped to his feet. "Yeah, you see it—that's double. Pay me my money."

Disappointed, Shocka said, "Come on, dawg, who you take me for? I'm forty-one years old. I been around the world once and shook everybody's hand twice. Shoot again. This time, shake the dice."

Screwing up his face, Casino said, "Oh, you got me mistaken, on dawgs."

"I'm not bout to argue with you," Shocka said. "When you shoot, shake the dice."

Being that Shocka was known for being a murderer, not one person spoke up on Casino's behalf.

“Dawg, I’m not rolling shit,” Casino asserted. “I shook the dice.” He looked for someone to back him and confirm the roll, but no one would make eye contact with him.

“Look, it’s simple—roll the dice or I’m taking the pot.”

“Man, stop playing with me.”

“Playing with you?” Shocka laughed. “Lil nigga, I’m not playing. Matter fact—get the fuck out my park. Fuck you talkin’ bout, bitch-ass nigga.”

“Bitch? Ayo, who you—”

Before Casino could finish his sentence, Shocka slapped him across the face. Embarrassed, he stood still, holding his jaw. He couldn’t believe he was just slapped in front of basically the entire neighborhood.

He began to walk away, but he knew he couldn’t let this go unsettled. He had to do something. He had no clue it was going to go this far, but it did, and if he simply left, he’d never be able to return. People would talk about him for the rest of his life. As his face stung, he thought about his older brother, Heron-Homm, and what he would say and do if he heard about him not doing nothing after getting slapped.

But what Heron-Homm thought wasn’t enough to push him.

He just wasn’t fortunate to have heart.

"Fuck this shit. It's not worth it," he muttered, spun around, and started walking away.

"Ah, man!" Someone in the crowd yelled. "That nigga is a bitch!" The mass of people laughed.

Casino, however, froze. *Naw, I'm a dawg, just like my brother,* he concluded and turned back around. He then lifted his T-shirt, freed the .380 Brusa Darian delivered to him, and pointed it at Shocka's chest. Those that were laughing ceased and now held their breath.

Shocka expressed no fear—not a hint. This wasn't the first time he had found himself at the wrong end of a gun, and he wasn't going to give Casino, a coward in his opinion, the satisfaction of seeing him afraid.

"You better shoot me," Shocka said, gritting his teeth. "Because if you don't, there ain't a dog that will find you."

Casino closed his eyes—and shot him.

When he reopened his eyes, Shocka was sprawled out on the ground, dead. Parents were running, guiding their children to safety. The mass also broke up—the ladies ran for their lives, and the men, if they had one, ran to recover the pistols they had stashed earlier. Meanwhile, Casino went into Shocka's pocket, retrieved what was rightfully his, then vanished.

13 ½ Anthony Legend

13 ½ 13 ½ 13 ½

Located in the C-11 police station, Detective Griffin and Detective Stratton sat in their office. On top of his cluttered desk, Griffin rested his feet and reclined in a chair, while Stratton sat at his desk properly, catching up on some paperwork.

The office was small, consisting of two metal file cabinets and one measly window with a view of a brick wall. Neither detective kept photos on their desk.

"Hey, Tom," Griffin said.

"Sup, buddy?"

"How much you wanna bet the Solo Crew had a hand in that shooting that resulted in the murder of that young lady and that fifteen-year-old—soon-to-be gang banger?"

"Are you fucking serious, dude? How you gonna say that about that kid? You don't know what he would've made of himself." Staring at Griffin, Stratton wondered if that was how he thought of all young Black men—like potential gangbangers.

"You know what, Tom? You're right. I apologize for that. But I still bet you it was the Solo Crew that did it."

Stratton laid his pen down, then said, "Dude, what is it with you and the Solo Crew? Why are you so obsessed with them? I'm starting to think your beef with them is beyond them breaking the law. Come on, Griff, what is it?"

When Griffin opened his mouth to speak, the dispatcher came through their radio. "We have shots fired in Dorchester. Location, Thetford Ave. Possible victim. Again, possible victim."

Dropping everything, the two detectives hurried to an unmarked cruiser and got in. Immediately, they both fastened their seatbelts, but rather than throwing the Ford's gear shift into drive and joining the race, Griffin hesitated.

"Tom," Griffin called, staring straight ahead. "I wanna get something off my chest. I think it's only fair that you know the truth."

"Then talk, Griff. We got a shooting in progress."

"The Solo Crew."

"What the fuck—what about 'em?"

"I was a rookie at the time, but they came over the bridge into Quincy, stealing bikes. And well, someone in their crew tried to steal this one bike, but the kid who owned it caught him in the act. In love with the fucking thing, the kid put up a fight for it, and in the midst of the scuffle, caught a blade to the heart. The kid died, Tom."

"Who was the kid, Griff?"

"My nephew."

13 ½ 13 ½ 13 ½

Raheem had a migraine from thinking. They needed a secure connect immediately. Inventory had shrunk, and very soon, they were going to need more product to fulfill orders.

Stressed and starving for some fresh air, he pried himself from the couch and went to the strip club, Secrets, to see Rain.

Courting Rain was never dull. She was challenging, which made Raheem want her even more. Her resistance forced him to do what he did best: think until he figured out a way to seduce her. It took patience more than anything, but with some strategic planning, he eventually won her over.

Golfers were in town for the season, so while they were away from their wives, they took advantage of the club. Under the spell of the goddesses, these proper, straight-backed white men took up most of the space and threw money.

Taking a seat at his usual table, Raheem scanned the club for Rain and saw her near the back, entertaining a customer. "Get ya money," he muttered, then ordered a drink.

The waitress returned, placing two shot glasses of Hennessy and a cold beer on the table.

"G.L.O.," Raheem said, handing her a tip. Left alone with his drinks and thoughts, he sighed.

On stage, a dancer was mastering the pole, but Raheem paid her no attention. He wasn't here for that. The only thing on his mind was finding a connect and getting more money.

"Hey, handsome. Would you like a dance?" Rain asked, sneaking up on Raheem and interrupting his thoughts.

To his left, Raheem looked up. "A dance from you?" he said. "Yeah, why not? I got some ones."

Flopping into Raheem's lap, Rain stroked his waves. "Now, you know I haven't been able to focus since I saw you walk in, right? You got me unfocused."

"Don't do that. Why you gotta blame me?"

"'Cause, fool, you the one to blame." She smiled, then continued, "What's up though? You coming home with me tonight?" Seductively, she bit her bottom lip. "So I can put you to bed," she added. "Then wake you and him up in the morning."

Amused, Raheem chuckled. "Yeah, I'm going home with you, nasty," he said. "You gonna have to follow me to my crib, though. I'ma drop off my whip and jump in yours."

"That's cool—and don't act like you don't like it when I get nasty."

"I love when you get nasty, Nasty."

"I know, that's why I said stop faking."

"Yeah, aight. You want a drink?"

"See—look at you. You want me to get real nasty. Yeah, I'd like one. Give me the money, I'll go get the drinks."

He gave her forty dollars. "You know what I like."

"Yeah, me." She smirked, getting up and heading to the bar. Wearing fishnet stockings and a thong that was hardly visible, Raheem watched her walk away, distracted by her curves. He was so focused on her that he didn't notice the woman approaching him.

"Excuse me, sir, where do I know you from?" the woman standing before him asked.

Raheem looked her over, then said, "You tell me."

Squinting, she pointed a finger at Raheem. "Now I remember. You the guy that saved my ass the other week at the airport. Yup, that's exactly where I know you from."

He looked at the woman again, this time real hard. "Oh shit, that was you. That was about three, four weeks ago."

"Was it? Oh God, time is flying. But look, I owe you big. If it wasn't for you, I'd be behind bars, probably for the rest of my life," she admitted, brushing a strand of hair from her face.

"Listen, you don't owe me nothing. Real niggas do real things."

"Well, so do real bitches," she assured him.

"And I dig all that," he began, standing up. "But what type of nigga would I be if I didn't tell you the police was on to you? In my book, that's half a rat. So rewarding me for doing what I was supposed to do is uncalled for."

Well, I be damned—a Black man with integrity. I had no idea they existed, the woman thought.

With a drink in each hand, Rain joined the duo and stood idle. As her eyes bounced from Raheem to the woman from the airport, she tried to figure out why he was talking to her boss. I know he's not trying to hook up with another girl that work in the same club as me, she pondered.

"Rose," the woman from the airport called. "You know this gentleman?"

Not sure whether to answer truthfully, Rain hesitated for a beat, then said, "Um." She glanced at Raheem for a clue. "Yes, I know him. He's my boyfriend."

"Hold up," Raheem cut in. "Y'all two know each other?"

"Why yes—I'm her boss," the woman disclosed and playfully smacked Rain's butt. Her cheek jumped.

"Wait a minute—you're her boss?" Raheem asked, shocked.

"Well, yes—I'm everybody's boss here." She swept her hand in mid-air. "My family owns this club."

This is crazy. One day, she's about to board a plane—I assume with drugs—but today, she's running a business. Who is this woman? Raheem wondered.

"But anyways," the mysterious woman continued, "Rose, this man right here—your boyfriend—is now family. He saved my life and, I must say, my family from enduring a lot of suffering. I'd like to repay him with loyalty. And I will." She turned to face Raheem. "I told my mother about the airport situation, and she would love to see you to thank you personally. So how about you come by my place tomorrow for dinner?"

"Seeing that you not gonna let me off the hook, I guess I don't have a choice."

"Okay—I'll take your number and text you the address."

After he gave the woman his cell phone number, he said, "My cousin will be joining me. Is that cool?"

"Your family is now our family. Does that answer your question?"

"Clearly."

"I just texted you the address. I'll see you around six," she said, smiling cunningly. "Oh, by the way—my name is Bella."

"Nice to meet you again, Bella, but on better terms this time. I'm Two-Times."

"Well, I'm happy I met you." Turning around, her chocolate-brown hair swung. "Rose, you better keep an eye on him." And with that, she was gone.

"That was different," Rain mentioned and handed Raheem his drink.

13 ½ 13 ½ 13 ½

Outside of Raheem and Heron-Homm's residence, Chubbs sat alone in a new Impala, inhaling a laced cigarette.

The problem Chubbs have with the cousins was over money. He didn't want them in his city making any, as if the Federal Reserve didn't print enough for everyone. Nevertheless, had it not been for Heron-Homm and Raheem, he would still be sleeping in the Impala—prior to his new one.

But in an effort to repay them, he slouched down in his seat when headlights belonging to a Buick Lacrosse descended the road and lit up the side of his car. As soon as the Buick parked and Raheem got out, an M3 white BMW pulled up right behind it and came to a complete stop. Then, the BMW's interior light came on, and Chubbs became furious.

"Now they want our women," Chubbs snarled aloud, putting a dot of cocaine between his thumb and snorting it.

Instantly, he felt the effects of the drug. "This nigga think he can come to my city," he muttered. "And fuck on my bitches."

It had been a while now since Raheem disappeared, and the BMW hadn't budged. This irked Chubbs—the indecency of leaving a woman waiting for such a long period, especially at three o'clock in the morning, was not how a man was supposed to treat a woman in his eyes.

The lady bought you time, and you keep her waiting. Alone. Chubbs thought, shaking his head in disapproval.

Reconsidering his decision, Chubbs thought about disregarding Rain's presence once Raheem reappeared. Groping his Kel-Tec 9mm, he had a vision of shooting Raheem. He fought hard to restrain himself from killing him here tonight—and succeeded in subduing the urge. The last thing he wanted to do was involve an innocent woman, so he let Raheem proceed with his life…

For now.

Um'a get'chu, fuck nigga. Um'a get'chu.

CHAPTER FOURTEEN

BOSTON BAGHDAD

It was early morning when Mega parked his Jeep along the curb of a side street and let Freaky climb inside. Behind the limousine-tinted windows, Freaky sat in the front seat while Flame and one other O.T.S. member occupied the back seats. Not sure whether or not they were aware of his activities, he became uneasy but held his composure.

I hope this bitch ain't running her mouth, he dwelled. But if his secret was no longer clandestine, he was fully prepared.

"Gun smoke," Mega began. "Kill my curiosity and tell me where you been."

"What you mean, where I been at?" Freaky answered, paying close attention to Mega's body language.

"He meant exactly what the fuck he asked you," Flame said.

Freaky scanned the car, looking at all three men in the process, then said, "What the fuck is up with all the hostility? Did I miss something?"

"Freak." Mega called and set the cell phone in his hand into the cup holder. "Can we trust you?"

Acting as if he was appalled by the question, Freaky said, "Are you serious?"

"Freaky, just answer the question—can we trust you?" With his finger, Mega demonstrated what he meant by *we* and swirled his finger around.

"Yeah, of course. But on dead dawgs, I can't believe after all I did for the tribe, niggas is acting like I'm suspect." Freaky stressed.

"Niggas ain't tryna hear that—explain why you haven't been to none of the meetings. And why hasn't no one seen or heard from you? And why can't niggas contact you? We just took a major loss out here, and we riding. But as we bending corners, we wondering where the fuck is Freak at. We could use your gun, but can't nobody even start to think where you at." Flame paused for a second before going on. "It never used to be like that. That's why we looking at you like you suspect. Either that, or you don't give a fuck about what happened to my lil brother and my wifey."

Freaky's heart skipped a beat after hearing Flame mention his brother.

"Come on, kinfolk. Why you had'a go there?" he said. "It really hurt my heart to know that you would even think like that. How can I not care about what happened to your wifey and bro? Ya lil bro was mine too. You think it didn't crush me to see you and ya loved ones in pain, suffering from the loss? Attending funerals back to back with you and listening to you blame yaself over and over? Nigga, that shit got to me. So yeah, I fell back to get my mind right." Poking himself in the chest with his index finger, he continued. "But what have I been doing to get my mind right? I been doing my homework. I been in traffic. That's what I been doing. That's where I been at. I'm for my tribe to the teeth, and that will never switch."

For a long second, silence consumed the car. Then Mega said, "That's all we needed to hear. Real nigga shit."

Gazing out the window, Freaky said, "Matter of fact, speaking of doing homework, I'm ready to turn it in." He turned his head from the window. "I got the drop on dawg who clipped Gun Smoke at the barbershop."

"You talking about that lil nigga Riot? Yeah, I got a whole clip with his name on it," said the O.T.S. member seated behind Mega.

"So tell us about the drop," Mega said.

"I been watching ole boy for a few weeks. I got his movements down pack. I know where he gonna be tonight. If y'all want, we can link up tonight and get him done."

"The fuck you talking about *if* we want to—ain't nothing else we'd rather do," Mega asserted.

"Nuff said. I'll hit y'all later."

With three fingers, Freaky shook everyone's hand. He then climbed out the Jeep, and Flame got back in the front and reclined the seat.

"Ayo," Mega said, putting the gear shift in drive. "Am I bugging, or did I hear that nigga Freaky right?"

"Yeah, you heard him right—kinfolk."

13 ½ 13 ½ 13 ½

Hoping to get Raheem off her mind, Tia figured she'd do some shopping and toured Copley Mall. From one department store to the next, she purchased items—basically attempting to buy happiness that would never emerge through material things.

Nothing in any store could make her as happy as Raheem does. And there isn't a fabric nor a patent in the world that could replace what they have together. Tia wants her man, a feeling a designer can't even create.

Shopping wasn't helping her mood, so she ended the spree and called Liya—who worked in the area. It was twelve o'clock in the afternoon and Liya's lunch break, so Tia asked her to have lunch with her. Liya agreed, and they made plans to meet at the food court in Faneuil Hall.

The food court was nearly empty. Between each customer, there were three or four tables separating the patrons. Hushed conversations could be easily heard.

Hungry and unable to wait, Tia ordered a chicken Caesar salad, paid the man behind the counter, then, with the salad in hand, strolled over to a clean round table and sat down. When she noticed Liya, she was walking toward her—her hips swaying from left to right in a Pledger' Devoe, French lace dress.

"Aye, bitch!" Liya shrieked, making Tia smile. She loved her friend and was glad they were able to have lunch together.

"Girl, you so ghetto," Tia expressed.

"So what. I miss you," Liya confessed. "But how was your trip? Come on, talk to me. I want to hear all the juicy stuff—don't leave nothing out."

Tia breathed in a deep breath. "That boy think I'm stupid," she blurted.

"When you say stupid, what do you mean? Why you say that?"

"First of all, the nigga tryna play me. He keep saying everything he does is for us. Like, nigga, please—save that shit." Tia moved her hair out of her face and continued. "I'm not benefiting from none of this nonsense. The only one getting something out of this is him."

"Did he tell you when he coming back to Boston?"

"Nope. And see, that's the thing—he never mentioned nothing about coming home. He been gone for way too long when it was supposed to be for a month. He acting like everything all good. In his head, I'm happy. The boy so dumb he really think he playing his role. It's just sad."

"That's a nigga for you," Liya said and clasped her hand on top of the table.

Tia took a bite of her salad, then said, "You not gonna get something to eat?"

"I brought lunch from home today. Im'a eat it when I get back to work."

"Oh, you on ya saving shit." She took another bite of her food. "So tell me why this bitch-ass nigga cheating on me."

The bottom of Liya's mouth dropped. "What? How you know?"

"How I know? Bitch, that's like a nigga asking you how you know you pregnant. Let me think… First, he wasn't tryna fuck like that. He haven't been in my pussy in months, and you not tryna dig all in my back?—Suspect! I had to damn near beg for the dick."

While Tia spoke, Liya listened intently.

"The first night, he put it down, though—I'm not gonna lie. But after that, he was acting funny. Okay, what else? Oh yeah, the whole time I was there, he kept his phone off, but he supposed to be getting money," she said sarcastically.

"Yeah, that's some sneaky shit, boo. I gotta call it as I see it."

"And my whole thing is this—why you turn ya phone off? He know his bitch—I'm not gonna come between the bread. But this how I know I'm not bugging—when he did turn the sucker on, he brought it to the bathroom."

Liya shook her head in disappointment. "Yeah, he getting messy, like no funny shit."

"But wait, listen to this." Tia sealed the salad and swept it to the side. "I followed his ass. Yup, I followed his ass and pretended I had to use the bathroom while he was in the shower and went through his phone. And guess what?"

"Girl, what?"

"I found text messages from some hoe named Rain."

"Get the fuck outta here. Raheem really outta pocket. I'm sorry, boo."

"He sure is outta pocket," she agreed. "But it's cool. I got just the tools to fix his ass. He don't even know. I'm gonna play like everything cool, but Im'a make him pay. Mark my words."

"I feel you this time."

"I sacrificed too much fucking with that boy, and he think he gonna make a fool outta me and break my heart. I'm supposed to be his wife. Watch—I got this nigga. Watch."

"Girl, you crazy."

"No, bitch—I'm dead serious."

13 ½ 13 ½ 13 ½

At the entrance of the property, security guarded Bella's apparent wealth. Heron-Homm and Raheem gave the guards their names. Once they were cleared, the guards allowed them to proceed through the wrought iron gate and ascend the paved road leading to a mammoth mansion. Visible cameras attached to the mansion monitored the premises.

In the driveway, an Aston Martin V8 Vantage GT and a Maserati Levante SUV sat. Turning into the driveway, Heron-Homm parked behind the two vehicles. They were getting out of the car when a thought crossed Raheem's mind: Somebody fucking the plug.

Raheem was sure he didn't have to, but he rang the doorbell anyway and waited for someone to answer. The dinner was scheduled for six o'clock, but they arrived fifteen minutes early.

Raheem thought it showed class.

The door swung open, revealing Bella—dressed modestly, her hair in a bun.

"Hey!" she said, smiling. "I'm glad you made it—please, come in. I'm sorry it took a bit to answer the door. I was on the west wing handling something, and honestly, I wasn't expecting you for another ten minutes."

She led Hommi and Raheem through the mansion.

"Who's your friend?"

"Um, sorry—where's my manners?" Raheem said. "Bella, this my cousin Hommi. I spoke of him at the club, remember?"

"Oh yes, yes, I do recall." Stopping in her tracks, she turned around and shook Hommi's hand. "Did your cousin tell you he saved my life?"

"He mentioned it, but he didn't go in depth," Hommi answered.

Bella smirked. "I see. A man who don't need to brag is a man who do what he do because it's supposed to be done—not because he want recognition."

Moving along, she led them to the backyard, served them drinks, and told them to have a seat and relax.

"Im'a go and get my mother. I'll be right back."

The backyard felt more like an island, with palm trees and a marble stone pathway leading to a man-made lake under a pinkish-blue sky.

When Bella returned, she introduced her mother to the two cousins.

"How are you gentlemen doing? I am di Ballerina."

Raheem and Hommi locked eyes.

"It's an honor to meet ju and ju cousin, Two-Times. Mi daughter tell mi ju saved her from di police. That was very noble of ju, and I wanted to meet ju and thank ju personally." Pausing, she glanced at Bella, then continued. "I wouldn't know what to do if mi child was arrested. And for saving her, I owe ju loyalty. So with that, let's migrate to the diner and have dinner. Mi chef prepared Frogmore seafood stew—ju'll love it."

In every other room, gold and crystal chandeliers hung from the ceiling. Each one caught Raheem's eye—including the expensive paintings on the walls and the staircase that outlined the first floor and spiraled up to the third. The mansion also possessed an elevator.

Once in the diner, they all took a seat at the table. Bella sat at the end, while Ballerina sat at the top. Hommi and Raheem sat across from each other.

Raheem glanced at Ballerina, moved by how striking she was. Not an age line etched her smooth face. Had it not been for Bella, her age would be mysterious. The mother and daughter looked more like sisters.

The dress gracing her curves caused the mind to wonder—did she work out rigorously, or had she had surgery?

While they waited on the food, a maid served drinks. Raheem appreciated the Chandon Imperial Brut Champagne, but he was hungry, and the scent of the food only made him hungrier. So, to distract himself and pass the time, he figured he'd make conversation.

"So…" Raheem began, "if you don't mind me asking, why do they call you the Ballerina?"

Smiling, Ballerina said, "Oh, that's simple." She glanced at Hommi, then regained eye contact with Raheem. "They call mi di Ballerina because I have so many—I dance on keys."

Raheem choked on his drink.

"What's di matter, Two-Times?" She smiled warmly. "Ju never heard or see mi kind?"

"No, it's not that—I just wasn't expecting you to say that… But this is a coincidence, because we're looking for a new connect. The people we been dealing with can't meet our demand."

"I see," Ballerina stated, clasping her hands. "Let's have dinner, and then we will talk."

Two maids brought out plates and set them in front of each person. Steam rose from the food. After refilling everyone's glasses, the maids disappeared.

"Let's make a toast," Ballerina suggested, raising her glass. "Let's toast to loyalty."

When all four glasses were mid-air, they all said, "Loyalty." Then, they drank.

Setting her glass back down on the table, Ballerina asked, "So, Two-Times—how long have you and ya cousin been in South Carolina?"

Raheem set his fork down and gave the question some thought.

"Well, we actually got a bunch of family out here, and we been coming back and forth from Boston since we was young. But as for me, I been out here this time, going on seven months now."

"And me," Hommi joined in, "I been out here for a while. I just did two and a half years on a five-year bid in a South Carolina prison and been on the pave now for a year and some change."

Ballerina listened carefully, then continued eating.

"How's the food?" Bella asked.

"This shit bomb," Hommi answered between bites, making Bella, Raheem, and Ballerina laugh.

Ballerina turned to Raheem, her tone shifting.

"Ju know what mi like and appreciate di most, Two-Times?" she asked, becoming serious. "And before ju answer, mi want ju to know—I thank ju from di heart, and ju are a hero in our eyes."

To show gratitude, Raheem nodded. "Ya welcome, and I'm happy I was able to elude any suffering your family would have had to endure. But to answer ya question—no, I can't say what you appreciate the most, but please enlighten me."

Ballerina washed her food down with champagne, then spoke.

"Mi like ju way of thinking. And mi appreciate di way we meet, because if we met under different terms, mi wouldn't trust ju—and people mi don't trust usually don't live too long."

"Slow down—are you threatening us?" Hommi interrupted.

"Threatening? Of course not." She waved her hand dismissively. "Ju and ju cousin, mi can trust. Mi not worried whether ju di feds or a snitch. Cops don't help criminals escape from cops. And snitches snitch—they don't put their balls on di line."

Listening, the two cousins grasped every word she spoke: She trust none. But she trust them.

Ballerina looked around the table. “Is everyone finished with their meal?” When she saw their plates were empty, she stood. “Good. Come, I would like to show ju two something.” They all got up from the table and followed Ballerina.

Leading the way, she took them to the west wing of the mansion, and together, they boarded an elevator. After taking it down one level, they got off and continued following Ballerina through a soundproof passage.

As they walked, Raheem thought about his gun and wished he had it on him. Hommi was thinking the same thing. He didn’t trust no Mexican. Especially a wealthy one.

When they reached the end of the passage and entered a brightly lit room, Raheem and Hommi immediately noticed the nude woman hanging from a beam by her wrists.

Ballerina studied their body language.

Neither spoke.

“Ju see dis young lady?” Ballerina asked, pointing at the woman—who hung above an open bag of bath salt, two chained Doberman Pinschers, and a skinny, bald Mexican man sitting on top of a bucket, sharpening a knife.

"Dis is a person mi don't trust," Ballerina disclosed, walking them a bit closer. "See, dis young lady right here is a snitch. She was supposed to be our eyes and ears in di airport. She was supposed to let mi daughter know if it was going to be a bust—but she said nothing. She kept silent, knowing di police was coming." She paused for emphasis, then continued. "She knew di government was going to bust mi only child, and dis bitch did nothing. In fact, she was in on it. But thank God for Two-Times… Thank God for ju kind."

Raheem glanced at Hommi and saw him shaking his head. Then, he looked at Bella and wondered if she was anything like her mother.

Ballerina addressed the Mexican man sharpening the knife in Spanish, and he stood.

"And dis is what we do to traitors," she said, flaring her nostrils.

Raheem caught Bella smirking.

I guess that answers my question, he thought.

But that wasn't the only thing he took heed of. Ballerina wasn't showing them how she punished disloyalty because she wanted witnesses. No, not at all. Her effort was meant to ensure the opposite.

Now that the Mexican man had orders, he grabbed the hanging woman's ankle with his bare hand and, one after the other, cut the skin completely off the bottom of her feet.

Unannounced, she screamed insanely.

And the Mexican man?

He tossed the skin to the dogs.

Mumbling from above, the woman begged for her torturer to end her life. But he wasn't quite done.

Grinning slyly, he scooped up a handful of bath salt and stuck it to the bottom of her left, skinless foot. Then, he reached into the bag again, grabbed another handful, and did the same to her right foot.

Screaming for mercy, she fainted.

Luckily for her, the five faces she saw before everything went black were the last faces she would ever see again.

Turning around, Ballerina faced Hommi and Raheem. Grinning like she had just watched a play with an excellent cast, she said, "What do ju two know 'bout montaga?"

CHAPTER FIFTEEN

BOSTON BAGHDAD

Behind Riot's girlfriend's house, Freaky, Mega, Flame, and one O.T.S. member sat in a stolen Toyota Camry on Intervale Street, waiting in the dark.

The only thing they could see in the car was the zeal in the white of each other's eyes. The only thing they heard was the humming sound of the electricity box at the corner.

Along the main road, drug dealers peddled their supply while crackheads found different ways to come up with money to feed their habit. Blue Hill Ave was infested with crackheads, so much so that it was nothing to see or witness damn near anything in the area.

Needless to say, not one man in the car gave a damn about who witnessed what. They all followed the same law: kill your man, and if somebody sees it—kill the witness.

After waiting a significant amount of time with no sign of Riot, Mega spoke up.

"Freak, I thought you knew the time this nigga got up to the time he got his dick sucked."

Mega peeked in the rearview mirror, wondering if Freaky was setting them up. All he saw was Flame's eyes—and they were begging for the word to murder Freaky.

Mega debated whether to give the okay but decided to hold off.

"Bro, I'm telling you, he gonna come out," Freaky stated. "I guess he taking his sweet time tonight. Life does that when it knows death is near."

"Man, fuck all that—let's just run in the spot and press play," Flame urged. "I'm not with none of this sitting duck shit we doing. How we know dawg don't already know we laying on him and called his niggas to come slide?"

"Dawg, chill. You thinking too hard," Freaky said. "He gonna come out, blind to everything. Trust me."

Come on, bring your ass out here, he encouraged silently.

13 ½ 13 ½ 13 ½

Technology intelligence broke into the cell phone D.T. Griffin recovered at the drug house with no problem.

The content—after investigating—led D.T. Griffin and Stratton right to Riot's girlfriend's house.

From the back seat of a cruiser, Griffin looked through a pair of binoculars, monitoring the storefront apartment building, hoping to spot the man of interest.

Stratton, on the other hand, sat behind the steering wheel, watching their surroundings. His gun occupied his lap.

13 ½ 13 ½ 13 ½

They say the crooked live long and the good die young. If true, that myth is getting rewritten tonight. The longer the wait, the stronger Mega's gut feeling got—telling him Freaky couldn't be trusted. Going with his instinct, he forwarded a text message to the O.T.S. member seated behind Freaky.

The text read: Clip 'em.

Unaware of the plot, Freaky rested his head against the headrest.

The man who received the message raised his gun.

13 ½ 13 ½ 13 ½

A dark-colored cat strutted across the street, crossing Stratton and Griffin's path before proceeding along the side of a house.

“Griff,” Stratton called. “You thought about what we’re gonna do when we see this kid? Are we bringing him up on charges?”

“Honestly? No,” Griffin admitted. “I haven’t thought of a plan on this one. But fuck charges—I’ll be happy just kicking the kid’s ass.”

“Then that’s the plan. I didn’t appreciate him shooting at me anyway.”

13 ½ 13 ½ 13 ½

Emerging from the back of the apartment building, Freaky recognized Riot by his distinct walk and shot forward.

“There he go right there!” Freaky announced. “I told y’all he was gonna show up.”

“You sure that’s him?” Mega asked.

“Positive!”

That’s all Mega needed to hear. “Kill.”

They all exited the car, guns drawn.

Hunched over, Freaky and the O.T.S. affiliate hugged the parked cars like shadows, moving quickly along the sidewalk, closing the gap between them and Riot. Hurrying along the street, Mega and Flame did the same.

Retaliation clouded each of their minds—except for Freaky's. For him, this was chess, and tonight's move was just another step in the game.

A move Riot caught—thanks to Rico's teaching.

13 ½ 13 ½ 13 ½

Riot was ready to leave his girlfriend's house for the night when he peeked out the blinds. From the window, he had a clear view of the beginning of Intervale Street.

That's when he noticed something unusual— a tan Toyota Camry he had never seen before.

Thinking maybe the car belonged to someone visiting a neighbor, he waited for the owner to return. That was at 11:30 p.m. By 1:14 a.m., he deemed the car suspicious, retrieved the extended clip from under the mattress, and stuck it in his .40 caliber. *Whoever in that car must got me mistaken for Forrest Gump,* he thought, looking over his shoulder, hoping he hadn't woken up his girl. Curled into a ball, she was still sound asleep. He was grateful—he wasn't in the mood for questions.

Exiting through the back door, Riot threw his hoodie over his head and took the stairs to the ground floor. *Don't let them know I peeped.* Walking to the corner he took a right onto Blue

Hill Ave. From Freaky's perspective, it looked like Riot was heading toward Grove Hall. Needless to say, that was part of the plan. What Riot actually did was press his back against the building and listen. Then, he heard four car doors shut. He peeked around the corner and spotted four goons—hunched over.

Two using the sidewalk.

Two using the street.

Squinting his eyes, Riot tried to see if he recognized any of them.

His heart dropped.

Freak?

Riot ducked back behind the building. Gripping his gun, he tried to make sense of what he saw.

Then, he took in a deep breath.

"I'll make sense of this later. Right now—they coming for me."

He cocked back the .40 caliber and stepped from around the corner.

13 ½ 13 ½ 13 ½

Not expecting to be fired on first, Mega, Freaky, Flame, and the O.T.S. affiliate dropped to the ground, then scurried for cover.

From their new position, all four men returned fire.

The gun battle lit up the area.

13 ½ 13 ½ 13 ½

"Ayo, Tom," Griffin called, pointing a finger. "Look at this."

Stratton turned around. "What the hell is he doing?" he asked. "He looking around the corner… But for what?"

"You wanna bust him?"

"Let's hold off. I wanna see what he's so interested in."

No sooner than Griffin answered, Riot pulled his piece from his hoodie pocket and started shooting.

"Oh fuck!" Stratton blurted. "We got a shooting in progress!" While Stratton dispatched, Griffin shot out of the cruiser. His Glock 19 led the way as he snuck behind a parked car and hid along the side. Not long after, Stratton joined him.

"There's more shooters… I'm not sure how many, but it's definitely a gunfight." He paused. "So look, this what we gonna do. I'ma come from around the car here and try to apprehend this kid. Cover me, aight?"

Stratton nodded. "I got your back."

Griffin crept around the car, then stopped at the rear bumper and surveyed the area. The seemingly endless road was clear, so he bolted across the street, gun raised. Meanwhile, Stratton extended his arms across the roof of the car, keeping his weapon steady. And since fate ain't written in print, he kept his eyes peeled for anything that would make him choose between life—or death. It was still a decent gap between them when Griffin yelled, "Freeze! You son of a bitch!" Had he been closer, maybe Riot would've heard him. But the gunshots muffled the order. And had he heard Griffin instead of feeling his presence, maybe he wouldn't have spun around—thinking Griffin was one of the four men—ready to kill.

A move he never got the chance to apply.

Before Riot could even pull the trigger, a bullet tore into his chest.

He did not fall.

He did not stumble.

In fact, he did not even know he was shot—yet.

This is real life.

But when Stratton fired another round and put a black hole in his head…

He dropped instantly.

This is real life.

There was no blood.

There were no fragments.

Just a motionless body.

Once again—this is real life.

Scowling, Griffin stood over the child and shook his head.

"Fucker," he mumbled.

Once Stratton joined him, he asked, "You alright?"

Griffin stared at him, then back at the lifeless lump of flesh.

"Yeah, pal. Thanks for asking." He kept staring. "You think he was gonna shoot me?"

"Think?" Stratton scoffed, rubbing his chin with the murder weapon. "You forgot what he's capable of? If I didn't take him down, it'd be two dead instead of one. And we can always use a great cop more than… scum."

"I guess you're right."

"I seen it in the little bastard's body language. He was on defense. You looked like offense."

"You gonna be alright?"

"Hey, fuck 'em. He's what I call a nigger. The legends die so he can have a fair opportunity—he squandered it. He gives my people a bad look. We better off without him."

"I absolutely agree."

Minutes before the area was crawling with cops, Mega, Freaky, and their two cronies fled the scene on foot.

Barely getting away.

CHAPTER SIXTEEN

Raheem and Heron-Homm sealed a deal with Ballerina, arranging to receive four kilos of top-quality heroin every month for eighty thousand a piece. But they only pay for two upfront—and in return, she'll give them another two on consignment. A price and a deal— Ballerina said herself, they only got because of Raheem's attributes. Thinking ahead, they moved into a new condo but kept the prior one as a safe house.

After getting their first four kilos, they used the extra space for production—transforming the four into eight using fentanyl. Then they packaged it, stamped it, and arranged to ship two kilos to Money-Making Rich and another two to Boston.

Smoking a cigar of weed, the sun shined down on Hommi and Raheem as they rode around Myrtle Beach, collecting money owed to them. The A/C clipped the ash from the cigar, blowing the smoke around the car.

"Cuzo," Hommi called.

"What's shakin'?" Raheem answered.

"Business is doing good."

"I'm hip. And it's 'bout to be a new month, so you know what that means."

"New money." Hommi hit the weed. "But besides that," he went on, "what's good with wifey? Y'all good?"

"Real talk, kinfolk. I don't even give a fuck whether we good or not no more." Instantly, he regretted saying that. He could only blame himself for this reality. Tia had been there for him when nobody else cared. *Damn... is this life really worth my relationship?* He questioned it—but quickly found a reason to say yes. "I think she fucking with someone anyway. No bullshit."

"Naw, kinfolk. Not T," Hommi said. "That girl can't live without you. You need to stop shittin' though, before you make her do some crazy shit. And you won't have nobody but ya'self to blame." He passed the cigar and made a turn.

Raheem thought about calling Tia but fought against it.

Truth be told, he missed her—he just didn't want to hear her complain.

"I'm not shittin', bro. I'm livin'," Raheem said. "It's like T wants a broke nigga. I told her to move out here so we could get a crib together, but she kept talkin' 'bout we need to 'work on our relationship' first. Like bitch, I been with you goin' on a decade—fuck you mean we gotta work on our relationship?"

Screwing up his face, Hommi said, "No funny shit, bro—fuck all that. That shit sound like a soap opera. If she not tryna live good and get with the program, then bitch, bye. Word! That shit just got me tight. We getting dope money—you could buy a whole new, badder bitch." Pulling into a Kangaroo gas station, he parked beside a pump. "Ayo," he said, as a question came to mind. "Did niggas find out who smoked the lil homie Riot yet?"

"I'm not gonna lie, it slipped my mind. I was supposed to been tell you the war report on that," Raheem admitted. "But basically, this is what it is—Riot was in the middle of a shootout with them kids, and the boys got involved somehow and ended up smacking the lil nigga."

Gripping the steering wheel, Hommi squeezed. "That shit is crazy." He took a second to digest the news, then said, "Niggas on it, right?"

"When have we ever not been on it? Get-back is mandatory. Two for one—you know that." Raheem paused, then added, "But on another note, I'm not sure if you knew Riot's situation, but his people basically abandoned him. All he had was the tribe, but them crackers don't see it that way. And since they don't, they won't render his body to us 'cause he's a minor. Niggas said the morgue wouldn't give them any information at all—about nothing. So as of now, we don't even know where his body at."

Hommi paused for a beat. "This shit is crazy. They can kill him but…" He exhaled sharply.

"Man, fuck all that. Somebody gotta die."

13 ½ 13 ½ 13 ½

The day had passed, and it was now late into the night.

Inside her bedroom, standing in front of a mirror with only a towel wrapped around her curves, Tia held a conversation on her phone.

"What do I have on?" she teased. "You would like to know, huh? Matter fact, what time is it?" She glanced at her phone, then put it back to her ear. "It's one twenty-two in the morning and ticking. Why don't you come over and see what I have on for yourself?"

"Damn," the person on the other end cursed. "I gotta make this last play real quick."

"Well, you better hurry up." While still on the phone, Tia received a text. Checking the screen, she noticed it was from earlier that afternoon. *Dumb-ass phone.* "Boo! Hold on for a second," she said, anxious to read the message.

Fr. Raheem: *I love you, sexy. 2-Times.*

Yeah, we gonna see about that, Tia thought.

"Boo, you there?"

"Yeah, I'm here," the caller responded.

"So what time you think you'd be home?"

CHAPTER SEVENTEEN

Heron-Homm and Raheem met with Ballerina first thing in the morning to go over some business ideas and to pick up their monthly goods.

In the middle of the meeting, Ballerina schooled them more on the heroin trade.

Along with the lessons, she gave them an instrument that allowed them to open and re-seal cans.

Once she recognized you as family, you could be sure you were gonna live like family.

Loyalty—in her book—was unspoken.

Ballerina was impressed by Raheem and Hommi's hustle and their thirst for success.

So much so that she deemed them sharks.

Those were the qualities it took to make it.

And she saw those characteristics in them, clear as day.

Before departing in a black stretch limousine, Ballerina rolled down the rear window and called her two apprentices over.

Granting her request, they now stood outside the rear door.

"Beside so that ju can take care of ju family," Ballerina began, "why do y'all want to be rich?"

Raheem answered first.

"Invincibility."

Ballerina removed her large designer glasses and pointed at Hommi.

"And ju?"

"I'm not gonna stunt, Miss B," Hommi said. "I wanna get rich just so I can give it away."

Ballerina pondered.

"So ju want to get rich to go broke?"

"Ya misunderstanding me." Hommi said shaking his head. "When I was growing up, everyone in my crib was broke," he began. "But even though we was fucked up, we held each other down. So imagine if we was rich—we woulda held each other up." He looked her in the eye. "I keep that at the forefront of my mind while I'm getting this bread—so that once I'm rich, my people are rich. 'Cause if we're all rich, I won't ever go broke." Without uttering another question, Ballerina rolled up the window, and the limousine's wheels began turning.

Resembling two doctors, wearing face masks and sky-blue gloves, Raheem and Hommi re-packaged the brown sugar they picked up earlier inside the safe house.

Now finished, they were cleaning. Hommi wiped down the table with disinfectant, while Raheem washed the utensils. But the opium scent refused to be manipulated from the air just yet. So,

Hommi went over to the window and cracked it. Suddenly, his phone rang. He checked the screen.

Caller Unknown. Hommi usually didn't answer blocked calls—which is why he was hesitant now. But for some odd reason, an unseen force compelled him to press send. *It's probably my lil' bro,* he thought.

"Talk nice or don't talk at all." He answered. The voice on the other end of the phone made Hommi's mind race. *What is this, a game? How the fuck she get my number?* He didn't have a long list of guesses. Aggravated, he shook his head.

Noticing Hommi's mood change, Raheem wondered: *What now?* Placing his hands under the running faucet, he rinsed the soap off.

After listening for most of the phone call, Hommi finally hung up.

"Who was that?" Raheem asked.\

"Ayo—you swung Ballerina my number?"

"My nigga, are you for real?" Raheem asked, offended. "You just broke my heart."

"I didn't mean it like that. I only asked you because of our mutual connection." Rubbing his hand over his face, Hommi ripped the mask off.

"I've been summoned."

"Dawg, what the fuck you talkin' 'bout?"

Trying to make sense of the phone call, Hommi didn't answer.

"Kinfolk," Raheem called. "Holla at me—what you mean you been summoned?"

Snapping out of his thoughts, Hommi said, "Ballerina, cuzo… The bitch Ballerina wanna see me. And she wanna see me tonight—alone." He looked at Raheem for answers.

"You ain't say or do some fly shit, did you?"

"Bro, that bitch is, for one—Mexican. For two—crazy. And for three—old, crazy, and Mexican with a whole lot of money. Why would I play with her? I'm not stupid."

"Then what you worried about?"

"I'm not worried, I'm just curious why she wanna see me alone. I ain't never met with her alone before, so what changed?"

Raheem came around the island. "You puttin' too much thought into it." He shrugged. "Quiet as kept, she might want you to lay down the D."

"I wouldn't borrow your dick to fuck her." Hommi said, making Raheem laugh. "Fuck around and hit her with the stick, next thing I know, I'm tied up and dawg in her basement cuttin' my shit off—pre-ordered by her. Yeah, I'm 150 twice. She gets nothin'."

"Nothin'!"

"You think this shit funny. All I know is, if anything happen to me, you better clip her."

"Here you go again, insultin' me. Let that be ya last time."

Hommi snatched the Backwoods pack off the table. "Yeah, whatever nigga," he said. "I gotta roll up. Bitch got me lightweight stressin'."

13 ½ 13 ½ 13 ½

Before Freaky stood Lil Gary and Bundy.

Bundy was average height, brown-skinned, with long cornrows and no facial hair. Lil Gary was brown-skinned, too—but his hair wasn't long, and he was short with a hard disposition. They were partners. And through the art of taking what wasn't theirs, they survived. According to the streets, they were accountable for many lives.

But anyway… On Harvard Street, behind a school-looking tenement building, they parked side by side. Bundy and Lil Gary stood along the side of their car. Opposite from them, Freaky posed the same position as they all went over some things and put them into perspective.

"So hold up, wait—time out." Bundy gestured for Freaky to stop talking. "You want us to rob ya cousin? Is that what you tellin' us?"

"Bro, lemme ask you somethin'," Freaky said. "Why you keep askin' me that? It's not like I'm tellin' y'all to smoke him. All I'm sayin' is, take his shit." Lil Gary and Bundy looked at each other. Without saying a word, they knew what each one was thinking: If down the road, someone try to rob us, he lined it up.

"Aight, my nigga."

Bundy's tone was leery.

"I'm just tryna make sure this is somethin' you *positively* sure you wanna go all the way through with. 'Cause at the end of the day, I don't give a fuck. And Lil G, I know for a fact, don't give two fucks."

"On dawgs." Lil Gary confirmed.

"So now that we're all aware and content with our decision, go 'head and continue explainin' the stick," Bundy said.

Freaky paused to think.

"Where was I? Oh yeah, his B.M…"

13 ½ 13 ½ 13 ½

Darkness had already dominated the sky when Hommi stopped at the entrance of Ballerina's front gate. In a midnight blue Dodge Charger, rental, he waited for security to let him through. Once allowed, he drove onto the property and got out the vehicle. While one guard—a Mexican man—pat-frisked him, the guard's partner—who was also Mexican—searched the inside of the car.

"You're all set, sir," one guard said after they completed their duties. "You may continue." Hommi climbed back in the car and drove off.

Steering with one hand, he dug in his pants with the other and retrieved the .25 automatic he had stashed in his boxer briefs. "Won't catch me drippin'," he mumbled.

At the front door, there was no need for Hommi to ring the bell. The butler—a narrow, old Mexican man—was already waiting for him in the threshold.

"The Ballerina awaits you," the butler said. "Please, sir, follow me."

Hommi entered the mansion.

Staying close behind the butler, they climbed the stairs up to the third level.

From there, the butler led Hommi through a carpeted hallway.

Inside Hommi's jacket pocket, he clutched the .25, wrapping his finger around the trigger.

For every door he spotted, because he anticipated an ambush, he aimed inconspicuously.

When they finally reached a closed door, the butler stopped.

"The Ballerina awaits you on the other side," he disclosed, then walked away.

Unaware of what lay behind the door, Hommi stared at it with uncertainty. He tried to guess what Ballerina was up to, but he came up with nothin'. He thought about leaving and browsed the area for cameras. He didn't see any. But that didn't mean he wasn't being watched. Regardless, Ballerina knew he was there. And if he left, he'd look like a complete coward. Sure of that, he went ahead and turned the knob, then opened the door.

Along with a bottle of wine sticking out of a bucket of ice, lit candles decorated a glass table, giving off a sweet vanilla scent. As the blue flames flickered, they danced in Hommi's eyes. Those same flames illuminated his stare—a stare that expressed confusion more than tension. The stress he had felt earlier simmered down.

On the floor, rose petals encircled the table. But then, there was the wall, made entirely of glass, enclosing the whole room. There was no need for interior lights--the moon and stars shining down were enough. From where Hommi stood, he could see the city lights. And the view was… Mesmerizing.

It wasn't until a gentle breeze brushed against his face that he realized the ceiling was nowhere to be found. Gazing up at the white moon, he felt just as huge. While Hommi was distracted, Ballerina appeared, wearing an all-white, custom-made Michael Costello gown with a thigh slit, smelling like Chanel perfume. The gown hugged every inch of her figure, Showing a perfect amount of cleavage. Her firm breasts sat up, and her hair was in a neat bun, leaving her elegant neck exposed.

Coming around the table, Ballerina stopped directly in front of Hommi and stared into his eyes.

"Ju thought I was going to kill ju, huh?"

Hommi let out a subtle laugh. "Naw. I thought I was gonna have to kill *you*."

Ballerina smirked cunningly. "I like ju confidence. Ju have heart." She placed her hand flat on Hommi's chest, then rubbed it. "But if mi were to die by ju hands... ur whole world dies."
Hommi's jaw twitched. "Did I hit a nerve?"

Lowering her voice, she continued, "No one should know ju button, señor. If I know ju button, I know ju move—I can control ju." She studied his face. "Disguise ju feelings. Ju feelings show what ju think." Pausing, she smirked. "But that's for another day—let's take a seat."

As they sat, Hommi took a peek at Ballerina's butt. Damn… that motherfucker look so soft, he thought.

Grabbing the wine bottle from the bucket of ice, Ballerina poured herself a drink. She then held up the moist bottle. "Would ju like?"

"Ah, yeah. I'll drink wit'cha." His tone and body language indicated inquiries.

"Mi sure ju want to know why ju here." She sipped her wine.

"I been looking for the answer for a couple of hours now. It better not be nothin' about crossing my kinfolk."

"Oh no, señor. Two-Times is family. He is di only reason ju family. But… to answer ju question—ju here to see mi."

"I see that—but why? I saw you this morning."

"Yes, mi know. And now ju see mi again—tonight." Smirking, she batted her long eyelashes.

"But again—why?"

"Because," she finished her drink. "Like ju, mi came up very poor. And when mi became rich, mi did what ju want to do for ju people. Mi know how ju feel, and mi know ju heart. How can mi not? Mi have di same kind in mi chest. Ju are special—like mi. That is why ju here."

While Ballerina refilled her glass, Hommi pondered.

Am I trippin'? Or is this old bitch shootin' at me?

"So this is all for me?" Hommi swept his hand through the air.

Seductively, Ballerina gazed at him.

"No—it's for us." She glanced at Hommi's glass. "Ju haven't touched ju drink. Ju gonna make a girl drink alone?"

Until she mentioned it, he had forgotten about the glass of wine.

"Now that would be rude," he said and gulped the beverage. "Pour me some more." Happily, Ballerina did as he said. "So, how did you manage to remove the roof?"

"With money," she answered. Then she leaned in. "But mi gonna get straight to di point. Di Ballerina not good with wanting something and not having it. Whatever it is that mi desire—mi get."

"And what is it that you want?"

Crossing her leg, she said, "Di Ballerina want ju. We are two of a kind."

Hommi's thoughts raced. *Wait till I tell this nigga Two-Times this shit.* He was elated inside—but kept his cool. "Can I smoke in here?"

"Ju can do whatever ju want."

Hommi removed a pack of Backwoods from his back pocket. As he rolled up, he dwelled.

"Ballerina," Hommi called. "You sure you ready for this? Matter fact—you sure you want this? I might be a little too much for you."

Ballerina held up one index finger, and waved it.

"There's nothing in dis world mi not ready for. And yes—mi sure I want ju. But under one condition. Ju dare not disrespect mi."

"How so?" Hommi cut in.

"By fucking with bitches. If ju are to fuck someone outside of mi— Ju better make sure she from a whole different state. Mi won't tolerate ju giving anyone a reason to feel like they on di same level as Di Ballerina, Di Queen. They will die. And ju—ju will have problems."

"That's intense."

"No, mi love. That's life of a boss. Mi have a reputation to uphold." She studied him. "Now tell mi—what do ju want to do? Ask ju-self, how do ju want to live?"

He thought about the question.

"What about ya peoples? You know they not gonna be feelin' you fuckin' wit' me."

Ballerina's expression didn't change. "Mi dear, do ju not yet understand who mi am?" She leaned forward. "Look at mi—listen closely. Mi make di rules. And mi break them if mi want to. Mi don't give a chicken's feather about what anyone think. Or what they have to say. If a soul question Di Ballerina… They dead by dawn."

Hommi found himself turned on by the callousness in her strong accent. *I gotta take this for the team,* he told himself. But in reality he was just making an excuse. An excuse to disregard a rule of his own and indulge in Ballerina's web.

"Baby." Hommi called, and Ballerina blushed.

"Yes, darlin'?"

"Heron-Homm and the Ballerina. I like the sound of that—it got a ring to it."

"Please, do tell mi what ju mean."

"I'm fuckin' with you."

"Kiss mi."

"Kiss you?"

She leaned across the table.

"Yes—now." Their lips met, and then their tongues locked. Hungrily, for some time, they kissed, but when their desire reached its peak and they had to have each other, Ballerina whispered, "Take me."

Hommi turned her around and bent her over the table. Caressing up the side of her thigh, he rose her gown over her lower back. Had she worn any panties, they would have been drenched.

Splitting Ballerina's soft, round cheeks apart like they filed for divorce, Hommi enfolded the back of her smooth neck with his right hand and entered her deeply.

Relieved, Ballerina moaned, feeling that they were now one.

Their lovemaking lasted late into the night. But little did Hommi know, Ballerina had never been so dominated—or satisfied. After tonight, she told herself, she wouldn't go without it any longer.

However, two rules had been broken tonight—by them both. Ballerina went against her upbringing by indulging in a sexual relationship with not only the help—but worse: a nigger.

And Hommi… he broke the rule of mixing business with pleasure.

An old adage says: If rules weren't necessary, it wouldn't be necessary to create them…

13 ½ 13 ½ 13 ½

Darkness still had early morning in its grasp while Lil Gary and Bundy waited inside a modest car at the top of Freaky's cousin's street. Keeping their eyes on Freaky's cousin's duplex home, they went over the plan…

Threw names back and forth, trying to think of someone who would buy their portion of the drugs after the robbery.

And talked about sports.

But when the sun's head peeked over the duplex, the talking ceased and, Bundy looked at his military watch.

"It's time," he said.

"Let's get paid." Lil Gary said.

They casually eased out the car, proceeded down the street, walked onto the driveway adjacent to the duplex, squeezed by a Land Rover, and strolled around back.

On opposite sides of the back door, they planted their backs against the house and clutched their guns.

Ten minutes came.

With their backs still against the door, ten minutes went.

After a total of twenty minutes, they heard footsteps and a feminine voice.

Lil Gary looked in the window next door. Besides the shades—they were unattended.

The door unlocking sounded.

Quickly, they pulled their weapons.

The golden knob turned.

They breathed through their noses, and tightened their grips.

The woman—whose voice they had heard—stepped outside and into sight.

Lil Gary raised his weapon and aimed his revolver at the little boy.

"You scream," Bundy began, "The kid is outta here." His warning was clear.

Out of fright, she almost dropped the child and had to regain control. Both her arms wrapped around the boy.

"Mommy. They got—"

"Shut him up," Bundy demanded.

"Be quiet for Mommy." She placed the boy's forehead against her chest.

Bundy gestured with his gun for the woman to go back upstairs. She knew—her obedience was the only thing that would protect her son.

So without resistance, she did as she was told. Close behind, Lil Gary and Bundy followed. Once at the top of the steps, Bundy retrieved the woman's keys and opened the door to the apartment.

"Ladies first," Bundy said.

The woman rolled her eyes and led them inside.

From the kitchen, they heard music playing in the background. They migrated to the nicely furnished living room.

"Take a seat, pretty lady," Lil Gary whispered in her ear. Her skin crawled with goosebumps. But still—she started to head for the couch.

"No," Lil Gary stopped her. "The floor."

She moved the hair from her face, tucking it behind her left ear. *Do what he say. It's my duty as a good mother to do as he say and protect my son.* She sat down on the carpeted floor. Her son sat in her lap.

Outside the living room, beyond a wall, there was a long hallway. While Lil Gary monitored their hostages, Bundy crept down the foyer until he reached the bedroom door where the music was blaring. He entered—aiming.

The end of Bundy's gun found its target first.

Freaky's cousin was on top of a towel, laying flat on the king-size bed…

In a compromising position.

In one hand, he held a dirty magazine. In the other…he held his dick masturbating.

Bundy shook his head as if the sight was comical. "Put down the snake," he ordered.

Freaky's cousin's heart skipped causing the magazine to slip out and fall to his waist. He partly raised up, threw the towel over his private, and accidentally knocked over the bottle of lotion beside him. His eyes moved frantically around the room. But then—they locked on Bundy. The unwanted guest.

"Who you?" Freaky's cousin questioned. "What you want?"

"Who I am don't matter. What I want? We can talk about that after you join ya family."

"My family?" he blurted.

"Yeah, nigga—ya family. Now get up and come on."

Freaky's cousin led the way to the living room, and although Bundy had a gun pointed at his back, he tried hard to think of a way to get out of the situation without getting his family killed. And without handing over a thing.

"Look, y'all," Bundy said, pushing Freaky's cousin into the living room.

"Daddy!"

Stumbling in, he noticed his family sitting on the floor, held at gunpoint.

The sight almost broke him. But he found it in himself to keep it together.

"Ayo," Bundy said while zip-tying Freaky's cousin's hands. "Would you believe I found this freaky-ass horny nigga whacking off to a magazine? Not even a porno—a fuckin' magazine."

Had Freaky's cousin looked at his girlfriend, he would have seen that she was disgusted. Embarrassed.

"Daddy, Daddy!" the little boy called. "Beat them up! They mean to me and Mommy!" Feeling less than a man, Freaky's cousin acted like he didn't hear his son.

"Shhh! Be quiet, baby," the mother whispered. "Be a good boy for Mommy."

"There's only one way Daddy can help you, lil' man," Lil Gary assured the child. Then he looked at Bundy. "Zip-tie her feet too."

Bundy finished the task. "Now, like I told you before—once we all together, I'll tell you what I want." Bundy squatted in front of Freaky's cousin. "But ya not stupid. You may be a pervert, but ya no dummy. You know what I want. You know why we're here. So why not make it easy on yaself and tell me what I wanna hear?"

Freaky's cousin looked up at him. "How I know after I tell you, y'all not gonna kill me and my family? Y'all didn't even wear a mask—I know how it go."

Bundy stood behind the mother and the little boy. "See, that's just the thing," he said. "You don't know. I'll tell you one thing though—you can try to play smart and make us search every inch of this place. And when we find the stash ourselves, we'll slump you, ya handsome son, and ya beautiful B.M. Or… you can save us the trouble, tell us now, and maybe we decide to let y'all live. At least ya B.M. and son. All I'm trying to say is…" Bundy's voice turned cold. "Don't leave this earth knowing you coulda saved ya family, but failed to."

Freaky's cousin's mind spun.

Bundy didn't want him to think. He wanted him to talk.

"And just so you know…" Bundy leaned in. "If you make us, I promise you—I'ma body you last. Or… not at all. I might let you live with that decision."

"What the hell you waitin' for?" the woman screamed. "Tell them what they wanna know! Be a man, Jamal! Save your family!"

"Aight! Aight!" he snapped, then breathed deeply. "It's in the deep freezer."

"What's in the deep freezer?"

"The…" He hesitated. "The money. The money is in the fish stick boxes."

"What about the white?"

"How you even know I got white?"

Bundy stared at him. "What about the white?"

"It's in the room… inside the safe in the closet."

"What's the code?"

"It's already unlocked." In despair, he dropped his head. "Fuck."

Bundy smirked. "If it makes you feel any better, you did the right thing, Jamal."

Bundy scraped his hands against the ice as he dug through the deep freezer, tossing frozen food onto the floor.

At the bottom, he spotted the blue fish stick boxes and started pulling them out one by one. He checked each box, and just like Jamal said.

Money. And, more money.

In the living room, Bundy set a black trash bag down and headed to the bedroom to retrieve the drugs.

Meanwhile, Jamal's son called for his father.

"Daddy! Daddy, save us!"

Jamal looked at his son. "It's gonna be alright."

"That's right, lil' man," Lil Gary said, smiling. "Everything'll be over in just a second. What's ya name, lil' man?"

The little boy refused to answer.

Instead, he stared hard, trying to make the meanest face possible.

"His name is Jaquan," the mother said.

"Jaquan." Lil Gary smirked. "Lil' tough guy, huh?"

In response Jaquan raised his hand and pointed.

"When I get big… I'ma kill you." His tiny fingers shaped like a gun. "Pow, pow."

"Oh my God, I'm so sorry," the mother gasped, covering her son's mouth.

Lil Gary waved her off. "No need to apologize. He's a soldier."

Bundy returned from the bedroom, carrying a pillowcase full of drugs. "Our work here is done."

"You sure?" Lil Gary asked. "What we doin' 'bout them?"

He nodded toward the hostages.

"You said…" Jamal spoke up before Bundy could answer. "You said you'd let us live if I told y'all where the shit was at."

"No I didn't." Bundy corrected him. "I told you, if you did the right thing, at least you'd die knowing you tried to save ya family." He glanced at Lil Gary. "Any suggestions?"

"I got one," Lil Gary announced.

He turned to Jaquan. "Crawl over to ya father and give him a hug."

As Jaquan did as he was told his mother started crying.

"Alright, Jaquan. Now crawl over there for me and cover ya eyes. You don't need to see this." Lil Gary pointed to a spot between his parents. Jaquan crawled over and covered his eyes with his tiny hands.

Lil Gary raised his gun.

Jamal and his girlfriend closed their eyes.

Lil Gary pulled the trigger.

Silence.

Jamal and his girlfriend opened their eyes. They were alive.

But Jaquan…Their beautiful boy lay between them. Lifeless.

The mother screamed.

"Why?"

Lil Gary's expression didn't change.

"Because he threatened me."

"He was just a child!" she sobbed.

"Who would've grown into a man."

"But why? He was only four years old!"

"The cycle." Bundy said.

When they left the apartment, they left it a morgue.

Later that evening, Lil Gary and Bundy met up with Freaky, and together, they divided fifty-nine thousand dollars and thirty-four ounces of cocaine.

"Now that wasn't too bad, was it?" Freaky said. "How my people? He good? He ain't put up no fight, did he?"

Silence.

"What's up with y'all? Y'all acting like y'all lost ya dog or some shit. My cousin smooth, right?"

Waiting on a reply, it dawned on him. "What happened?"

"Nigga, you know what happened," Lil Gary said.

Freaky screwed up his face. "Naw, nigga, I don't know a motherfuckin' thing. How 'bout you enlighten me?"

"We smacked him," Lil Gary said. "And his bitch. And their son. And on some real shit, if you gave a fuck that much about ya peoples, you would'a never fed him to us. You put him on our plate and you gassed the lick. What we took out that crib wasn't worth three lives. But you sent us the lick anyway. So miss me with that 'I give a fuck' role. You know how we give it up."

Freaky kept quiet. He had no comeback. No legs to stand on. He didn't want to admit it, but Lil Gary was right. And what happened earlier today? That was now a secret. Another secret he was gonna have to live with. And die with. Fuck it. It is what it is. Either you the come-up, or you the one coming up. He told himself.

After splitting from Bundy and Lil Gary, Freaky made a call from his car.

"Yo." Rico answered.

"What's shakin', kinfolk? Where you at?" Freaky asked.

"Um in the Terrace."

"Okay, good. Listen, my mans—"

"—Yo," Rico interrupted. "Just come chop it with me in person."

"Aight. I'll be there in a second."

"Um here." Rico hung up.

Freaky took a right into Norfolk Terrace and parked. He got out the car, walked up to the apartment, used a key to unlock the door, and stepped inside.

In the kitchen, he spotted Rico and Casino. Rico was over the table, handling two kilos of heroin, while Casino stood by watching.

Freaky was surprised to see Casino, but he kept quiet. At least for now.

"What's really good?" he said.

Rico looked over his shoulder and saw Freaky standing in the doorway.

"You light-weight spooked a nigga," Rico admitted. "Hold up—I'm comin' over there to holla at you now." He rinsed his hands. Then, the two of them went into a side room.

"It's a good thing you called me," Rico said. "Two-Times and Hommi just sent more work, and I need ya help bustin' it all down. This nigga Knox out with his shorty, and we gotta get this shit done ASAP. Kinfolks said they need the money straight, and we got a deadline. I'm not trippin', though. We got enough chicken to cover the next four bricks, but fuck that, I think it's smart to stay ahead." He glanced at Freaky. "And another thing—no more talkin' crazy over these phones, bro. For real. But anyway—what was you sayin' on the jack?"

"Oh yeah, my man got some white on deck right now for the low-low. And it's some fish scale. You tryin' to go half with me and grab it?" Freaky asked.

"How much work is it?"

"Twelve ounces."

"What's the tag?"

"Eight."

"You seen it?"

"You know that."

"Hard or soft?"

"Soft."

"So that's twenty-four hard."

"Easy."

"Yeah, I'll fuck with you. When you tryna make the move?"

"Immediately. Dawg said first come, first serve."

"I'ma call my bitch and tell her to count up my half. I need you to go grab it, though."

"That ain't 'bout nothin'," Freaky assured him.

Rico was in the process of leaving when Freaky called him. Stopping, he turned around. "What's up, bro?"

"What's up with the lil' nigga Casino?" Freaky asked. "I never knew he was on it."

"He wasn't, but the streets always been in him. You ain't hip? Casino is Hommi's lil' brother. Yeah, bro, he's family. And ever since I lost my baby boy Riot, he the only lil' nigga I see potential in. So he gonna be around from now on."

"Say no more. I wasn't questionin' ya judgment. Ya welfare is my only concern. Ya like a brother. Matter fact—you are my brother. So the company you keep matters to me."

"The love is mutual," Rico assured. "But let me grab my jack so I can call wifey and get the ball rollin'."

"While you do that, I'ma front you the bread so we don't miss the lick. On my way back, I'll grab ya half."

"Real nigga."

"C'mon, dawg—"

"—Nah, for real. I appreciate you puttin' me in the loop."

"Man, I'm gone—solo." Freaky said and left the apartment.

CHAPTER EIGHTEEN

FEBRUARY

Looking to buy a car, Raheem traveled to the dealership that sold his favorite brand—Jaguar. Accompanying him was no one other than Heron-Homm.

After checking out two cars he liked, he was still undecided when he laid eyes on a Jaguar XK. Immediately, he asked the dealer—an old Albanian man with silver hair—for the key and climbed inside. The leather seats filled his nose.

While inspecting the sports car, Raheem brought up a conversation he'd been waiting to have with Hommi. And quickly, it got heated.

"Dawg, you fucking the plug is risky. That shit could come between business. What don't you understand?" Raheem questioned while playing with buttons and switches.

"What is there to understand? If anything, hitting it should make business better. She'll give us whatever we want off the strength," Hommi argued.

"Yeah, well, I don't want it like that. We don't need a handout. Next thing you know, the bitch gonna be talking about how we owe her. I'd rather put my bread up and build my own empire. I'm not about to build her another empire off my labor. I'm not putting in no more than I have to. I'm not a worker—I'm a boss."

"Cuzo, you sound crazy."

"I sound crazy?" Raheem laughed. "How? You breaking all types of laws, but I sound crazy? You on some L7, square-from-Delaware shit."

"Sqquarree froomm Delaawarree," Hommi mocked. "What are you, a pimp now?"

"Naw, nigga, I ain't no pimp, but I am a businessman, and businessmen don't mix business with pleasure."

Hearing the confrontation outside his office, the old Albanian man got up out of his chair and started walking toward the Jaguar XK.

"Fucking gangsters don't know how to act in a place of business. Just ignorant," he mumbled the whole way over—before quickly switching up his attitude.

"Excuse me, gentlemen, is everything alright? Would one of you like to make a purchase?" Raheem saw the salesman's expression. It clearly showed he had no patience.

"Nah. I'm all—"

"—Yeah, my man's buying it," Hommi said, cutting Raheem off.

"Kinfolk, I don't need this right now."

"Yeah, aight—you getting it. Don't trip, it ain't coming out ya pockets."

"Then whose pockets it coming out of?"

"Mine. Now fall back so I can call my bitch and tell her I want it. Consider it a gift."

Getting out the car, Hommi got on his phone, while Raheem, on the flip side, stared at his back with disgust.

13 ½ 13 ½ 13 ½

10:53 P.M. – LIQUOR STORE

It was cold outside, but before the liquor store closed for the night, Mega had to manage two things at once.

One—hurry inside before the old man locked the door.

Two—keep up with the conversation on his phone.

"Hold up," Mega said, sliding into the store. "What was that?"

"I said yes," the voice on the other end replied.

"On dawgs?" Mega questioned.

"Why would I lie?"

"How you know this?"

"Don't worry about it," the voice said, coyly.

"What?! Who you talkin' to? I'll still bust that ass. Don't think you too grown—I raised you."

The voice chuckled.

"Okay, okay. One of my girlfriends talk to him. That's how I know."

"Oh, aight. I thought you was about to say you was fuckin' with dawg. I would'a killed you. But anyway, did he say anything to you?"

Silence.

"Hello?" Mega said.

"No—no, he don't know who I am."

"Aight. But look, stay clear from dawg. If ya friend bring him around, get ghost. I ain't playin'. I ain't tryin' to repeat the past. Be safe, I'll call you later. Love you."

"Love you too."

"Next!" The cashier called out, and Mega stepped up to the counter, pocketing his phone.

"Lemme get a fifth of Pledge."

13 ½ 13 ½ 13 ½

HIGHWAY 93 – NIGHT DRIVE

Veering onto the ramp, then swinging onto the highway, Rico navigated north on Route 93 toward the Underbar. To help him cope with his sins, he mixed pineapple juice with Cîroc in a red plastic cup and took a sip from time to time.

Glancing at the star-lit sky, he cracked all four windows a notch and breathed in the air, slowly. I am my city, he told himself.

He got off at his exit, reached for his cup of alcohol, and noticed it was empty.

"Yo, pour some more drink in my cup, baby boy."

"I got'cha," Casino replied.

Rico had been keeping Casino close. He wasn't Riot. And Rico wasn't trying to replace Riot, but he missed their bond.

Rico is a killer. Riot was a killer. They were both killers who murdered killers. Casino, though, was merely Rico's cousin. Had he been anything more, Rico didn't see it yet. He'd heard about the incident Casino was involved in at the park, but he knew Shocka. He could see Shocka forcing a coward to take his life. That encounter wasn't enough for Rico to proclaim Casino as anything—cousin or not. He needed more. That's why Casino was around. He wanted to feel him out.

Look in his eyes. See how he carried himself. And if he had to, teach him how he was supposed to carry himself.

Rico took a sip of Ciroc, then placed the cup back in the cup holder. Damn, Riot I miss you, baby boy. You bump into them niggas we sent up there yet? Don't trip, we're not done riding, but no matter how many of them kids we clip, none of them gonna amount to you, he thought.

"So," Rico began. "How you feel, baby boy?" he asked Casino.

"Shit, I feel good. Um getting money with the tribe, everything I put on is designer, niggas know me when they see me, and um out here fucking the baddest bitches in the town. I feel respected, to keep it three-hunnit."

"Respected," Rico said and glanced in the rearview mirror. "Kinfolk, listen, don't confuse dick riding with respect. Niggas may respect ya money or where you're from, but wolves don't respect and will never respect you until you gain respect as an individual. You must earn respect, and that doesn't happen overnight. It take time to win, but no time to lose."

Thinking, Casino made no attempt to respond. I know how um'a gain my respect… with my gun.

Rico took a left onto Tremont Street and pulled over in front of the club. Looking through the windshield, he and Casino watched as beautiful women and well-dressed men began to pour out of the establishment and onto the cobblestone street.

"Let's get out and see what the night has to offer," Rico said, grabbing his cup and climbing out of the car. Coming around, he then sat on the hood of the car. Meanwhile, Casino positioned his back against the passenger door and stuffed marijuana in a Dutch Master.

In midair, different erotic fragrances playfully wrestled. And the silence that once was is now filled with English and foreign chatter, drunk laughter, and impatient taxi drivers honking their horns.

"Yo, Casino, pick ya head up and look at this bad thing coming up on ya right, giving you the goggly eyes," Rico said. Casino scanned the wave of people until his eyes landed on the petite beauty with slits for eyes, a funky short hairstyle, and small pink lips guarding a set of pretty white teeth. As far as her complexion, she's very light. But gracing her figure, she wore a sleeveless, blue, white, and gold Yves Saint Laurent dress. And to match, she sported all-white Gucci boots that cut off beneath the knee. Damn, Casino thought. Word, she's bad.

Not allowing her to sway along, he gently took her by her manicured hand and said, "Now you know I can't let you do that."

"Do what?" she asked, smiling.

"Walk by without stopping you," Casino answered. "Can I walk with you?"

"I don't know—could you?"

"I can do whatever I want."

"Then why you ask?"

"Again, 'cause I can do whatever I want. What about you?"

"I'm grown, so yeah, I can do whatever I please." Full of mischief, she gazed at Casino. "But I want to do whatever it is you want to do tonight." Unable to hold his composure, Casino's mouth turned into the letter U.

"Is that right?" he challenged.

"Yup," she said with sass.

"Time out. Rewind—what's ya name?"

"Vivi."

"Vivi, huh. What's ya nationality?"

"I'm Taiwanese and Jamaican."

Cold snack, Casino thought before saying, "Let me get ya number."

"Let me see your phone." Unlocking his cell phone, Casino handed it over. Vivi stored her phone number, then handed the phone back.

"You know ya mine now, right." Casino said, making a statement.

"You think so? How you know I'm even interested in all that?"

"Ya eyes say." His charm made her beam. "But where ya ride at? You here by yaself?"

"No. My girlfriends."

"Hold up for a second." Holding his hand up, palm first, Casino listened closely and heard a dispute. One of the voices in the argument sounded familiar and forced him to turn around and look: Some distance away, on the ball of his toes and looking up at a Black man with hair like wool, Rico exchanged heated words. Casino gave Vivi his back, not uttering a single word.

"Nah—check ya bitch. I didn't force her to stop and talk," Rico said, pointing at a Brazilian woman among a crowd of spectators.

"I don't have to check shit, bro. I'm checking you," said the man with hair like wool.

Rico chuckled. "Um telling you, dawg, this ain't what you want. What you doing in my city—going to school? Playing sports? Do that. Um giving you an out. Keep it pushing before ya night turn into a nightmare."

"I don't care for your empty threats. We can throw down right here."

Nearing the altercation, Casino pulled—the hood attached to the Polo hoodie he was wearing—over his head and tugged on the two strings. He then drew the .40 caliber pistol off of his narrow waist without drawing any attention. Niggas gonna respect me. In his head, he repeated those words over and over.

Stepping on the scene, Casino walked up on the side of the man arguing with Rico and threw the piece to the side of his head. Then instantly, like some kind of trick, the man's world disappeared.

Talib, the student of UMass, the young man with hair like wool—he never saw it coming. And his girlfriend, she never saw him again. In fact, she never even knew his name. She literally met him that night.

After fleeing from what turned into a crime scene, Rico and Casino checked into a hotel in Summerville. The hotel was seedy, but it was good enough to serve its purpose.

In the corner of the room, Casino slouched in a brown chair. His facial expression was blank. Rico, on the other hand, went back and forth, pacing the carpeted floor. I swear, I hope this lil nigga didn't kill that dude. Secretly, he hoped the student Casino shot sustained his life.

"Yo," Rico called, now standing across from Casino. "What the fuck was you thinking back there?" So upset, Casino had no idea what to expect from his cousin. He'd heard so many stories of what Rico was capable of, he made a mental note to watch what he said.

"I don't know what you mean," he began. "That clown was talking nasty to you, so I felt like he had to go. I was just trying to hold you down."

"First, I don't need you to hold me down—I'm Rico. And secondly, holding me down ain't catching a body in front of a whole fucking club, dumb nigga. We don't move like that. What if ya on camera clapping dawg, then jumping in my whip? You don't think, and in this life, you have to think."

Casino bit his tongue, but inwardly he said: Can this dude hear himself? His whole rep is off not thinking, but here he is trying to school me. I don't give a fuck where we at, a nigga disrespect, um offing him. Fuck thinking—I can give two fucks about life.

"You feel what um saying?" Rico continued.

"Yeah," Casino answered. "And you 300 percent right."

CHAPTER NINETEEN

As the sun began to rotate and cause the sky to shift to a pinkish-purple hue, a sleek, all-black Jaguar purred in front of Raheem's girlfriend's two-bedroom home. Life that only belonged to the night was in the midst of awakening. And just like the nightlife, so was Raheem's dick.

Stretched over the gearshift—without either hand—Rain's head moved up and down in Raheem's lap, surrounded by leather the color of peanut butter. Once Raheem was at full length, she took his hand and placed it on the back of her head. Breathing in his bottom lip, Raheem pressed his foot behind the gas pedal to keep from stomping down on it.

When Raheem finally came, Rain moaned and picked up her pace until he had no more natural resources to feed her. Smiling, she asked, "How was it?"

"What did I do to deserve that? Or should I say, how much do I owe you?"

"Shut up," she said, playfully hitting Raheem. "Disrespectful, for real. Seriously though, it's something about big cars, the smell of new leather, and a fly-ass man in it. Especially when it's my man."

"You make a nigga wanna cop some new shit every day now," Raheem said, and Rain laughed. "Shit, you laughing. I'm dead ass."

"You a fool. Oh yeah, baby, before I forget, I got some money for you." From out of a Fendi handbag, she pulled two neat stacks. "Here, Daddy."

"How much is this?"

"Eight thousand."

Reaching across, Raheem tossed the two stacks in the glove compartment. "First bomb head, now eight grand. You tryna make a nigga fall in love with your ass, huh?"

"Actually—no, I'm not," Rain answered. "A man with feelings ain't the man for me. What I'd like to do is get you to see that I'm down for your crown."

"You got some game on you," he said, smirking.

"I don't run game on you. You too smart—you recognize it."

Raheem was glad Rain recognized his intelligence because he liked her. But had she thought she could deceive him, she would've been too much of a risk. And if he thought someone ran the chance of being a risk, then in his book, they were expendable.

Raheem's phone rang. Picking it up, he looked at the screen. "What it do?" he answered.

"Yo, what's up? It's Money-Making Rich."

"I'm hip. What the lick read?"

"You already know—money!"

"Dawgs," Raheem agreed. He pressed speaker and set the phone in his lap. "But how you? How the BM doing?"

"Aw, man, she's healthy, bro. Due any day now. Thanks for asking," Money-Making Rich said, speaking in code.

"You don't have to thank me, bro. You thank strangers. We family. But look, I'm kinda in the middle of something. I'ma send a few gifts for the baby shower."

"Say no more—preciate you. Out." He hung up.

"Daddy."

"Rain, what's up?" Raheem asked.

"Earlier, I told you that a man with feelings ain't the man for me—"

"We already went through this—"

"I know, but basically, what I was trying to say is, I'm not looking for you to love me. But I do want you to know that I love you, and my goal is to prove it to you, every single day."

"Rain, let me tell you something… Love is just a stimulus. It's something that rouses the mind and your emotions temporarily. I don't trust love. You can fall asleep loving someone, then turn over in the morning hating them. You hear me?" Rain nodded. "Fuck a feeling. Where I'm dropping you off at?"

For a brief moment, she stared at Raheem, then cut her eyes. "The club, jerk."

13 ½ 13 ½ 13 ½

It was morning, and through car speakers, the song *I'll Hold You Down* by DJ Khaled played low as Hommi made his way to South Carolina's Prison for Women.

When Hommi first came to South Carolina to visit his mother's side of the family, he ended up meeting the female version of himself…

It was at a cookout one of his cousins brought him to. He thought it was more like a bonfire, but once he laid eyes on Christina, he didn't care what his surroundings looked like any longer. So that he wouldn't look desperate, he waited for the right time to approach her.

The perfect moment came much later in the day when they both were at the cooler. Hommi grabbed a beer, and Christina, afterward, bent forward and pulled out a wine cooler. Straightening her back, they locked eyes.

"And what's your name?" Hommi asked.

"Who, me?" Christina pointed to herself. "My name is Kash."

"Why they call you Kash?"

"'Cause that's all I'm about."

"Cash."

"With a K, but exactly," she confirmed.

Hommi wondered what she meant by being all about cash until one day, when he was in desperate need of money, she told him she knew someone he could rob. Now, Christina wasn't the prettiest girl Hommi ever saw, but she was appealing—and in his mind, made for him.

After the first robbery, they went on a spree. Christina set the robberies up, and Hommi executed them. For nearly a year, that's how they survived.

Then, one day, a robbery went south quick, and Hommi had to shoot their way out—killing the man they intended to rob and grazing Christina in the process, leaving DNA at the scene.

That night, they skipped town and went into hiding, switching hotels every other day. They kept it up for eight months before the stress of being on the run ate them alive and forced them back to King Street—the worst mistake they could've made.

Two weeks later, state police kicked in the door of their apartment with a body warrant for Christina. She was charged with first-degree murder and home invasion.

The DA was certain she wasn't alone during the crime, but because she wouldn't cooperate, once a jury found her guilty, they argued for a harsh sentence. The judge—after expressing his thoughts and promising leniency—handed down an eighteen-year sentence.

Christina never let her chin drop.

Hommi, however, immediately scraped up some money and hired her an appellate lawyer.

But for not siding with the prosecutor, Hommi said: "A lawyer ain't enough. I owe her my life."

Just as Hommi parked in the prison's parking lot, his cell phone rang. Checking the screen, he saw it was Raheem.

"Yo?"

"Where you at?" Raheem asked, trying to disguise the urgency in his tone.

"I'm at the prison, about to head inside and see Kash. Why? What's good? You straight?" He noticed the tension in Raheem's voice.

"Dig this, kinfolk, enjoy your visit. Tell Kash I said keep her head up. But when you leave, come straight to the condo."

“Nuff said.”

“Out.” Raheem pressed end.

It wasn’t long, but Hommi ransacked his brain, trying to figure out what was so urgent. Coming up with nothing, he pushed the conversation aside and got out of the car.

I’ll deal with that when I get there. Right now, it’s all about wifey, he thought, heading inside the prison.

13 ½ 13 ½ 13 ½

There, in the middle of the safehouse, Raheem stood with his gun in hand—furious. He couldn’t believe what he was seeing, as if what he was staring at wasn’t reality.

The safehouse had been broken into and left in a chaotic state. Luckily, they had moved the money a month ago, but without having to check, Raheem knew whoever broke in had made off with a little fortune in heroin.

On dead dawgs, whoever robbed us better have made amends with God, Raheem thought as he retrieved his cell phone from his pants pocket and texted Chief.

From Raheem: Ayo, as soon as you see this, come to the condo.

Chief: On my way now, bruh.

While waiting for Chief, Raheem figured he might as well clean up and headed toward the kitchen. He was more upset about the break-in than he was about the drugs. The drugs could be replaced, but once someone violates you—you've been violated. There's no getting that back. It's a feeling you're going to have to live with, even after getting revenge.

He tried to imagine who had robbed them but couldn't picture a living soul. Then he wondered—besides him, Hommi, and Chief—who knew about the safehouse?

Not yet done running through the list of names in his head, he heard a hard knock at the door. Quickly, he dumped the grains of rice he had scooped up off the floor into a trash bag and headed toward the door.

Since he wasn't expecting anyone besides Chief right now, he opened the door…

Mistake.

Every time Hommi came to visit Christina, it felt like he was meeting her for the first time all over again. His stomach would get butterflies, and his heart and mind would start racing—like they were competing with each other.

At the vending machine, he bought himself a bottle of water and Christina's favorite snacks, then headed over to the row and seat he was assigned to. No different from previous visits, this one was gonna be hard too.

Knowing that Christina was doing so much time because of him—and for him—ate him up inside.

Like usual, the visiting room was crowded and loud. All around, babies were crying, visitors were crying, and couples were arguing. In fact, four chairs down from Hommi, two C.O.s were breaking up a heated dispute between a lesbian couple.

Beginning to get annoyed, Hommi glanced toward the entrance just in time to see Christina walk in.

It was like a breath of fresh air.

Not paying anybody else any attention, Christina blushed the whole way to her seat. She didn't even hear her friend from the institution say hi as she walked past.

"Hey, babe." Christina hugged Hommi tight. "Oh my God, I missed you so much."

Hommi kissed her, then said, "I miss you too, light skin." Sitting across from each other, they held hands. "So, how you doing?"

"Better now that you're here," Christina said. "Why you so late today? You usually here around eleven."

"Yeah, I'm hip. But on my way in, Two-Times called me. He said what's up too. Our quick convo made me the last visitor in line."

"Tell Two-Times don't be getting in the way of my time. Y'all got all day to talk. I know that line had to suck, though."

"It did, but if I had to go through a line twice as long just to see your brown eyes, I'd do it. You worth it."

Cautiously, Christina groped Hommi's dick. "I'm worth it, baby?" Lust replaced the white in her eyes.

Hommi straightened his back and scanned the room.

"Babe, stop making it hot," Christina said.

To let her fondle him like she always did during visits, Hommi leaned forward.

"Your horny ass ain't changed at all."

"Shit, I'm even worse. But why you acting brand new?" She squeezed his dick. "You fucking with someone, huh? You giving another bitch a chance to fulfill my spot?"

Silence.

"Hommi, you hear me?" She squeezed tighter. "I'm doing eighteen years. You know I don't care about you getting your shit off. But actually fucking with another bitch is totally different—and out of the question. So, what bum ass bitch is out there trying to fill my pumps?"

"You bugging. What makes you think I'm fucking with someone? And how did we go from you playing with the dick to all this?"

"It don't matter how we got here—we here now. Keep it real. You at least owe me the truth."

"Damn, baby, I came here to make you happy, not for this."

"Then make me happy, nigga, and answer my question."

"First, let go of my dick."

She looked Hommi up and down. "My dick," she corrected, then let go.

"Ayo, did your appeal lawyer come see you yet? I just dropped some bread on her last week."

Christina waved off the question. "What's her name?" She stressed through clenched teeth. "What is it?" she pressed on. "We don't keep it three-hunnit with each other no more?"

Cocking her head sideways, she stared at Hommi and waited.

Hommi thought about their relationship—how it was built on trust and how he would never tarnish that. He couldn't imagine Christina not trusting him or second-guessing his love for her.

Here it is, I owe this girl my life, but all she want from me is the truth.

"Her name is…" He hesitated. "Her name is Ballerina."

Christina smiled. "I'm so glad you told me the truth, like always. Because I already know. The streets talk, and so do these walls, babe—you know that. You shoulda known I was gonna hear about it. Everybody know you mine from S.C. to A.T.L. Plus, the bitch is making it known that y'all together and you not to be touched."

"Word?" Hommi said, surprised.

"Yeah, word. You need to tell her to pipe down. But we'll touch on that in a second. I got a question… Do you love her?"

Looking at Hommi, her eyes turned into slits.

"Fuck no, I don't love her," he said automatically. "And on some dawg shit, I'm using her. It ain't a bone in my body that love her. Dawgs."

"Using her for what—pussy?"

"Pussy, Kash? Are you serious? The bitch is a connect. A real live connect from Mexico. And she pitching me and cuzo bricks like we play baseball."

"So, I got nothing to worry about? Look me in the eyes when you answer."

Holding eye contact, he answered, "Kash, you got nothing to worry about. Ain't no bitch come before you. I don't even put myself before you."

"You sure?"

Hommi went to speak but noticed a C.O. watching them. *What the fuck this clown in my mug for?* he wondered but quickly brushed it off and looked back at Christina.

"I'm positive. On my niggas."

"That's all I needed to hear. Get that money, Daddy." She caressed his hand. "Did you bring me my pack? These hoes fiending on the yard."

"Yeah, I got you. Just be careful with this shit." Hommi warned.

"Promise me one thing."

"What's that?"

"Don't ever tell that woman you love her."

13 ½ 13 ½ 13 ½

Aimed at his face, Raheem looked down the .223 rifle, thinking: Damn, today is my day. I didn't even get the chance to do right by wifey. Who the fuck is this nigga anyway?

"Got yo fuck ass. Bring me to the money. Hurry up," Chubb said, shaking the rifle.

Raheem backpedaled slowly as Chubb stepped inside the condo.

13 ½ 13 ½ 13 ½

When Chief received Raheem's text and saw it was urgent, he flew to the safehouse. Never had Hommi or Raheem hit him up under urgent circumstances before, so it was clear something was wrong.

Chief pulled up, jumped out the car, and ran to the front door. He was about to knock when he noticed it was left slightly open—a red flag.

Instantly suspicious, he pulled out his gun—a .357 Mag, Ruger. Pressing the weapon close to his side to keep it concealed, he leaned forward, listening for any noise from inside…

"Mutherfucker." Chief mumbled the curse under his breath the second he heard Chubb's voice. For a moment, he didn't move, just thinking.

What if Two-Times and Hommi think I got something to do with this shit?

Shaking off the thought, he eased into the safehouse, moving quietly, and ducked behind the island separating the living room from the kitchen.

Chubb's back was to the door, so he didn't see Chief sneak in.

Raheem, however, did.

Playing along with the robbery, Raheem silently thanked God.

Chief listened as Chubb barked, “So where the money, bitch nigga? Teach you New York niggas a lesson ‘bout coming to my city—where the money at?”

“Behind you, in the closet to your right,” Raheem answered.

Chief peeked over the island and locked eyes with Raheem—who shot him a murderous look.

Catching the signal, Chief ducked.

“Don’t you move,” Chubb ordered. “And the money better be in here. I looked already earlier and didn’t see a bitch-ass thing.”

The second Chubb walked to the closet and the opportunity presented itself, Chief leaped up and cracked him over the head with the butt of his gun.

Chubb hit the floor—out cold.

But Raheem wasn’t done. He ran over and stomped Chubb out until he got tired and his foot started hurting.

When Chubb regained consciousness, his head was inside a toilet bowl. Raheem had the rifle now, and Chubb was terrified.

Squirming in Chief's grip, Chubb started begging for his life. "Please, mane, don't kill me. Come on—I can't breathe," he coughed, water dripping down his face.

Raheem told him to stop begging, then cracked him across the jaw with the stock—again and again.

Even though Chubb and Chief were childhood friends, Chief had no interest in saving him, but he knew Chubb's whole family, and someday, he'd have to look Chubb's mother in the face when she ask, Chief, what happened to my son?

Chief sighed. "Aye, mane. He had enough. He learned his lesson by now. Why don't we just let his ol' fuck ass go?"

Raheem shot Chief an insane look. "Then what?" Raheem snapped. "Next thing we know, the whole fucking city trying us." The thought hit him all at once. "You had something to do with this? Huh, Chief?"

"Come on, mane—"

"Nah, fuck all that." Raheem cut him off. "Did you or did you not set us up?"

"Two-Times, listen to me, mane. I would never—"

"Dawg, fuck all that. I ain't trying to hear that bullshit. Did you"

Chief shot Chubb in the back of the head—three times. Inwardly, he told himself: You left me no choice, fool.

"Smart move," Raheem said, then pulled his own trigger.

The rifle exploded.

Bullets ripped through Chubb's body, shell casings flipping as they hit the tile floor.

"I wouldn't have felt right if only you clapped him," Raheem muttered. "Here, hold this." He handed Chief the .223. "I gotta hit Hommi real quick—tell him not to come here."

He left Chief in the bathroom.

Taking it upon himself, Chief dug through Chubb's pockets and found a car key in the back pocket.

He walked into the hallway and held it up for Raheem to see.

"How much you wanna bet the work he took is in his car?"

"I bet you, if it's there, you can have it."

"Bet. What we doing about the body?"

"I'ma show you right after I grab some blankets and trash bags."

13 ½ 13 ½ 13 ½

After getting the warning text from Raheem not to come to the safehouse, Hommi detoured to Ballerina's place—just in time to walk into an argument.

"Why was you at a woman's prison today?" Ballerina demanded.

Hommi started seeing what Raheem meant at the dealership.

"Bitch, how you know where I was at? You had somebody following me, you crazy bitch?"

"What ju call mi?" Ballerina dared him to say it again. "Mi got people everywhere, where ju least expect. Mi told ju, ju don't wanna play wid mi."

The C.O. in the visiting room. I knew something was funny. "No bullshit, you really one crazy bitch."

SLAP.

Ballerina smacked the shit out of him.

Hommi grabbed her arms and threw her on the bed.

"Ayo, who the fuck you putting your hands on?"

Hommi was pissed.

Ballerina, though?

She was shocked.

And she wasn't sure if she wanted to kill him or fuck him.

Hearing the commotion, Ballerina's guards stormed in—eight Mexican men, all aiming assault rifles at Hommi.

Ballerina jumped up and ordered them to stand down.

They didn't.

"Mi said to stand down!" she barked.

They still ignored her.

Lifting her long skirt, Ballerina pulled out a four-shot Dillinger and murdered the commanding officer.

Blood flowed from the hole in his head.

"Now," Ballerina said, stepping over the body. "Clean up dis mess—den get out."

As boots shuffled, obeying her orders, the men scowled.

They couldn't believe their boss spilled Mexican blood for a Black.

To them, it was weakness.

And they wouldn't forget it.

CHAPTER TWENTY

BOSTON BAGHDAD: MAY

"Finally, good weather," Freaky said.

"Niggas is stuntin' this summer. Let the streets see for themselves they ain't fuckin' with Solo," Rico said.

Driving, Rico went from cookout to cookout. Today was the nicest day this month had offered, and a lot of locals were tired of being cooped up inside. For those looking for some fresh air and company, they gathered up family and friends and fired up the grill.

Although Rico was enjoying the weather and having a good time crashing cookouts with Freaky, something about today didn't feel right.

Everything, for some reason, stuck out. Every time he turned around, the sun was shining directly on him. Earlier, when he first woke up, his mother was heavy on his mind.

He always thought about his mother—but something was different this morning.

It was like she was trying to tell him something.

Catching the red light at the intersection of Morton Street and Norfolk, he brought the car to a stop and looked to the right and noticed Freaky's visor close.

Reaching across, Rico snatched it open.

"Come on, bro," he said. "You drippin'. What, you want them kids to see you through the windshield and fuck around and score?"

"My fault, my nigg. But that's what we here for—if one of us drippin', we pull each other's coat."

Rico pulled off when the light turned green.

He didn't say another word.

They'd been through too much to still have to pull each other's coat.

13 ½ 13 ½ 13 ½

As Mega drove, he put Flame and another O.T.S. member, Frog, on to how Freaky was an imposter.

In the midst of telling them about all the scandals Freaky had a hand in, he pulled up to a red light and cursed himself for forgetting to take the right turn onto a side street—one that would've let him hit Norfolk without having to go through the light.

"No funny shit, gun-smoke, I been hip to Freaky. Everything you sayin' add up. Like, it only make sense and explain why he been M.I.A.," Flame said.

"On dawgs," Mega agreed.

"Ain't this 'bout a bitch," Frog muttered.

"What happened?" Mega asked.

"Speak of the fuckin' devil—there go the slime ball right there," Frog said, leaning forward from the back seat, pointing.

"Where?" Looking every which way, Mega and Flame asked at the same time.

"Right there, in the Benz. I think he peeped niggas too, 'cause he just dropped his visor."

"You sure that's him, gun-smoke?" Flame asked.

"Dawg, I know them braids anywhere." Frog nodded.

"Yeah, that's him," Mega confirmed.

"Word," Flame said. "Spin the bend. It's about time we clip this bird."

13 ½ 13 ½ 13 ½

A cell phone rang.

"Is that your jack or mine?" Freaky asked.

"That's your phone bitin'," Rico answered.

Grabbing the phone from the cup holder, Freaky answered without looking at the screen.

"Talk."

"Where you at?" the caller asked.

"Who is this?"

"Nigga—it's Jetta."

"Oh, my fault. Relax, though."

"Who else would it be callin' you, Freaky?"

"Jetta, on dawgs, miss me with all that."

"Anyways—where you at?"

"Around."

"Well, I made yo' ass a plate. Come get it. You know I gotta make sure ya grown ass is fed."

"Aight. I'm on my way."

"Okay. I love you."

Freaky had never told her he loved her before. So instead of saying it back, he simply pressed end and disconnected the call.

"Ayo, gun—" Freaky almost slipped and called Rico gun-smoke but caught himself.

Turning down the radio, Rico said, "What you say, bro?"

"Nah, I was sayin' slide through Topliff real quick so I can check this bitch."

"Aight," Rico said and took a left turn.

During the drive, he was deep in thought.

So deep, he wasn't even aware who was lurking in the rearview mirror.

Neither was Freaky.

He was too busy texting.

13 ½ 13 ½ 13 ½

After spotting Freaky, Mega turned onto a narrow backstreet—sped down, then swung around the next street over.

Now, he was right behind the gray Mercedes.

"Ayo, one of y'all got some gloves?" Frog asked.

"Nope."

"Nah."

Frog kicked off his sneakers and started peeling off his socks.

"The fuck you doin' back there?" Flame asked, looking over his shoulder.

"Shit, 'bout to use my socks as gloves. Fuckin' with Freak, shit might get sticky. And if the boys get on me and I gotta toss the slammer, I ain't tryin' to leave prints."

"I don't even give a fuck," Flame said. "I'll do a natty for smacking this snake."

When Mega turned onto Topliff Street, the houses blocked the sun, shading the road.

Hitting the brakes, he let Rico park first, then continued driving.

"Ayo, there go that sucker-ass nigga Rico right there. Freak ridin' with him," Flame said.

"Now we seen it with our own eyes," Mega added.

"I can't believe this clown," Flame muttered. "Take the right and pull over so I can get out," he said, cocking his gun. "I'm 'bout to let my gun smoke."

Frog and Flame got out the car.

13 ½ 13 ½ 13 ½

Rico parallel-parked between two cars. Something he hardly ever did, but had to—there was nowhere else to park.

From a packed yard, women sat drinking, kids ran between legs, and music blasted.

Nearby, a group of men stood around tables, eating ribs covered in barbecue sauce, watching either a card game or a game of dominoes.

The number of people at the cookout was ludicrous—the whole sidewalk was flooded with men and women holding red cups, smiling, laughing, dancing.

Freaky looked for Jetta. He didn't see her. He tried calling her, but no service.

"Yo," he tapped Rico's shoulder.

"What I tell you 'bout puttin' ya filthy paws on a fly nigga like myself?" Rico said.

"Here go this conceited shit. Let me see ya jack."

Rico pointed to the cup holder.

"Ya hands broke or somethin'? It's right there."

Grabbing the phone, Freaky dialed Jetta's number. After three rings she answered.

"It's Freaky."

"Why you callin' me from a random number?" Jetta asked, annoyed.

"That's irrelevant," Freaky said. "I'm out front."

"Okay, I'm coming now. Don't your boy—the one you always with—want a plate?"

Looking over at Rico, Freaky saw he wasn't paying attention.

"Nah, he smooth," he muttered, lowering his voice.

"And don't be worryin' about another nigga—the fuck wrong with you? I hate that friendly shit."

"Sorry. I won't do it again," she said and Freaky hung up.

Rico may have been in a world of his own, but he didn't miss the brown-skinned man with braids going down the side of his head.

Looking him over, Rico thought to himself:

This nigga look too tough for a cookout.

Still eyeing the man, he noticed the dude had on sweatpants. Rico checked his left pocket for a gun print. Not seeing one, he then tried to see if anything was weighing his pants down.

After a quick observation, Rico told himself:

He ain't strapped.

And with that, he dismissed the brown-skinned man as a threat. In the seat next to him, Freaky toyed with his cell phone, trying to find service. Had he been watching his and Rico's back—instead of focusing on his phone—he would've recognized his once-accomplice coming...

And maybe, just maybe, saved some lives.

13 ½ 13 ½ 13 ½

Flame maneuvered through a crowd of people on the sidewalk.

From a distance, he spotted a light-skinned female with freckles and red hair walking up to the Mercedes that Rico and Freaky were sitting in. She had a plate wrapped in aluminum foil.

Flame hoped she was still there by the time he started shooting.

Along with Freaky, he wanted to kill her too.

Ever since he lost his brother and girlfriend to the streets, he had lost all value for innocent lives.

The red-haired girl began walking away from the Mercedes.

"Jetta, bring ya ass back over here."

Freaky called her back over, and she stuck her head through the window and kissed him.

Flame freed his gun from his waist.

What a God, he thought.

The brown-skinned man with the braids was none other than Frog.

As he made his way across the street, he saw Rico, laid back in the driver's seat of the Mercedes.

He took a deep breath—

Then, in the same motion of spinning around, he lifted up his shirt and pulled the Tech-9 from between the leather belt wrapped around his torso.

When Rico became aware of his new position, he was staring down a barrel.

Fuck! He said inwardly.

"O.T.S.!" Frog roared and began firing.

Bullets tore through the car.

"Pull off! Pull off!" Freaky yelled.

Rico slammed the gear shift into drive, ready to flee—

But crashed into the car's rear bumper in front of him.

Flame and Frog lit the car up, shooting Rico and Freaky in broad daylight, raping the innocence from the children's laughter and family gatherings.

They ceased all movement, all conversations, and sent chills. The street was silent but the smell of gunpowder still lingered.

As mothers and fathers whisked their children away, a female lay sprawled out on the sidewalk.

Dead.

Her sneakers had come off, and her feet were scraped.

Poor Jetta.

Inside the car, Rico and Freaky looked slumped over—unresponsive.

Blood stained the interior. It nearly filled the cup holders. The dashboard and door panels were spray-painted red.

The car sat on all flats, riddled with bullet holes.

All the windows were shot out, shell casings decorated the street and sidewalk.

Time passed.

The gunshots had stopped.

Then movement.

Rico gained consciousness.

Slowly, he opened his door.

Immediately, shattered glass fell onto the pavement—followed by the blood spilling from his mouth.

It was getting dark.

Death was taking the place of life, but Rico told himself to fight.

And he did.

But he was too weak to get out of the car.

So, knowing his next breath might be his last, he did the only thing he could do…

"Call a fuckin' ambulance!"

He screamed for help.

CHAPTER TWENTY-ONE

On a dirt road, parked outside a drug house that looked more like a shed in Kingstreet County, Raheem waited alone in the car while Heron-Hommi executed a deal.

As he waited, he received a call from his brother.

"Yo!" Darian blurted out. "They hit, bro."

Raheem only caught Yo and bro.

"What you say?"

"They…" Darian sniffled. "They—they shot, bro."

"Bro? What the fuck you talkin' about? Calm down and tell me what you talkin' 'bout."

"Rico."

"What about 'em?"

"They clapped him."

"What?" Raheem's back straightened. "Where? When? Who shot him? Fuck you mean they—who the fuck is they?"

"Them kids."

Darian took a shaky breath.

"And they hit him bad. He's undergoing surgery now, but the doctor said…" Darian's voice cracked. "They don't expect him to make it."

Tears raced down Raheem's face.

"Nah…" he uttered. "I'm not hearing that." He wiped his face. "Tell whoever—if my brother die, everybody in that hospital die."

"I don't know what to do, bro—what should I do?"

"You ain't hear me? I just told you."

"But what else?"

"Don't get booked. I'll be there tomorrow morning."

"Aight… hurry up. I need you here," Darian admitted.

"I'm on my way. Soldiers only live once." The phone line went dead.

Hommi climbed into the car. Raheem was in a daze.

Tears were still flowing.

"Who we gotta bury?" Hommi asked.

"Who we should've buried already—them kids."

"I'm hip, but what make you say that? What's wrong?"

"Rico."

"What about him?"

"He's in surgery right now."

"Nah… not my nigga."

Hommi clenched his fists. "What happened? What he in surgery for?"

"Them kids caught up with him."

"Fuck." Hommi slammed his fist against the door panel. "What's the word on him?"

"Knox said the doc told him—" Raheem hesitated.

"They don't think… he gonna pull through."

Hommi stayed silent.

"I'm leaving for the city tonight."

"I'm rolling."

"Nah, you gotta stay here and hold it down. I got this—"

"Nigga, who the fuck you talkin' to?" Hommi cut him off. "Fuck this shit. The tribe come before this bread."

Raheem took a deep breath.

"Kinfolk, I know that. You ain't gotta tell me that. But that same bread we put the family before, that's the same bread the tribe gonna need to win this war." Raheem stared at him. "I need you to think outside the box. Fund this war. I got the rest."

Hommi held out three fingers, and Raheem locked his three fingers with his.

"I love you, cuzo," Hommi said, looking him dead in the eyes. "So make it back."

Raheem nodded.

Assuring him—

He would.

CHAPTER TWENTY-TWO

BOSTON BAGHDAD

Raheem watched over his younger brother. Tears dropped from his eyes, rolling onto his knuckles as he held onto the rail of the hospital bed. The sight of his brother's condition enraged him.

Rico's skin had a gray tint, his body reduced to flesh and bones.

Fat tubes stuck out from everywhere.

Two separate tubes ran under both armpits.

One was in his stomach.

Another protruded from the center of his neck and upper back.

A thin one ran through his dick.

And two more—the same size—were inserted into each nostril.

Raheem's heart was in pieces.

He could imagine his mother turning over in her grave. *I was supposed to protect y'all,* Raheem reminded himself.

It was a promise he made to his mother.

Rico had suffered eight bullet wounds and had been in a coma for a week.

For every single one of those days, Honest, Darian, Raheem, and Rain had been by his side.

Not one second was guaranteed to Rico.

He had to fight if he wanted to live.

Every day was nerve-wracking.

The hospital staff thought Rico was strong as hell—most victims who suffered the same type of wounds either arrived dead or didn't make it past the first day.

But Rico made it to the next week.

The fight, though, was far from over.

I gotta get my family out this game... out this life... out this repeated cycle.

And I gotta do it fast.

Seeing his brother laid up in a hospital bed, shot up, did something to him.

He needed to talk to the only person he could be himself with.

He still couldn't believe how far he and Tia had grown apart.

He always thought he'd marry her someday.

How did I let it get to this point where I can't even call my bitch for comfort?

For a long minute, he thought about his own question—

Then he said, "Rain. Come on."

Rain got up from her chair and strolled over to his side.

"Where you goin', kinfolk?" Darian asked.

"Outta here. I gotta get out this room for a minute," Raheem answered.

"Be safe—you back in Baghdad. Call me if you need me."

Raheem looked at Honest. "You need anything?" he asked.

"No, I'm fine." Her answer was a lie.

But Raheem took her word for it and left Boston Medical Center with Rain.

Walking down Harrison Street, Raheem and Rain got into a four-door Volvo 6.0—a rental he had picked up from the airport.

Starting up the car, he told Rain, "Roll up."

While she rolled a blunt, he made a call.

"Owoo," Hommi answered.

"What it do?" Raheem asked.

"Same ol' shit. What's shakin'?"

"This shit crazy, no bullshit. They got my boy all fucked up."

"I'm sorry to hear that, cuzo. How he doin' though?"

Tapping the blinker down, Raheem pulled into traffic and made a right turn.

"He been in a coma for a week now, but he comin' around. Lil nigga three-hunnit."

Now on Massachusetts Avenue, he kept straight toward the DoubleTree Hotel.

"Yo, let me ask you this—did you find out who the culprit is?" Hommi asked.

"Mega, dawg."

Rain had just finished rolling up the blunt.

She handed it to Raheem and, hearing the conversation, wished she could do more.

I swear, I hope while we're here, I can prove my loyalty.

"Yeah, cuzo, dawg's time way overdue," Hommi said.

"You ain't never lied. But, yo—I'ma hit you back later."

"Aight, bet."

They hung up.

Rain saw the stress on Raheem's face.

She hated seeing him like this.

And she wished, more than anything, she could ease his pain.

Taking a right turn, Raheem pulled up to the hotel entrance.

He peeled off a few hundred-dollar bills from a thick fold of money and handed them to Rain.

"I'll be back," he told her.

She didn't want to add to his stress, so she did exactly what he expected of her.

"Okay, baby," she said.

"Be safe, please. Ya streets are dangerous."

She got out of the car.

13 ½ 13 ½ 13 ½

Raheem stood on Tia's grandparents' porch, butterflies in his stomach.

Once he got himself together, he rang the doorbell twice.

Shortly after, the door swung open—

Tia's grandmother stood in the threshold, smiling.

"Hey, Raheem. How you been? Give me a hug."

"Hi, Grandma. I been alright," Raheem said, hugging her.

"Where Tia at?"

"Oh, Tia don't stay here no more. She moved some time ago."

Raheem's face twisted.

"You outta all people didn't know that?"

"Nah," he said, confused. "I wasn't aware of that."

"Baby, how not?"

"I don't know, Grandma. But it was good seein' you. Let me go—I'ma just call her."

"You got her new number?"

Raheem froze. *New number?*

"No, Grandma, I don't have the number."

"Let me get it for you. Are you two okay?"

"Yeah, we good. We just gotta get some things in order."

"You two better get it together," she said, shuffling off to grab the number.

When she returned, she handed it to him.

"Here you go."

"Thank you, Grandma."

Raheem gave her a big hug and a kiss on the cheek, then left.

13 ½ 13 ½ 13 ½

The next day, Raheem called a meeting and held it in the inner city.

Rain had accompanied him but stayed in the car.

She was clueless about what the pow-wow was concerning but could probably guess.

Sure that it would be a while before Raheem came back, she reclined her seat and relaxed under the A.C.

Soon, she got hungry.

She had a craving for Caribbean food. There was only one restaurant in Myrtle Beach that served Caribbean food, but their dishes taste like soul food with a bunch of spices.

She texted Raheem.

From: Rain: *Daddy, I'm hungry. Where can I get some bomb Caribbean food?*

Raheem texted back the address to a popular restaurant.

Following the GPS directions, she pulled up to Flames. As soon as she arrived, she noticed the restaurant was crowded.

Damn, they packed. Their food must be good.

Excited, she got out and stepped inside. Immediately, the smell had her nose in heaven.

On her left, a long line of customers waited to place their orders. On her right, several round tables were occupied by patrons eating their food.

At one of the tables, Rain noticed a big, light-skinned man—So light, he could almost pass for white. But his facial structure and features told her otherwise.

She noticed his brown freckles, braids down his back, and white-gold grills.

Up North is kinda weird, she thought. *But I like it.* In the presence of the freckled man were two grimy-looking dudes. But besides his freckles, something about him stood out the most to Rain.

Rain and Freckles locked eyes. Quickly, she looked away and strolled over to the line, but she could still feel his eyes on her.

"Aye, ma!" Freckles called. "I saw you peekin'!"

Rain paid him no mind.

Freckles, however, could tell she wasn't a native and he had to have her first.

"What's up, ma? You don't speak to real niggas?" He smirked. "My name Mega—the realest nigga you gon' find. What's ya name, ma?"

Instantly, Rain had a flashback of Raheem's phone call yesterday.

Her heart skipped.

Mega dawg. Rain reminisced, then said, "Mega? That's cute. My name is Rose."

Mega got up, walked over to her, and said, "You not from here, huh?"

"I am… but I'm not."

"Which one is it?" Mega asked, laughing.

"I mean…" Rain smiled. "Now that I met you? I wanna say I am." They both laughed.

"I see you got a sense of humor. If you don't mind—what's ya number?" He licked his lips. "I'd like to get to know you."

Grinning, Rain said, "Give me yours. You gon' take your time callin' me."

Mega liked that she was direct. He handed her his number.

Rain, on the other hand, was thinking about Raheem and how he was gonna love her for this.

"I'ma call you tonight… see what you doin' tomorrow," Rain said.

Mega grinned. "Shit, I can answer that question now—I'm doin' you."

Rain smirked. "No, boo." She placed her palm flat against Mega's chest. "I'm doin' you."

CHAPTER TWENTY-THREE

"Aye, Griff," Stratton called. "Come check this out."

In the evidence room, D.T. Griffin and Stratton examined surveillance footage of the shooting in front of Underbar.

For Griffin to get a better look, Stratton scooted back in his chair and pointed at the monitor.

"Where you know that walk from?" he asked.

Griffin studied the screen, then said, "I don't know. You tell me."

Stratton looked at him sideways. "Are you serious, dude? That's the kid Casino."

Griffin leaned in. Squinted. Then—"That is that fuckin' prick. But…" He kept watching. "You can't see his face. Or who he's gettin' in the car with."

"That's true," Stratton admitted. "But at least we got a break in the case. And I think he's a wannabe. Maybe we can get him to talk."

"Maybe." Griffin exhaled. "But them Solo dudes. They a tough crew to crack, though, Tom."

"True. But he's a poser. I know one when I see one."

"You do know Casino is Heron-Homm's younger brother, right?" Griffin folded his arms. "I think he'd know better."

"You may be right. But for what it's worth…It's worth a try."

Griffin nodded. "You got me there."

13 ½ 13 ½ 13 ½

Rain showers came and went since sunrise.

But still, everyone was in position.

Two days ago—When Rain first showed Raheem the picture of Mega in her phone—she immediately explained the coincidence. And her reason for entertaining him. At first, Raheem was skeptical. But by the time she finished explaining the run-in the leery thoughts left his head and he was grateful for Rain's quick thinking.

He knew what he had to do.

And so did Rain.

She had put herself in position for this exact moment.

Raheem told her—

"Set up a date."

"So what you wanna do?" Mega asked.

He was driving, giving Rain a tour of the city.

"Whatever!" Rain answered. "But before we get too busy can we stop by my aunt's place? I gotta pick up some money for my pockets."

"Pick up some money?" Mega smirked. "Ma, I am your money for ya pockets."

Straight trick, Rain thought.

She said, "I appreciate you. But I like to keep a little somethin' of my own. Just in case you get missin' on me."

"Missin'?" Mega looked at her sideways. "Ma, I'm not goin' nowhere, and neither are you. But if it makes wifey feel better— Where your peoples stay at?"

"Wifey, huh?" Rain smirked. "You know where 53 Esmond Street is?"

Mega grinned. "Come on, ma. I am these streets. You talkin' 'bout the buildings. Let's slide through there real quick." He made an illegal U-turn—

Completely oblivious to the unmarked cruiser parked nearby.

The cops had been watching. So, as soon as he made the traffic violation—the sirens flashed.

Mega's stomach dropped.

He looked in the rearview mirror.

Fuck.

He thought about his suspended license.

And the gun on him.

I can't get caught with another slammer.

I'm already on my second subsequent.

After considering his circumstances he came out of his shirt and stepped on the gas.

Rain's eyes widened.

I know this dude don't have me in a stolen car...

She didn't know what the fuck was going on, but she secured her seatbelt.

Mega swerved around cars—

Speeding up Quincy Street, heading toward Humboldt Ave.

He honked his horn, trying to clear the road.

He also simultaneously called his sister.

As her phone rang he passed a mob of kids on the sidewalk—

They cheered him on.

One of them pushed his bike in front of the police car—

Then ran.

Finally, his sister answered.

"Yo, sis!" he blurted. "Where you at?"

"Why the hell are you yellin'? I'm on my way to see my man. Why? What's all that noise in the background?"

"I'm gettin' chased. I need you to meet me. Where you at?"

Running a red light and cutting through Warren Street, a public bus nearly crashed into the speeding BMW. Rain screamed, covering her eyes with her palms.

"Who the fuck is that screamin'?" Mega's sister asked.

"Fuck all that—where you at?"

"I'm on Blue Hill Ave and Seaver Street. What about you?"

Mega glanced at a street sign, then looked in his rearview mirror. He still had company.

I gotta shake these niggas, he thought.

"Listen, I'm 'bout to take a left on Humboldt now. Meet me on Hutchington. Park on the left-hand side of the strip. Have your window rolled all the way down. I'ma throw the blick in your whip and keep it movin'. Got it?"

"Aight, I'll be there in two minutes," she assured him.

"Make it one." Hanging up, he accidentally dropped his phone. It hit the floor and rolled under his seat.

On the opposite side of the road, Mega sped up. He was doing close to 80 MPH, maneuvering swiftly through traffic, causing two police cars to crash, setting off a chain reaction of collisions.

After putting three blocks behind him, he turned onto Hutchington Street. His sister's car wasn't there yet. Figuring she hadn't made it yet, he kept going, planning to double back. That turned out to be a blessing because the cops weren't sure which way he went. They took a left. Mega, however, took a right and was coming down Hutchington again.

This time, he spotted his sister's car. Pulling up alongside it, he threw his piece through the window, then kept going.

The hair on Honest's arms rose, but not because of the gun now resting on her passenger seat.

What is he doin' with her?

Her mind raced for answers, and she knew this wasn't a coincidence.

Her brother was being set up.

I gotta tell him.

Although police swarmed the area, Mega managed to find a safe place to hide, letting the heat die down. He reclined his seat and told Rain to do the same.

"Now that was crazy."

Rain's hands shook. She held them up. "Look. My nerves are bad right now."

Mega laughed. To him, it was funny. Had he not been laughing he could have heard the phone vibrating under the seat.

Rain had no clue—she was one phone call away from being exposed. Everything happened so fast she never had the chance to see Honest.

And she would forever have to live with that mistake.

While Mega and Rain waited for the smoke to clear, they talked about everything.

Mega was determined to win her over.

But he wasn't the only one.

Because while Mega was trying to win Rain over, Rain was trying to prove her love and loyalty to Raheem.

"Damn, I know you don't want to chill with me any longer, huh?" Rain asked.

"Why would you say that?" Mega said.

"I don't know. I just feel like I'm bad luck. The first day you hang with me you get into a police chase."

"That's not ya fault. Don't trip about that. We good."

Mega assured.

"So can we still stop by my aunties house?" She asked, bashfully.

"Yeah, anything for you." Throwing the car in drive, Mega headed to Esmond Street.

As Raheem sat and waited on Esmond Street, he received a text from Rain. She told him she and Mega were on their way, but she didn't know how far away they were.

Raheem passed the info to Darian and Casino. He was itching to see Mega and the white in his eyes. For so many nights, he had dreamed about this day. And now—it was finally happening.

For Raheem, this felt like he was about to have sex with a woman he'd been anticipating all his life.

Raheem looked out the window. By the reddish-brick building, Darian crouched behind some trash barrels.

Looking straight ahead, he asked Casino—who was lying flat across the backseat—

"Yo. You ready to die?"

Casino rubbed the handle of his gun with his thumb. Thought for a moment. Then said, "No."

Raheem nodded. "Good. Cause anyone ready to die ain't ready to kill."

Pondering, he wondered what Raheem would do if he told him he wanted out.

Would he kill me?

Or would he tell my brother? Shit, that's almost the same as smacking me. You know what — I don't even want to find out. Now that I'm here — I just have to deal with it. Fuck it.

Unbeknownst to Casino Raheem could feel his nervousness as well as smell it. Rico had told Raheem some time ago that Casino was thorough, but the conversation they had and the vibe coming off Casino wasn't adding up. From being in the streets for so long Raheem knew that Casino wanted out, but it wasn't going to happen.

Raheem made a promise. Cousin or not, if this lil nigga come back to this car and his blick isn't empty… Finally, my dream has come true.

Mega's BMW turn onto Esmond street.

For the third time today, it was raining cats and dogs.

Raindrops hit the roof of the car, making a dull sound.

"You can park right there," Rain said.

"What?"

"I said, park right there." She pointed at an open spot. "I won't get that wet running inside."

"Aight. I got'cha."

Mega parked. Hearing his phone vibrating he leaned forward to grab it from under the seat. Rain got out, but instead of heading inside the building, she made a detour and crossed the street and she climbed into Raheem's car.

Honest's name showed twenty-nine times in Mega's call log. Concerned, he called her back. She picked up on the first ring. "Bro!" Honest blurted. "Get away from that chick you with! She's setting you up!" Mega could barely process what she said. He was about to tell her to repeat herself. But the words got caught in his throat. Because at that moment it all made sense. Raheem and Casino were running toward him.

Weapons drawn.

Mega dropped his phone and went for his gun-- then froze. He forgot—he didn't have it. *Fuck.* He hurdled over the console, tried to escape out the passenger door. But then—he spotted Darian.

God... whether it's heaven or hell—all I ask is that you reunite me with my gun-smokes.

For one final moment, it was just the rain.

Then—gunshots.

The storm intensified.

The triggers eased.

Raheem exhaled.

"Solo."

Then—he walked away.

At peace.

13 ½ 13 ½ 13 ½

Honest trembled.

The tears that seeped from her eyelids stained her face.

Although Mega dropped his phone, she remained on the line and listened.

She wished she hadn't—because listening to Mega die in agony and not being able to help him was something she would have to live with for the rest of her life.

But she was also glad she did—because had she not, she wouldn't have known who was responsible for murdering her brother.

Mega.

13 ½ 13 ½ 13 ½

Detectives Griffin and Stratton stood on Esmond Street, supervising the crime scene. Police had shut down six blocks in both directions, barricading every street to collect evidence and interview witnesses.

After removing Mega's corpse from his vehicle, he was identified, placed in a body bag, and transported straight to the morgue. There was no saving him.

Underneath the rain, forensics collected a little over eighty shell casings while a crowd of concerned neighbors stood nearby, watching. One woman took a picture of the crime scene with her phone and uploaded it to Facebook. Another woman even captured a photo of Mega being placed in the body bag and posted it on social media.

Detective Stratton made sure Mega's car was properly inventoried before signaling the tow truck driver to take it to police headquarters. He scanned his surroundings and spotted Griffin examining a shell casing. Adjusting his holster, Stratton walked over to see what he was thinking.

"What's on your mind?"

"Indictments," Griffin answered. "These fuckers are running around my city with guns, shooting each other with no regard, like we're in fucking Baghdad or something."

"Who do you think is responsible for this?" Stratton asked.

Griffin studied the shell casing in his palm. "Well, judging by the caliber of the weapons, who got shot two weeks ago, and who was shot today—plus how many times he was hit—I'd have to put my money on—"

"Solo," Stratton finished.

Griffin tossed the F&N shell casing to Stratton. "You're learning. Come on, the newscast is here. Let's get this interview out the way."

13 ½ 13 ½ 13 ½

The following day, Honest sat beside Rico's hospital bed, lost in a trance. The cold room made her shiver, but her body barely reacted.

Dark circles ringed her eyes from lack of sleep. She looked a mess—because she felt like a mess. She didn't care about life as of now.

Her brother's last cry haunted her.

Her loyalty to Rico tormented her.

She told herself she should kill Rico.

It would only be fair.

She betrayed them both.

Maybe taking him out would be the only way to wash herself clean of her sins.

In her mind, she owed both Mega and Rico her loyalty.

But if she killed Rico—at the very least, she'd be honoring Mega.

For her brother.

For her sanity, Honest grabbed the pillow from under Rico's feet, tucked it under her arm, and stood over him. Slowly, she leaned forward, pressing soft kisses onto his face.

"I love you, baby," she whispered, over and over.

Tears rolled down her cheeks.

She gripped the pillow with both hands, inched it toward his face, then sat it over his nose and mouth. She watched his heart rate spike.

Honest wasn't in her right mind. If she had been, she never would have tried to harm him.

And thankfully—for the unexpected visit—she wouldn't.

"Boston Police," Detective Griffin announced, barging into Rico's room with Stratton. "We're here to speak to Rashard Grant regarding an ongoing investigation—" Griffin stopped mid-sentence. His brows furrowed as he eyed Honest. "What the hell are you doing?"

Her body stiffened.

Thinking quickly, Honest turned and forced a nervous smile. "Oh, hey! How y'all doing?" She swallowed, shifting the pillow behind her. "I was just fixing his pillow under his head. The nurse told me to move his head frequently, so he doesn't develop bald spots."

Her voice cracked.

Her eyes wandered.

Griffin wasn't buying it. He took a slow glance around the room.

"He's lucky to have someone in his corner," Griffin said with a hint of sarcasm.

Stratton smirked.

"But anyway… how is he? Still in a coma?"

"Yes," Honest replied quickly. "But we're expecting him to wake up any day now."

"Well, alright." Griffin retrieved a business card from his jacket and handed it to her. "Give me a call when he wakes up. I'd appreciate it."

He turned to leave—then suddenly stopped. "I didn't get your name. Mind if I have it?" He pulled out a pocket-sized notebook.

Honest broke eye contact—then forced herself to look him in the eyes again.

"My name?" She cleared her throat. "My name is Honest Dixon."

Griffin lifted his gaze from his notepad. "Did you say Honest Dixon?"

"Yes, sir, that's correct."

From the corner of his eye, Griffin glanced at Stratton. Then back at Honest. "Okay. That'll be all. Take care of our boy for us."

Honest looked at Rico.

"Of course, sir. He'll be fine."

As Griffin and Stratton left the hospital, Griffin's mind raced. Something in his gut told him something wasn't right.

"We gotta keep our eyes on that girl, Tom."

"You think so?" Stratton asked.

"I know so."

CHAPTER TWENTY-FOUR

When you're no longer a threat, you see who your real friends are. If the people who claimed to love Mega had shown up at his funeral, there would've been hundreds at his burial.

But there weren't.

Only four or five friends.

A handful of older family members.

And Honest.

She stood at the edge of Mega's grave, watching as the undertaker lowered his state-issued casket six feet into darkness.

Above them, the sun broke through the thick clouds, shining directly on the coffin.

Conflicted, Honest didn't know what to do. She didn't even know how to feel. But she did know she loved her brother. And inside, she was hurting.

Three muscular men, armed with shovels, began tossing fresh dirt over Mega's casket.

Honest watched. Then made a decision.

She would bury her secrets with her brother.

As the dirt rained down, she spoke inwardly:

I guess I might as well tell you the truth...

Now that you're above us all—able to see everything under the sun—your baby sister can't hide nothing from you no more.

I never meant to keep anything from you...

It's just that... when I should've told you—when I would've—I didn't even know.

And by the time I found out... I was already in love.

She inhaled deeply.

I didn't know what to say when you asked me if I saw who shot me. And how did I—out of all people—end up caught in a crossfire?

How does someone tell their brother... that the person who shot them... was him?

That it was his bullets... meant for Rico... that hit me?

How was I supposed to explain that I was sitting inside your enemy's car? That the place you thought was his apartment... was really ours?

I know I'll never hear your answer... but I pray you forgive me. I never meant for it to be like this. I just wanted a man like my big brother.

What I didn't realize... was that a man like you... is just another real one. Another gangster. Another man willing to go against the odds—even if those odds...

Was you.

I'm sorry, bro.

I love you.

But, I love him too.

"Honest!"

Hearing her name, she snapped out of her thoughts and looked around. Seeing who had called her, she said,

"Hey, Uncle Rob!"

Once in reach, she gave her uncle a hug. She hadn't seen him since the feds picked him up for his role in a Hobbs Act case.

Rob—known in the streets as Black Reign—was her mother's brother. And while he took his uncle role seriously, the family blamed him for how Mega turned out.

To those who didn't know him, or weren't alive long enough to understand his history, his name made little sense.

Why would a light-skinned man call himself Black Reign?

It wasn't until he learned about the knowledge of self—acquired through the teachings of the Five Percent Nation of Islam while locked up in M.C.I. Cedar Junction Walpole—that it became clear.

He believed his origin was supreme. That the Black man is God.

But in the streets, Black represented the essence of darkness that followed him wherever he went.

And Reign?

That symbolized the obstacles he had conquered growing up in the ghettos of Providence, Rhode Island.

Black Reign was one of the last old-school gangsters left. And he fed off that.

Before he earned his righteous name, people called him The Cop Killer—not just for what he did to get locked up, but for how he handled cops in general.

Overprotective of his loved ones, he had zero tolerance when it came to family and their safety.

After doing seventeen years straight, lifting weights the entire time, he was built like a rock.

His early thirties had taken his hair, so ever since, he kept a bald head.

His eyes—solid black—held the souls of many men.

If you had questions about a brother, a son, or a father… you might just find the answers buried deep in the pit of his gaze.

"What's up, young lady?" Black Reign said. "How you been?"

"Well, besides this recent tragedy with my brother, I'm good," Honest answered.

"Yeah, I know." Black Reign breathed in deeply, his broad chest expanding as he exhaled slowly. "I hope the ones who did this got life insurance… 'cause death is near." He paused. "But anyway—do you miss your uncle?"

Forcing a smile, Honest nodded.

"Of course. When did you get out?"

"Two months ago. The feds sat me down for a couple years, but I beat my case at trial." He smirked. "Glad to be home. But I ain't feeling what happened to my nephew. Not one bit." Black Reign rubbed a hand over his head. "This ain't going unsettled."

Tensing up, Honest broke eye contact.

It was hard to look him in the eyes knowing her sins.

"Honest," he said, "I'm up here. Why you staring at the ground?"

"I was just thinking," she muttered.

Black Reign grilled her suspiciously.

"Honest," he said slowly, his voice dipping into something dark.

"What's the family's number one rule?"

She swallowed hard. Her fingers toyed with the fabric of her dress.

"Family first until our lives disperse," she recited. "I'll die of thirst before I lie with a foe."

Black Reign smirked. Then, he pulled her into a hug. "You know I know, right?" He whispered it against her ear.

Instantly, she jumped back.

His eyes burned into hers. "No need to be afraid," he said, his tone smooth. "You're my niece. I love you. Always been my favorite. But you know…" His voice lowered. "If you go against the family… you go against the odds." He gave her a moment. "Your mother—my sister—deserves to know that the person who killed her son ain't walking free. You get what I'm saying?"

Honest nodded, but in her head, she screamed at God.

Why?

Why has my life fallen apart—so fast?

God didn't answer.

But Black Reign did.

"You know what must be done."

CHAPTER TWENTY-FIVE

A thousand-volt lightbulb flickered above the suspect's head, making sweat drip down the back of his neck.

Anxiety clawed at his stomach.

Nerves twisted into knots.

He had no idea why the SWAT team kicked in his door at four in the morning—yanked him out of bed at gunpoint—dragged him to Boston PD headquarters, and left him sitting in a cold-ass room for hours with nothing except…

A steel desk.

A single chair.

A lightbulb swaying from the ceiling.

And his own damn thoughts.

They had forgotten about him. Or at least, it felt that way. But then—the door creaked open. Two men entered. Dark suits.

Cologne that smelled like power.

Arrogance oozing from their presence.

"Good afternoon, Mr. Adams. I'm Detective Griffin." He nodded at his partner.

"This here is Detective Stratton." Griffin flashed a smirk. "We're sorry to keep you waiting." He let that settle. Then chuckled.

"You know what? Let me quit lying. We're not sorry at all."

He stopped pacing.

His cold stare pinned Adams to the chair.

"You know what I hate?"

Adams didn't answer.

Griffin smirked.

"Pests."

He leaned forward, gripping the edge of the table.

"And you, Mr. Adams… are a pest."

Adams swallowed.

"We're exterminators," Griffin continued.

"You know what exterminators do to pests?"

Adams said nothing.

"Do you even know why you're here?"

Silence.

"You don't?"

Griffin's voice dropped.

"Murder."

The word hit like a bullet.

"For first-degree murder."

The room spun.

Adams' forehead dropped onto his folded arms.

Griffin leaned in.

"You really thought you were gonna get away with shooting and killing a college student outside a club in downtown Boston?" He sneered. "You thought the cameras wouldn't catch you? Thought we wouldn't see you jump into Rico's car?"

Adams' breath hitched.

Rico's words echoed in his head.

"We don't move like that. What if the police check them cameras? Real niggas don't move like that."

Adams hyperventilated.

Stratton took a step forward.

"You need some water, son?"

Adams nodded. "And a lawyer."

Stratton turned to Griffin and told him to follow him in the hallway. In a low voice, he said, "Well, he exercised his rights. What now?"

Griffin scoffed. "You heard him ask for a lawyer?" He pointed at himself. "Because I didn't." He smirked.

"Fuck his rights. If we call his lawyer, we gotta let him walk. And if we let him walk, he's gonna know we're bluffing.

He'll think we're some clowns in a suit." Griffin straightened. "I ain't lettin' that kid leave this precinct. Not until I'm done with him." Griffin's eyes darkened. "He's a coward. I know his type."

Stratton clutched Griffin's shoulders with both hands and locked eyes with him.

"Griff, I get it. But we gotta be real careful. Let's not forget—these dudes are making money. We don't need some shark of a lawyer chewing at our hamstrings. Last thing we need is this kid's statements coming back to bite us in the ass, and next thing you know, these dudes are back on the streets after an appeal. Don't be overzealous."

Griffin sighed. "Look, just give me a couple more minutes with him. If he doesn't crack, I'll back off. Deal?"

He extended his hand. Stratton hesitated, then shook it.

"Deal."

Back inside the interrogation room, Stratton spoke first.

"Listen, kid. I don't give a fuck that we're both Black—I ain't playing with you. We know it all. So if you wanna help yourself, help us. Because if you don't our intel will be front and center at your open-and-shut trial."

Casino swallowed hard, his throat dry.

Stratton leaned in.

"You know what? Let me just lay it on the table for you, Casino."

Hearing his street name made his heart skip a beat.

Stratton noticed.

"You fucked up," Stratton continued. "I mean, you really fucked up. You're on camera—clear as day—blowing a man's head off. And don't get me wrong, I sympathize. I'd do the same for my partner—hell, let alone my cousin."

Griffin pushed off the wall and took over.

"That's right, Casino. We know you only did it for your cousin Rico. And, honestly. You're obligated to protect family. But in the state of Massachusetts murder is first-degree. And you committed it."

He turned to Stratton.

"Hey, Tom, what do they call it?"

"A smack, Griff."

"That's it, Casino—a smack."

Griffin smirked, mocking. "Do you know how much time you do for a smack, Casino?"

Silence.

"Life." He let it sink in. "Life like Eddie and Martin, you fucking dickhead."

Casino felt like he was about to vomit. Although Rico had warned him about this part of the game, he never thought he'd end up here.

Griffin leaned forward. "Let me ask you something." He placed a finger on his lips, pretending to think. "Why'd you shoot that kid and jump right into the car? That was stupid. And we know the car belonged to Rico—we just can't prove it 'cause the light over the license plate wasn't working." He shook his head, feigning disappointment. "But you, on the other hand? You're crystal-clear on camera, gunning a man down like a fucking dog."

Casino's mind raced.

It's over. These crackers got me by the balls. I ain't going out like Willy Lump Lump.

"Look, kid," Griffin said, voice softer now. "We're giving you one chance to save yourself."

He paused, then tapped his fingers on the desk.

"You can finally think about yourself for once. Do the right thing. Go home to that gorgeous girl of yours—what was her name again?"

He snapped his fingers.

"Oh, right—Vivi."

Casino's stomach churned.

"But if not." Griffin shrugged. "We'll just take you to the back and book you. It's up to you."

Casino lifted his head.

His hands were clammy.

Sweat traced his top lip, rolling down from his armpits to his ribs.

He looked at Griffin.

Then swung his head toward Stratton.

But everything around them spun.

He tried to control his breathing. In… out…

Then, barely above a whisper, he choked out,

"I'll tell on—"

Before he could finish, his stomach lurched, and he threw up.

The first symptom of treason.

CHAPTER TWENTY-SIX

The day Honest had been waiting for had finally arrived.

After months in the hospital, on August 3rd, Rico was finally getting discharged.

First thing in the morning, Honest was at the hospital to pick up her man.

And not just because she wanted to.

Because she had to.

Her uncle was applying extreme pressure on her.

Inside the elevator, she thought about the love she had for Rico and how she didn't want anything to happen to him.

But being a Dixon came with a duty.

She whispered under her breath.

"I'll never forgive myself for this."

The elevator dinged.

Doors slid open.

She stepped out onto the glossy white floor, making her way through the hall to Rico's room.

She took a deep breath before walking in.

"Hey, babe."

Rico was sitting up, watching TV.

The second he saw her, his face lit up.

"There she go! What's up, baby? I been waiting on you since five this morning."

She smiled, masking the guilt tearing her apart.

"So, that must mean you're ready."

"I stay ready, so I don't gotta get ready," he smirked. "Let's blow this joint."

Shaking her head, she helped him out of bed and into the wheelchair beside it.

"I swear, boy—you haven't changed a bit."

"Why would I? I got the baddest, most loyal chick in the Bean, dawgs."

Honest's throat tightened.

Her eyes swelled.

Rico kept talking, oblivious.

"This shit feels like wrapping up a bid, no bullshit. I'm just glad I don't gotta deal with no more needles or none of that dumb shit."

He laughed, shaking his head.

"You ever had to get a shot in the ass-cheek every day, at the same time? That shit'll drive a man crazy."

Honest forced a smile, pushing his wheelchair toward the exit.

She lifted him into the car, struggling.

"Damn, babe—you heavy."

Rico laughed.

"Heavy? Girl, I woke up one-twenty. I lost damn near seventy pounds!"

Honest sighed.

"Don't worry, mommy gonna fatten you right up."

"I know that, bighead. That's why I love you."

He rubbed the back of her head, and she swatted his hand away, pouting.

"Stop talking 'bout my head."

He grinned.

"Okay, let's get the fuck up outta here."

Honest pressed the gas, exiting the parking lot. The whole ride, while Rico slept, Honest's mind spiraled. *I know I should hate Rico. I should want him dead. But I don't. Now that Mega's gone... he's all I got. He's my family. He's my beginning... and my end.* But loyalty ran deep in her blood. And Black Reign was waiting.

Inside Honest's Living Room…

The lights were off.

The curtains shut tight.

Black Reign sat on the couch, calm.

Dressed head-to-toe in army fatigues, he waited.

He sniffed a line of heroin.

What he wanted for his niece was for her to see, with her own eyes, what loyalty was—and what loyalty looked like.

So, he waited.

Thirty minutes passed.

Then an hour.

Black Reign snorted another line of brown powder.

Ninety minutes passed.

One hundred and twenty minutes.

Two hours.

He wasn't stupid.

He knew when games were being played.

So, he made a call.

Rico watched as Honest stuffed luggage on top of luggage into the backseat of her C-Class Benz.

She was moving fast, eyes darting around like she was being hunted.

Something was seriously wrong.

And Rico wasn't about to ignore it.

The second she climbed into the driver's seat, he went straight at her.

"You got something you wanna tell me?"

Honest froze—just for a split second.

Her throat felt dry as sandpaper.

She grabbed her bottle of Poland Spring, took a sip.

Rico's stare burned through her.

"Huh, Honest? What's going on?" His voice sharpened. "Why the fuck we outside some storage unit, stuffing luggage in the V? Like we on the run or some shit."

Honest turned and gaze out the window.

"My uncle," she said simply.

"Ya uncle?" Rico frowned. "What the fuck do ya uncle got to do with anything?"

She hesitated, then exhaled.

"I think it's time I tell you the truth."

Rico's jaw tightened.

"Oh, you think it's time to tell me the truth?" His voice edged toward anger. "Nah, fuck all that—start making sense."

Honest turned, her eyes glossy.

"Mega. He's my older brother."

Rico's face dropped.

Honest lowered her head, hands covering her face as sobs escaped.

Rico stared at her through slits, his mind racing.

This whole time… I been sleeping with the enemy?

How the fuck did I miss that? What was this hoe's intention? Before he could speak, her phone rang. Without thinking, she answered—on speaker.

"Hello."

A deep, slow voice came through the speaker.

"So, you chose to go against the grain, I see."

Rico's eyes snapped to the phone, then back to Honest.

"What are you talking about?" she asked, voice unsteady.

Black Reign smirked on the other end.

"Honest, you know exactly what I'm talking about. I gave you a chance to do the right thing. I told you to bring your boyfriend to me." His voice turned sharp. "But instead, you took my gesture for granted. You left me in your apartment—with no intentions of coming back."

Rico's mind clicked.

The setup.

The betrayal.

And now, the consequences.

"Unc, I don't know what you're talking about," Honest lied. She stared at Rico, pleading silently.

"They ain't discharge him from the hospital yet," she rushed out. "He's still there. The doc said he needs a few more days under their care. Ain't nothing I can do."

Silence.

Then, Black Reign's tone changed.

"Honest."

"Yes, Unc?"

"Your name should be Liar."

"But Unc—"

"But nothing." His voice turned ice cold. "You chose your path. Now run."

Click.

Rico's gaze locked on Honest.

"What the fuck was that?"

Her hands gripped the steering wheel, knuckles turning white. Nervously, she swallowed. She had no choice now. She had to tell him everything.

"While you were in a coma," she whispered, "your brother killed my brother—Mega."

Rico didn't blink.

"And now my crazy ass uncle, Black Reign, wants you dead. "Her hands shook as she continued. "He tried to make me set you up—but I won't. I love you."

Silence.

Rico's face remained stone cold.

"So Mega was ya brother, huh?"

Honest nodded.

"How?"

She took a deep breath.

"We have the same mother."

Rico pinched the bridge of his nose, his mind spinning.

"So this whole time," he muttered, "this whole fucking time we been together, dawg been ya brother?"

Honest looked at him, desperate.

"I booked us a hotel. So we can lay low. So you can get healthy." Her manicured hand gently rested on his knee. "Please… just let me explain on the way there."

Rico exhaled sharply, jaw clenched.

Then, after a long pause, he gestured to the road.

"Drive."

Inside the Car…

Honest began to confess.

"I grew up sheltered. My brother never let me see the streets. Never let me know violence existed."

Rico listened silently.

"I never knew people fought, shot, and killed each other. Mega kept his street life far from me." She glanced at Rico. "When I met you, I had no clue y'all were enemies." Her voice cracked. "And I didn't find out until after I got shot."

Rico's stomach turned.

"I remember Mega asking me who shot me." Her eyes swelled up. "And I lied. I told him I didn't know." Her breath hitched. "But I did know." She clenched the wheel, voice trembling. "I watched my own brother shoot me—while trying to shoot you."

Silence.

"I didn't know what to do," she whispered. "I was in love with you."

Tears spilled down her cheeks.

"I just want to stay out of it. Because for what it's worth—our love, our life, and our future—is worth more than any of this."

Rico wiped her tears away.

Inside, his mind was at war.

She had every opportunity to set him up—but she didn't.

She chose him.

She chose their life together over her own family.

Damn... if that ain't loyalty, I don't know what is.

Rico took a deep breath.

Then, looking straight ahead, he said,

"I love you, Hon."

And after a beat—

"On dawgs, I'm with you."

13 ½ 13 ½ 13 ½

In a pair of boy shorts and a tank top, Tia stood over the stove, prepping a plate of food. The aroma filled the air as she set the plate on the table.

Her paramour inhaled deeply, eyes lighting up.

"Thank you, baby. I really appreciate you."

"You're welcome. But let me help you."

Tia picked up the knife, dicing the pork chop into bite-sized pieces before feeding him.

Once he finished, she helped him into bed.

"Good looking, ma. I love you."

After kissing him softly on the lips, she whispered, "How can I not love you back? Now get some rest. Mommy needs you to get better."

CHAPTER TWENTY-SEVEN

Raheem dropped everything the moment he heard homicide had kicked in Darian's door and arrested him for murder. Without wasting time, he called one of his close friends in Boston.

"Lisa, I need you to visit him," he said. "I'm back in South Carolina. I can't make it right away."

Lisa agreed.

"All I need you to do," he told her, "is go up to Nashua Street Jail—find out what's going on."

The next day, while hanging around the house, Raheem's phone rang.

It was Lisa.

"Talk to me."

She wasted no time.

"It's true," she said. "They booked him for Mega's body."

Raheem's stomach tightened.

How the fuck is he the only one booked? If they know Knox was involved, then they gotta know about me and Casino, too. This shit don't add up.

"You sure nobody else got picked up?"

"Only Knox," Lisa said.

"Did Knox say anything about me?"

Lisa hesitated.

"The police said they'd rather have you than him. But they'll settle for him."

Raheem's jaw clenched.

Lisa kept talking.

"And just so you know," she said, "he looks stressed."

Raheem sighed.

"I feel him. Getting booked for a smack it some shit to stress about."

"He told me to tell you to grab his money from his girl and get him a lawyer."

"That goes without saying. But what's his bail?"

"He ain't got one."

"Fuck." Raheem closed his eyes for a second, then exhaled. "I gotta get my lil nigga outta there."

Lisa hesitated again.

"Oh, and…"

"What?"

Lisa sighed.

"This is some crazy shit, Raheem. But Knox told me to tell you something."

Raheem pressed the phone to his ear.

"Say it."

Lisa's voice lowered.

"He said… *Foxwoods.*"

Raheem's eyes darkened.

"Foxwoods," he repeated.

Lisa nodded.

"He said you'd know what that means. He also said he sent you what you need to your P.O. Box—so you can see it for yourself."

Raheem's fist clenched. He already knew. But hearing it confirmed made his blood boil.

"Bitch ass nigga," Raheem muttered under his breath.

Lisa cut in.

"Look, Two-Times," she said, "I don't want shit to do with this. Y'all be on—"

"You ain't gotta worry about nothing," Raheem assured her.

Lisa paused.

"Alright. Imma take your word for it."

"You good. I appreciate you."

"Yeah, yeah. You owe me."

They hung up.

Raheem sat in silence. His hands gripped the phone, knuckles white. His own cousin.

Casino.

His right-hand man's little brother had snitched on his own family.

Why, nigga? Why would you rat like we wasn't gonna find out? How do I tell Hommi this shit? Or should I tell him at all?

Raheem shook his head.

This lil nigga fucked up. Can't nobody be trusted in this game.

Raheem grabbed a Backwoods and started rolling up.

As he broke the weed down, his mind raced.

I failed.

Again.

My mother always told me—if anything ever happened to her, I was supposed to protect my brothers by all means.

And once again, I failed her.

First Rico got shot.

Now Knox is in jail for a body.

I just wanted to get us out the hood—make my moms proud... but look.

Look at this bullshit.

His jaw clenched.

What would my moms say right now? Knowing her, probably nothing.

She believed in tough love.

He shook his head.

I let the money blind me. I lost everything—for these dead, racist presidents. Money brought nothing but fake bitches and snakes around me…And pushed away the ones who really loved me.

His blunt was rolled up now. He lit it. Took a deep pull. *I got caught up in this life… and I lost myself. But I'm tired of this shit. This game don't bring nothing but death, jealousy, disloyalty, and treason. Only a fool ignores the signs. And I ain't no fool. I got enough bread stacked up to make smart moves…I still got my health…I still got my freedom…It's time to cash out.*

Raheem took another pull, then let the smoke ease out.

He could see it now.

Cash out.

Get wifey back.

Start a family.

Make his moms proud.

But first…

I gotta get Knox home.

"Yo, you good, cuzo?"

Raheem snapped out of it.

Hommi had stormed into the living room—a towel wrapped around his waist, a gun in his hand.

"I thought I heard you yelling," he said.

Raheem exhaled.

"Nah, kinfolk. I ain't good."

Hommi squinted.

"What's wrong?"

Raheem took a slow pull from his blunt.

"Knox is jammed."

Hommi's face dropped.

"For a man-down?"

Raheem nodded.

"Get the fuck outta here," Hommi muttered, palming his face. "How much cuzo's bail?"

"No bail."

"Fuck."

"We need to cop him a lawyer ASAP."

"The best one money can buy," Hommi agreed. He rubbed his face. "Who's body they charge him with?"

"Mega."

"Awe man that's wack. How the dicks know he had something to do with it though? Like, what made them bag him?

Matter fact don't even tell me, let me guess, someone is ratting. I bet you it's a rat. Let me hit that blunt. I got a headache."

Raheem handed Hommi the Backwoods.

"I don't even know, bro. Knox didn't say if somebody told or not, but I doubt it. It was only kinfolks on that M.I., but if somebody is talking, you'll be the first to know."

Life is crazy. Here it is his own brother ratted, and I can't bring myself to tell him. I know my dawg, it will crush Hommi if he found out Casino told on family. Shit—period. He'd rather I spare him the humiliation and handle it myself.

Yeah, I'm done with this shit.

This game don't do nothing but destroy you.

Raheem stood up, folding his arms across his chest.

"I'm falling back from the game," he said.

"What? What you mean?"

"I'm fading to black. Niggas can have this shit. Real nigga shit."

"Hold up, let me go put some clothes on," Hommi said, disappearing into his room. When he came back, he was dressed and ready for war.

"Yo, cuzo," he started. "You not leaving me out here by myself. Like, who the fuck am I supposed to rock with? Who gon' watch my back? You ain't think of that, did you? Yeah, exactly.

You talking crazy. And what's your reason for fading? That bitch, huh? Man, fuck that bitch. You can do so much better. We don't need no hoe—we got each other, we got it all. You could have a bitch ten times better. You Two-Times, nigga. Fuck that bitch."

He slid open the glass door leading to the balcony, motioning toward the luxury cars filling the private parking lot below.

"Fuck that hoe. Look at our whips. Look at our crib. Look at our life! Cuzo, you can't pull out on me—you all I got out here."

"Hommi," Raheem cut in. "You gon' be good without me. You got the connect. You and Chief got the beach. You got enough work and support to expand. And you still got the drive for this. I don't. This ain't just for Tee. This is for my moms. She wanted better for me. I want her to rest in peace. I'll always be here for you—that'll never change. But it's time for me to step away while I still got the chance. I want a family, kinfolk. And more than anything? I want to overcome. I love you, dawg, but I gotta do this for me."

He paused for a moment, taking a deep breath.

"I'm flying back up top by the end of the week."

Hommi looked away, staring off into the distance before turning back to Raheem. He raised his finger, pointing.

"Ya chips." Then he turned his back and headed to his room. "B.B.L.-U.B.L.," he muttered over his shoulder before shutting the door.

Little did Hommi know—Raheem was doing this for him, too.

CHAPTER TWENTY-EIGHT

Due to a layover, Raheem sat in JFK Airport's waiting area, talking on the phone with Tia.

Took a whole lot of sweet-talking for her to give him another chance, but once he got it he was on his way home.

But first—he had to make sure Darian had a fighting chance to dodge a life sentence.

"What you doing, daddy?" Tia asked.

"Shit, in the crib thinking about you," Raheem lied. He didn't want her to know he'll be in town late tonight.

What he had to do required focus—and Tia was a distraction.

So instead of telling her he'd be in Boston tonight, he told her he'd be home the next day.

"Mmm, what you thinking 'bout?"

"Those soft lips around my joint."

"Uhh, you won't be getting none of that for a long time."

"It's all good," he chuckled. "I'm just happy to have my baby back. The extra shit gon' fall into place."

His flight got announced over the intercom.

"Aye, baby—Hommi hitting me on the other line. I'm supposed to meet him. Let me take this call. I'll hit you back when I'm done busting this move."

"Okay, just make sure you call me back. At least to say goodnight."

"I got you," Raheem said, then pressed end.

Tia sat at her kitchen table, staring at her phone with a smirk.

"All flight attendants aboard plane, huh?"

Shaking her head, she laughed to herself. So, he already on his way? Still wanna play games with a bitch.

Let's play.

CHAPTER TWENTY-NINE

The sound of the P.97 A.G. Ruger cocking back made him freeze. Not a bone could move, not a thought could process.

The silhouette told him all he needed to know.

More afraid of the man than the weapon—he knew death was near.

But he leaned on DNA to save him.

"Why'd you do it?"

"Why I do what?"

13 ½ 13 ½ 13 ½

Ever since Rico and Freaky got shot and Darian got arrested, money had been scarce. Not just slow—damn near gone.

And not just that—the drug game itself was drying up.

Desperate for cash, Casino took the last third of a kilo he had left, broke it down into ten-dollar slips, and headed to the Combat Zone.

A dangerous move.

The Combat Zone ain't for everybody. The junkies here? Treacherous. The drug force? On a warpath. But the risk? Worth it.

Especially for Casino, who was trying to flip his last product and get the fuck out of town before the streets found out what he already knew—

He snitched. An act he wished to God he could take back. Since that moment, he hadn't been the same. Couldn't stand the sight of himself. Couldn't even look in a mirror or catch his own reflection in a window. So, he kept all the lights off in his apartment.

Standing on the corner of Beacon Street, paranoia creeping up his spine, he spotted a suspicious car parked across the street.

Lights off—but he could see the engine running.

He watched it. Studied it. Debated—

Is that the boys?

Is that the jakes watching me?

Fuck it. Time to go.

Casino walked off.

13 ½ 13 ½ 13 ½

Behind the wheel of the suspicious car, Raheem strained his neck, tracking Casino's every move.

Then an idea hit him.

Rolling down his window, he called over a young drug addict—one who still had some sex appeal.

She obeyed the command.

"Hey, big daddy. What you looking for?" She flashed a crooked smile. "Thirty for head. Fifty for the pussy. Seventy-five for the ass."

"Slow down, ma," Raheem smirked. "Ain't nobody looking for none of that."

Her grin faltered.

"But listen," he continued. "I'm willing to pay you—for less. And it ain't got nothing to do with sex."

She squinted. "Then what is it?"

"First, let me ask you this. That dude on the corner just now. Dark hoodie. You see him?"

"You talking about the dude across the street?" She glanced over her shoulder. "Yeah, I seen him. He been coming around for a week or so."

Raheem nodded.

"Cool. Now listen—Imma give you a hundred dollars. Take fifty and buy some work off him. The other fifty's for your pocket, aight?"

"That's it?" She grinned. "Shit—consider it done."

She turned to walk off.

"Wait," Raheem called her back. "Take him to one of your special spots—where you'd usually do a date at."

She winked. "Got'cha."

13 ½ 13 ½ 13 ½

Casino strolled through the Boston Commons, lost in his own head.

Paranoid as fuck.

A voice called out behind him.

"Hey!"

He turned, spotting the same young drug addict from earlier.

"Sup?" he asked, cautious.

"You working?" She licked her lips. "I'm tryna cop."

Casino eyed her. Something felt off.

"Didn't I just see you on Beacon Street?" He glanced around for the suspicious car.

"Yeah, that was me."

"You a cop," he stated. "Get the fuck away from me. I ain't got shit for you."

He turned to walk off.

The girl looked offended—like he just insulted her whole existence.

"Ayo, hold up!" she called out.

Casino kept walking.

"Ayo, I'll suck ya dick!"

He stopped.

Slowly, he turned back. "What the fuck you just say?"

"I said, I'll suck ya dick—to prove I ain't no undercover."

He checked his watch. Almost 2:30 AM.

"Aight, bet," he shrugged. "But I ain't paying you for shit."

"That's fine," she snapped. "I just don't want nobody thinking I'm not who I say I am."

"Cool," Casino nodded. "Lead the way."

She smiled. "Follow me."

13 ½ 13 ½ 13 ½

Raheem clenched his jaw. What the fuck is this bitch doing? He had told her to bring Casino to a cut—a quiet spot. Not lead him straight to him. Hiding behind a thick tree in the Commons, dressed in all black, Raheem took a deep breath.

I should've known this dopehead was gonna pull some slick shit.

Fuck it. It is what it is. Soon as Casino gets close, I'm pushing his shit back.

Raheem gripped his gun tighter.

Since yesterday, he had been studying Casino's movements. And now? He was tired. Time to put this shit to rest.

Just as Raheem was about to ambush him, Casino suddenly turned back around and followed the girl.

Raheem exhaled. He put his gun away. He then, started following them both—again.

13 ½ 13 ½ 13 ½

The young drug addict led Casino to the end of a dark alleyway between two abandoned stores—a perfect spot.

She dropped to her knees.

"You still think I'm an undercover?" she asked, looking up at him.

"Just keep sucking that dick," Casino muttered, grabbing a handful of her hair.

She kept going.

Casino closed his eyes. Letting go—for the first time in a long time. He needed this.

"A nigga been stressing lately," he admitted.

She got up, wiping her mouth.

"I'm happy to ease your stress," she smirked. "But don't ever mix me up again."

As she reached down, she grabbed his stash. Casino, still zipping his pants, didn't even notice. Then— The sound of a gun cocking made him freeze. He turned, his face going pale. Raheem raised the Ruger.

"Why'd you do it?"

Casino's throat went dry.

"Why I do what?"

"Tell on family?"

Casino swallowed.

"Cuz... they made me."

Raheem's jaw tightened.

"And so did you."

The alley lit up seven times.

CHAPTER THIRTY

Parked outside Tia's apartment, Raheem reclined his seat, threw his right forearm over his eyes, and sighed.

Damn... these streets will turn you into a cold-blooded monster. Who would've ever thought I'd have to smoke my own lil' cousin 'cause he couldn't hold water? After all these years of keeping it three-hunnit—look at me now. I got my own DNA on my hands. And I'm back to square one—with nothing worth speaking of. I ain't get shit out this life, but pain and betrayal. Instead of love, I got hate. Instead of loyalty, I got deceit. What a fool I am. Or should I say, what a fool I was? Because I'm done. I paid my debt. Now it's time to move forward. It's over, Ma. I'm finally done. I'm done with this life, and I'm ready to live. Not just for myself, but for you too. It's about time your son gave you some grandkids—with the woman I love.

But through it all, Ma...I'm grateful. Blessed to have been through all this and still be able to walk away from the game—with some money and a second chance.

Raheem pulled out his phone and called Tia.

13 ½ 13 ½ 13 ½

Hearing her phone ring, Tia's company walked into her bedroom and sat on the bed beside her.

She glanced at the screen. The name she'd been waiting for. She answered.

"Hello."

"What you doing?" Raheem asked. "Was you thinking about me?"

"You know I was," she said. "I can't not think about you."

"Well, guess what?"

"What?"

"Daddy's home."

"For real?"

"Yeah, I'm downstairs. Unlock the door, I'm on my way up."

"Okay, Daddy," she smiled. "I can't wait to see your handsome face."

"I can't wait to see you too."

Raheem hung up.

Tia jumped up, slipping her phone into her back pocket. She turned to look at Freaky.

13 ½ 13 ½ 13 ½

Raheem smirked as he hung up with Tia. He still couldn't believe he almost lost her. Damn, I can't wait to hold her.

He exhaled.

"Let me hurry up before my baby start trippin'," he muttered, he reached under the seat for his pistol. Suddenly, his phone rang again which startled him. He glanced at the phone. Tia. He chuckled. I know this crazy girl like the back of my hand.

He answered. "You must really miss ya man," he laughed.

Silence.

"Tee? You there?"

13 ½ 13 ½ 13 ½

Freaky took Tia's hand and guided her to sit back down beside him.

"So, what he say?"

"He told me to unlock the door. He's on his way upstairs," she said.

"Aight, cool." Freaky got up but paused at the door. "When he gets up here, make him comfortable." He shot her a look. "If you gotta—give him some pussy."

Tia stiffened.

"I'ma be in the next room," Freaky added, stepping out.

Then he reappeared. "My fault," he kissed her on the forehead. "I love you."

"You love me?" Tia questioned.

"More than any nigga could."

And with that, he left.

Tia sat there.

Heart pounding.

13 ½ 13 ½ 13 ½

Raheem sat staring at his phone.

Not moving.

Not blinking.

Just... processing.

Because what Tia didn't know—was when she sat down, her phone accidentally called Raheem back.

And he had just heard everything.

Every. Single. Word.

THE END

13 ½

ABOUT THE AUTHOR

I was born and raised in Boston Massachusetts. My life is a reflection of some readers, but as real as all.

www.ingramcontent.com/pod-product-compliance
Lightning Source LLC
Chambersburg PA
CBHW020527110726
47899CB00004B/1278
* 9 7 8 1 6 3 7 5 1 5 3 5 8 *